Praise for Lisa Brace's novels

'*Swim* is a powerful novel about skill, courage and determination. I was completely invested.
Lisa Brace's writing moves seamlessly between tension, poignancy and humour in a compelling story. The perfect book for this year.'
Gill Thompson
'A beautifully told and tightly plotted read. Compelling, emotional and a true book for Olympic year.'
D.E. White
'Lisa Brace writes vibrant, strong, fun and well-rounded characters. A great read and a wholly satisfying ending.'
Sue Fortin
'A beautifully written, wonderfully astute examination of modern society that teaches us what's most important in life.'
A.A Chaudhuri

'A brilliantly heart-warming and refreshing story. I couldn't put it down.'
Anna Jefferson
'Tender, poignant, relevant and gripping.'
Amazon reviewer

Swim

THE ASTONISHING TALE OF LUCY MORTON

LISA BRACE

BLUE PIER BOOKS

For the women in my life; my mum, my sister, my daughter,
my nieces and my nan.
And the men who support us.

Prologue

July 1924, Paris

'Ready.'

The crowd began cheering, the noise was the loudest thing I'd heard since my Olympic trials back in Blackpool.

'Set.'

I arched my back in preparation to dive in and winced at the pain that raged through my body.

The pistol rang out and I instinctively dived in, just as I had hundreds and hundreds of times before. The water was cold but familiar.

My whole body wanted to fight me. It didn't want to push through the water, it felt like I was swimming through cement and my limbs had forgotten how to work. Trying and failing to find my rhythm, I misjudged my breathing and inhaled a mouthful of pool water which caused me to choke. Water streamed out of my nose and mouth and I watched as the American began to pull away from me.

Just swim.

The phrase reverberated as I continued in the water and breathed through the pain, the way I had every time I'd gone into the sea or the pool. This time I felt like I was reliving every moment I'd been in the water.

It's no one's race but yours, Lucy. Mr Swarbrick's voice came into my head and I realised he was right. I was not in this to lose against the American. I was in it to win for me.

The strength of belief coursed through me, I began to ignore the pains and the cement water and instead made peace with the pool. I would do the best for me.

I kicked hard. The third length disappeared and I was on the fourth and final fifty metres in the two hundred metre race. Reaching into myself for something else, I kicked again and I felt it this time. I could do this. The American had slowed, not a lot but just enough for me to be in hot pursuit of her, and gold.

I pushed with everything I had left and powered down the water.

This is for Mother. This is for Father. This is for Alice. This is for Harry. This is for Mr Swarbrick. This is for Joan who can't swim. This is for all the little girls who watched me in the heats in Blackpool, cheering me on. This is for me age ten. This is for me age sixteen. This is for me age nineteen.

This is for me now.

I threw my hands down on the side and looked up. I couldn't see anything.

'Who's won?' I shouted at the umpire nearest to me. 'Who's won?' I repeated, turning to Irene who'd only just come in and couldn't help. She just shook her head.

As I waited to hear the result that could change my life, I thought back to where it had all began.

Chapter One

APRIL 1908, BLACKPOOL

I almost died the first time I tried to swim.

Not during the lesson at the indoor swimming baths where we gripped tightly onto the side and kicked until a white foam surrounded our group of ten-year-old girls. All of whom had been told to go swimming or face the dunce hat once again.

Not whilst we tentatively pushed from the side for a brief moment, gasping at the freezing cold salty water that enclosed our heads if we didn't move our legs as quickly as the baths superintendent, Mr Gerrards, had told us to.

No. I almost died as I walked away from the baths, talking to my friend Lorna. I was telling her she should be a mermaid because she took to water so well. I remember the rough tiles underneath my feet, little particles of grit that the teachers had brought in on their shoes grinding into my heels, making me wince. I had turned to tell Lorna that I planned to swim the following week, when one of my feet met something slippery and the next minute I'd plunged into the water.

The world went blacky blue and I wondered, momentarily, if Mrs Phillips, the headmistress, would have been so keen on me trying swimming if she'd known this was how my life would end.

Her voice echoed in my head as I tried to work out where the surface was, kicking and throwing my arms out wildly.

'I have always felt that where there are facilities, every physically fit child should learn to swim,' she'd told me a few days before as I'd swung my legs in the high, dark oak chair in her office.

Again.

I was a regular visitor to that office due to my teacher and I having differing views on what constituted 'good' work.

'I have taken lessons myself; indeed, I think I'm rather good at it,' she had smiled at me, 'and I've encouraged my staff to do the same. I shall be suggesting it to the students I think will benefit most from it.'

Her voice had begun to disappear as I started to lose consciousness.

'You, Miss Morton, are one of those girls.'

'Thank you, Miss.'

'Don't thank me,' her voice echoed in my thoughts, 'you're the biggest dunce in school. Swimming might brighten your ideas up a bit.'

***

'Then he lifted you out of the water and swam back with you to the side.' Lorna reported my near-death experience to me as though I wasn't involved. If you believed her, I was under the water for minutes, not seconds, and they all thought I had drowned.

But the bit where Harry rescued me was true. I don't remember the rescue, but I do remember being laid on the side of the pool and coughing my guts up, spitting water over myself and him. He was crouched over me, his brown hair splashing droplets onto my face, a look of concern over his. My swim class had formed a circle around us.

'Are you all right?' he'd whispered, his hand on my forehead.

I'd nodded, my throat burning from coughing.

'Thank goodness. You gave us all a jolly fright.' He'd smiled at me. 'Make sure she's wrapped in a towel and gets changed soon,' he had directed Lorna who had solemnly nodded up at him as he'd unfolded himself from his crouching position.

Now we were sat by the pool, dressed, but drinking hot chocolates. Mr Gerrards had poured them out of his Thermos flask – he probably felt guilty he hadn't been on the side of the pool when I fell in. Apparently he'd gone on ahead to talk to a different class and wasn't watching us. Harry shouldn't have been down by the pool as it was women and children only, but I'm glad he had been.

'Hey there, kiddo, are you feeling better?' Harry had stopped by, his body, as he stood over us, blocking the light a little.

'Much better, thank you,' I managed, my throat still sore. 'What were you doing down here?' Harry grinned at me and crossed his arms. I noticed his brown hair had flecks of gold in it.

'Never you mind, just glad you're better. Righto, I best be off.' He stopped for a moment. 'Unless you're planning on falling in again?' I shook my head vigorously. 'See you around then.' He nodded at Lorna and we watched as he left.

'He's quite a dish,' Lorna whispered as he walked away and I giggled, pulling a face.

'Don't be silly. He's about twelve. We're ten.' I smiled at her and saw her eyes had gone wistful.

'Well, two years isn't that much of a difference. Think about it, when I'm twenty-one and he's twenty-three it'll be fine.' She grinned at me and I groaned.

'Only eleven years to go then,' I replied and we began to laugh hard, tears rolling down our eyes until we realised other swimmers were looking at us.

'Shush, we're upsetting the lessons.' Lorna said, giggling, and we both tried super hard not to laugh. I noticed Lorna had a drop of chocolate on her chin and I hoped I didn't, and that Harry hadn't seen it if I did.

'Girls, I think that's probably enough.' Mrs Phillips had appeared out of nowhere, though her bag and towel suggested she was going for a dip herself. She hadn't been there when Mr Gerrards had been teaching us. 'Lucy, are you feeling better?' She looked at me severely.

'Yes, Miss.'

'Good. I hope we'll be seeing you next week – not put you off?' She looked a touch concerned.

'I'll be here next week. I need to learn not to drown, Miss,' I replied and grinned. She smiled tightly and nodded, before walking away.

'Off you go now.'

We did as we were told, heading home full of the drama, so that when I returned home to Brighton Cottage – to my mother stirring a pot full of something delicious on the stovetop in the scullery – the fear had disappeared and I'd been left with just a tale to tell.

'How was it?' she asked, whilst simultaneously holding out her hand for my costume, throwing another vegetable into the pot and shooing my younger sister, Alice, out of the way of the stove. I handed her my things whilst trying, and failing, to nab a carrot to munch on without her seeing.

'It was a bit,' I shook my head like a dog, showering Alice and Mother with droplets, 'wet.'

'Oh you, stop that,' my mother shrieked, trying to grab a linen cloth from the side and rubbing it over my head. 'It would be worrying if it wasn't wet, wouldn't it? No, I mean, how did it feel? Was it nice?' She looked at me seriously. She had never learnt to swim and had been unsure whether I should learn when I came home with my letter to Father from Mrs Phillips saying I needed to.

Father had sided with Mrs Phillips and had said to Mother that it might be my only answer as I had no subject at school that I excelled at.

Mother was still waiting to hear my response and I considered it carefully, whilst I helped myself to a hunk of bread smothered in butter that she'd left out for me.

'It was a strange sensation. When you get a moment when your whole body floats in the water without your help, you feel,' I scrabbled for the right word, 'weightless.'

Mother pinched her non-existent side a little.

'Oh, what I'd give to feel like that,' she smiled, 'not all of us are born with long legs and a slight frame.' She stepped forward to embrace me. 'Not everyone is as lucky as you, my girl.'

She paused there for a moment and I breathed in her unmistakeably Mother scent, a mixture of her face cream, furniture polish and cooking. Warm scents of honey and thyme.

'I can't wait to go back,' my voice was muffled into her chest, 'it was ever such good fun. Can I go next week?' Mother pushed me to arm's length and studied my face, smiling. 'Yes, of course – now run along and get ready for tea.'

Chapter Two

APRIL 1908, BLACKPOOL

The following week, as I walked along Brunswick Street to Reads Baths, I watched a gull flying ever higher into the air. I was thinking how it would be marvellous to have wings and soar above the streets, when someone called out my name. I had spun around to locate the voice, scanning the street this way and that but I couldn't locate it – a mother pushing a large perambulator walked past me, crooning to her crying child, but it wasn't her.

Then I heard the voice again and looked behind to see Harry walking quickly up the street to me. He was a good foot taller than me and I had to crane my head up to look at him properly when he stopped and stood over me.

'Oi, Lucky Lucy, wait up.' I stopped and clutched my bag closely to me. I didn't want to be late for my second lesson but he had saved my life so I felt I owed him a minute. As he made his way towards me, I realised he had no intention of stopping so I quickened my step and fell in line with his strides. It wasn't easy. I may have been tall for my age, but his steps were far longer than mine and quite quickly I began to tire.

'You're going to have to slow down if you want to walk *with* me,' I huffed and exhaled. Harry laughed and slowed to a more acceptable pace.

'Sorry, that was thoughtless of me. Better?'

I nodded.

'So, how are you? Any other death-defying stunts this week?' he asked, a slight smile playing on his lips. I knew he was ribbing me, just like my sister did.

'No. Thank you. A highly uneventful week, well, apart from...' I faltered. I didn't know Harry, I didn't know how much I should be talking to him.

He raised his eyebrows at me.

'Apart from what? Let me guess, did you jump off of a building? No, I know, you decided to try and drive a motorcar? What a hoot.' He laughed at his own joke and I jabbed him in the ribs.

'No, actually. And now you've said those things it's nothing like as exciting,' I admitted, uncertainly.

'Go on, I'm interested now.'

'It's just that I find school quite dull. I'm a bit of a, well, *dunce*, truth be told. This week, I don't know if it was because I knew I'd be swimming today or what but, well, I was less of a dunce,' I admitted nervously, unsure if I'd said too much.

Harry smiled as we neared the baths.

'Well, that sounds like a good week. Not falling-out-of-a-plane exciting, but a good week.'

I grinned at him.

'Are you swimming today?'

He shook his head and I sensed an air of disappointment coming from him, a feeling echoed by myself.

'No. I usually swim during the week – I'm getting ready for competitions. I was only at the baths last week as I was picking up a couple of things. I'm running a few errands for my father today. Anyway, once you've got the hang of not drowning they'll probably get you competing too – quite a few of the Christ Church School girls do.'

I laughed happily at the ambitious nature of the idea.

'Me? Compete? I'll see how lesson number two goes first I think.'

Harry smiled and waved goodbye as I went into the baths.

'They'll have you competing, you mark my words. See you around, Lucky.'

Chapter Three
APRIL 1910, BLACKPOOL

I took to swimming like a duck to a swimming pool, that's how Mother described it. I loved the water. Somehow it just made sense to me, to my body. This was how I was meant to move.

After a couple of years of Saturday morning lessons, my father, on listening to my teacher who said I was more than proficient in the strokes he was teaching, took the decision to move my lessons to Cocker Street Baths under the tutelage of Professor Faraday. Father dropped me off outside the grandly decorated entrance for my first lesson and as he made to leave I grabbed him, realising I needed to share the worry I'd had for the last few days.

'What if he doesn't think I'm any good? What if I'm dreadful?'

Father shook his head.

'You won't be dreadful – you're good, Lucy, that's why you're here. And anyway, what's the worst that could happen? Just enjoy it.'

As it turned out, the worst that could happen was to find a cockroach in my shoe when I returned from my entirely uneventful first lesson. When I squealed, one of the girls in a cubicle next to me laughed, not unkindly, and yelled over the side, 'I suggest you bring a bag next time. Bloody blighters try to get in all the time. You need to tie your clothes in a bag and that'll keep them safe.'

I stepped out at the same time as her and smiled a little awkwardly when she saw me.

'Lucy isn't it?'

I nodded and she held out her hand in greeting.

'Greta, nice to meet you.'

'And you.' I smiled, more confidently this time, at the older girl. She had the freckliest face I'd ever seen and, as if that wasn't enough, she had a shock of ginger hair. Greta definitely stood out.

'You're very good,' she nodded in my direction as I wrung my hair out. Salty droplets fell off me. That was one of the negatives to swimming as often as I did, my skin was so itchy from being in the salty water all the time and my hair felt taut and dry.

'Thanks, so are you.' I'd watched Greta dive in. She looked how I imagined the Olympic swimmers did. She was so graceful she just sort of slipped into the pool with barely a splash, then elegantly pulled her way down and up the length of it. Actually, she reminded me of one of the seals we saw at the circus in the tower last summer.

Greta was studying me keenly.

'Has old Faraday taught you the Australian crawl yet?'

I nodded vigorously.

'Yes, we began it this week. It feels awkward though,' I admitted as we slowly began to walk from the cubicles towards the exit. 'My arms didn't want to go in the directions he was shouting at me to go.'

Greta beamed.

'Oh, but that's marvellous – he wouldn't be teaching you that if he didn't have a belief in you.' She clapped her hands together. 'There's a competition in a month, the Christ Church team are going in. It's the biggest one we've entered so far. But we need a crawl swimmer in the under twelves category. Fancy it?'

Her eyes shone with excitement and I felt caught up with her enthusiasm. Before I could say anything though, she laughed.

'Gosh, silly me – I forgot to say, I'm the captain of the team. Not just a random swimmer trying to get you to compete, that would be odd.'

I giggled at her awkwardness. She didn't seem like she was fifteen.

'I'd love to. That would be fun.'

'Yahoo, marvellous!'

I laughed again as Greta punched the air.

'Mind you, you'll have to step up practice. Come down three times a week and we'll have it licked,' she looked elated. 'I can just feel a certificate coming for you.'

I grinned at the prospect of doing well, then worried for a moment whether Mother and Father would mind me doing more practice. Greta misplaced my concern to be a financial one.

'Don't worry, as you're on the team you can swim whenever you want – other than when the men are in though, of course,' she snorted.

'Of course,' I grinned as we reached the street.

'Righto, I'm this way – cheerio, see you at school,' she yelled as she grabbed her bicycle. I waved and turned around, promptly crashing into Harry.

'Watch it,' he yelled, pushing me away. 'Oh, hullo, it's you.' He smiled at me and held me at arm's length. 'Well. If it isn't Lucky Lucy. How's tricks?' He grinned and I couldn't help but be swept up with his infectious smile. It had been quite a few weeks since I'd last bumped into Harry and, whether I liked it or not, despite my own infatuation with him since the day he saved me – some eighteen months or so ago – he seemed fine to go weeks without us seeing each other, whereas for me it would feel like agony.

The flustering this time meant I realised he'd asked me a question I hadn't answered and there was a difficult silence.

'Jolly good, thanks.' I paused as he looked pleased. 'In fact, I've just been asked to compete in a month,' I whispered, unable to believe it.

Harry smiled so broadly it was impossible not to return it.

'Well that's just brilliant, good work.' He hesitated, measuring his words. 'Tell you what, why don't we celebrate? You could come to my house.' He pointed down a side street. 'It's just a little way down there. Mother does a great bacon sandwich.'

My own mother was expecting me back for breakfast but Harry's exuberance was too enticing. And if I was honest, I'd missed him. It had been such a long time since I'd last seen him I'd begun to wonder if he was a figment of my imagination.

'Go on.' He raised his eyebrows at me and rattled a pocket full of loose change. I nodded.

'Atta girl. Good choice.' He looked around where we were standing. 'Did you bring a bicycle?'

'It's this one.' I pointed to my rusted dark-green steed that was propped up against the wall and began to walk over to collect it.

'Allow me.' Harry smiled, taking the bike from the wall and beginning to walk down the street with it. I felt a small flip-flop come from the flutter of butterflies in my stomach, which I knew was silly because he was fourteen and wouldn't be interested in me in the slightest.

But still. It felt nice walking beside him, listening to him telling me about his job as a trainee carpenter.

'Have you done much swimming lately?' I asked as I realised I'd not seen him near the pool for a while. Harry's face clouded a little and his smile dropped for the first time since we'd bumped into each other.

'Ah, no. Sadly, I've had to halt it – for the time being you know? I don't have much time to swim, between working and looking after my little sister Agatha when Mother is working – she's got a housekeeping job. It pays well but we don't see her much.'

He looked so rueful, I tried to think of something to cheer him up.

'I don't suppose you know anything about the crawl, do you?' I looked at him a little hopelessly. 'I'm a bit worried everyone will think I'll be better at something than I actually am, I've only practised it a few times, and it's really tricky.' I knew I was rushing all my words out but he seemed to be really listening to me and it felt nice to be listened to. Walking along a street with a handsome boy who was listening attentively to me, as though I was the most important thing in the world. 'I know I have time to practice and Greta says I can do it as much as I like—'

'Oh, Greta's great, she'll be good to listen to – I used to swim with her brother actually,' Harry interrupted, and I noticed a whisper of jealousy coming from me. I didn't want to talk about Greta. Even if she was great.

'Anyway, I need to learn it. Otherwise I'll come last and no one will let me compete again.' We'd arrived at a house that looked as though it had been squeezed in the middle of two others, and Harry leant my bicycle against the wall outside. Then he opened the front door for me and brought me into the tiny house.

The windows were steamed with the trail of a thousand cups of tea and there was a strong smell of fried eggs in the air. I realised I was ravenous and Harry, on seeing me licking my lips, laughed.

'I did wonder if you ever ate – there's nothing of you, Lucky. You need to make sure you eat after any training or you'll be one of those women who faint all the time.' He took my hand and pulled me into the kitchen where his mother was stood at the stove with a steaming kettle, straight off the boil.

'You're back quickly.' She turned and saw me and when she did I went red from head to foot. 'I know you, you're one of the Morton girls aren't you?' I nodded, but before I could speak, she'd pulled out a chair and pushed me into it. 'You've been at the baths by the looks of you, sit by the fire to warm up and dry out and I'll fix you something. What'll it be?'

When she smiled, lines appeared all around her eyes, small ravines which spoke of years of work and a lot of laughter.

'I'll have a bacon sandwich and a tea.' Harry grinned. 'And she'll have one too, with a glass of milk.' He turned his smile to me. 'We're trying to fatten her up a bit.' His mother laughed.

'Yes, well, there's not much of you – it'll be all that swimming. Your mother was telling Mrs Brown in the butchers about you. She seems very proud. Though...' Harry's mother stopped short of finishing her sentence and Harry looked at her with concern.

'Though what?'

She shook her head, turned away to the stove and began dropping thick slices of bacon into a pan. The smell made my mouth water and I heard my stomach growl loudly.

'Come on, Mother, say what you were going to say. I'm sure Lucy won't mind.' He looked at me and I shrugged, focused on just one thing. She could say anything she liked if she was going to put those rashers between the thick slices of bread I could see her preparing.

She shook her head again as though wrestling with what to say.

'It's just,' she started, 'there's no future in it. Is there?' Harry and I looked confused at her and she continued, aiming her words at the sizzling frying pan. 'Swimming. There's no future. Certainly not for a girl. Don't get me wrong, I'm sure you enjoy it. But you won't get a husband swimming. Will you?' she asked me and I realised I was wrong, there were some things she could say which would put me off my food. I felt hot. And it wasn't the close proximity of the fire.

'Well, what if she didn't want to marry?' Harry asked and his mother laughed. Her shoulders moved as she continued to cook.

'Want? There's no want in it, Harry. Darling, sweet Harry. You'll see soon enough. Our futures are set out for us. She'll get to be a wife and a mother and hopefully her husband will do right by her. But she won't be swimming for much longer – you're what, Lucy? Nearly thirteen? By the time you're eighteen your parents will want you settled down and out of their hair.'

There was silence as she removed the bacon from the pan and poured some of the dripping on the bread before handing it to me.

'Eat up.'

I sat in silence, listening to the fire crackling in the grate and munching on my sandwich, but now I had no appetite. Harry was quiet too, astonishingly for him.

'Mother, things are changing, you know. Women are going to get the vote – I've been hearing about the suffragettes, they're fighting for you – for Lucy.' He looked at me.

His mother sighed deeply.

'Yes, and maybe they'll get it. But if they do I'm not sure many of us actually want it. They're going about it in the wrong way if you ask me, but yes, maybe women will get the vote. Maybe that will give us more freedom but,' she turned and looked forcefully at me, 'Lucy, don't forget about your studies. Even if you find it hard, make sure you keep up your studies.'

'I will, Mrs Heaton, I promise. I don't like the home-making lessons though, they're ever so dreary – I'd rather learn from Mother,' I replied, half-truthfully. I didn't enjoy any of it really, but I wanted her to like me and it worked, I think, because she smiled.

'Good. You need to learn whilst you can, then when you meet your future husband he may even be impressed by your intellect.' She smiled again, a little sadly, and then rearranged her apron over her stomach, causing me to see the bump protruding out.

She caught me staring.

'Ah, didn't Harry say? I'm expecting. Again. Hopefully this time the young 'un will see its first birthday.' She looked sad again. 'But that's why you're so wonderful, Harry, working so there's a little more food on the table this time round. Well done, love, I'm very proud of you. You're a good provider.' She messed his hair.

'Oi. Leave me to eat my sandwich. Or I won't be able to get out again,' Harry grinned. 'I'll be so hungry I won't get to the shop on time.'

I laughed and he reddened a little.

'Watch it, Lucky, not everyone gets one of these sandwiches.' I laughed again and we shared a smile.

Mrs Heaton looked strangely at me and nodded her head a little.

'Be sure to come any time Lucy. Any time at all.'

Chapter Four

MAY 1910, BLACKPOOL

I t was the day before the competition, a Friday.

Mother called Alice and I downstairs, her shout floating up the three flights of stairs to the top of the house where we shared a room full of girlish knick-knacks and night-time ghost stories. I should have noticed the quiver in her voice but I didn't register it until I was in the kitchen. She was sat at the table, in itself a sign that something was wrong. Mother was never still. She was either cooking, or sewing, or ironing, or listening to the radio or busy with something. But today she was sat at the table, clasping my father's hand.

'Lucy, Alice, come. Sit. There's something we need to tell you.' She looked at Father as though drawing strength from his silence.

She reached for my hand and Alice held my other.

'The King is dead.'

I could hear the solid oak clock ticking outside in the hall. I counted the seconds, trying to understand what she'd said.

'What does that mean to my competition?' I blurted out, seeing the look of hurt which crossed my mother's face as soon as I spoke.

'Lucy, it's hardly the time to discuss swimming competitions,' my father admonished, looking pityingly at me, and I hung my head in deep regret.

'I'm so sorry, I didn't mean it. I didn't, Mother.' I tried to catch her eye to try and make her understand it was an accident. 'Really.' I searched for words. 'It was just such a shock. What happens now?'

Mother smiled a watery grimace towards me across the table.

'Nothing to us, nothing changes. But his son, George, will be our new King now. There will be celebrations for him soon – in fact, I think we shall organise a street party. But for now, there will be a few days of mourning and that does mean, in answer to your earlier question,' she tutted under her breath, 'that the competition is cancelled tomorrow. I'm sorry.'

'Oh.' I exhaled the word out and felt deflated. Sorry for the King, of course. But sorry for me too.

My father patted my hand.

'There'll be other opportunities. I know there will—' He was stopped from finishing his sentence when there was a thudding on the front door. He got up hastily.

'It's all right, I'll see who it is and send them away. I know you're not receiving anyone,' he said to my mother.

They loved each other, I knew they did, but they rarely showed care towards each other. Today he seemed to truly care for her.

I listened to the clock ticking again, then Father returned to the kitchen, his face white. And Harry was behind him.

'Harry, everything all right?' I asked, as he came in, removing his flat cap and smoothing his hair down. He looked at me sadly, and scrunched the hat between his hands.

'What is it?' my mother prompted.

'I'm sorry, Lucy, but he – he's dead,' Harry finished lamely, still wringing the hat as though the answer was in the material.

'The King? I know, Mother told me. But why are you here?' I asked, confused as he stood there, looking younger without his hat on. I knew we were to feel sadness at the passing of a monarch but I wasn't sure why Harry had brought his grief to our home.

My father came over and put his hand on my shoulder. I could feel the weight of his hand pushing through to me. It was reassuring and yet also felt like I was being pinned into place. I watched as Harry continued wringing his hat. When he spoke, it was quiet, as though he didn't want to impart the information to me. 'Lucy, I'm sorry. Professor Faraday has passed away.'

Chapter Five

June 1910, Blackpool

The baths were closed for a fortnight following the death of both men and I couldn't admit I was grieving far more for the loss of my inspirational teacher than the King.

But following the funeral of King Edward VII, and the inauguration of King George V, life began to be more normal. School resumed and, after a hiatus to respect Mr Faraday, the baths reopened and Mr Swarbrick, the replacement superintendent of the baths, became my new teacher.

He wasn't convinced by the crawl Mr Faraday had been teaching.

'No Lucy,' his moustache quivered as he spoke. 'I can't see it catching on. Breaststroke is much better – far more efficient. We'll work on that and the backstroke. I see those becoming your best strokes and there are plenty of competitions you can compete in with those,' he explained before my first session with him.

'But, sir, Professor Faraday said—' I wanted to tell him it was the future, but with my old coach gone I didn't have much experience to draw on to disagree with his argument. Besides, I just wanted to swim. Mr Swarbrick puffed himself up. His tall, lean body encased in a smart three-piece suit. The effect was, I believed, one of a grey oblong.

'Come along Miss Morton, into the pool. I think we should make a start on backstroke – it's pretty tricky to pick up, but I should think a girl like yourself will manage,' he remarked, as he walked over briskly, leaning a little heavily on a walking cane. I wondered why he needed it but Mother and Father had always said never to ask *those* sorts of questions.

I dove into the water, fully immersing myself. I tended to find it better to attack it that way than how some of the other girls approached it – lowering themselves slowly in with teeth chattering and goose-bumps on their arms.

'Right, with backstroke you must give yourself a good push, but then it's about the arms.' Mr Swarbrick demonstrated both his arms going round at the same time, his suit straining when he swung his arms overhead – the sight made me want to laugh but the stroke looked straightforward.

'When you're ready, Miss Morton.' He looked at me expectantly.

'Righto.'

I pushed away with my feet from the side and began to bring my arms over my head whilst ferociously kicking my legs, but the momentum pushed my head into the water and caused me to inhale a good portion of the swimming pool. Coughing and spluttering, I made my way to the side and Mr Swarbrick looked at me.

'What are you doing hanging off the side? Go on, off you go.'

'Righto.'

The same thing happened. And again. And again.

Exhausted, I pulled myself up out onto the side, my breath coming in huge shuddering gasps whilst my body prickled with tiredness and cold.

'It's... so... hard...' My teeth chattered as I tried to speak. Mr Swarbrick passed me a cup of tea.

'Drink, it'll warm you up.' He smiled.

I took a sip. The tea was sweet and hot and began to do its job, reviving me with its magical properties. I even began to feel a little more energised and Mr Swarbrick could tell.

'This stroke is meant to be hard. If everyone could do it where would the fun be? Now, when you push off make sure you're keeping the rest of your body nice and straight. Taut, like this.' He lay beside me, his jacket and trousers getting wet as he demonstrated on the side of the pool and I stifled a giggle at a grown-up acting so strangely. 'Keep your stomach tight and then, over the head, like this – see?' He demonstrated the move, his arms crashing into the tiled surface. 'And then keep going, like a windmill. Now. Into the pool, before you seize up.'

I did as I was bid and lowered myself into the water, trying to ignore the cold.

'Now push off.'

I pushed, the water flowed against my head, trying to force me down but I brought my arms over and over as quickly as I could, my legs kicking and for one brief moment I moved, but the fire in my shoulders was building and soon I'd gone under once again.

Swimming on the bottom of the pool to get myself to the end, I tried to imagine giving up swimming.

I could.

I could stop now and never need to practise this stupid stroke ever again. But then who would I be?

Chances were I'd be that dunce in the corner again. I'd been surprising them at school lately, it appeared swimming had unlocked something in me. I was beginning to work better, learning what I could. If I stopped swimming that could mean the end of school going well.

And Harry may stop turning up at the baths every now and then.

I reached the end and held onto the side.

'When you're ready Miss Morton.'

I took a deep breath.

'Righto.'

Chapter Six

OCTOBER 1910, BLACKPOOL

'Let's see it then.' Harry leant over to look at my certificate and I beamed up at him.

'It says "Lucy Morton swam 100 yards in less than 180 seconds". Well I think we knew you could do that,' he said ruffling my hair.

'Aw, you leave her be, Harry,' my mother lightly clipped him around the ear. 'We're very proud of her, she and the other Christ Church School girls have done really well.'

It was the first time Blackpool Council had given out official swimming certificates and I was incredibly proud of mine. I kept looking at it on the kitchen table. The weak autumn light made it look golden. A gold ticket.

'I think this deserves a little treat.' Harry grinned at me. 'Mrs Morton, would it be all right for your daughter to accompany me to the pleasure beach? I'd take good care of her.' He looked kindly towards me and I tried not to show how very, very much I wanted this to happen. My mother, however, looked like she already knew.

'I should think so. But you need to have her back by dinner time. I can't have my daughter out in the evening with a young man, we have to think of her reputation.' She looked at me in a particular way which made me redden.

'Yes, Mrs M, I promise. We'll just take a walk along the promenade, maybe enjoy an ice cream and then I'll return her.' He smiled again, this time at me, and my insides felt as though a cage of butterflies had taken up residence.

'Off you go then.' Mother smiled indulgently, then stopped and felt around in one of the biscuit tins on the side. 'Here,' she handed me a coin and looked a little guilty, 'enjoy yourself.'

'Mother, I can't. That's yours—' I broke off as she held a finger up.

'Shush now. That's between you and I, isn't it? No one else needs to know.'

I leant in and kissed her briefly on the cheek. She smelt of baking and polish, and home.

'Thank you.'

'Enjoy yourself.' She smiled to me, then turned to Harry. 'Look after her.' He nodded and waited whilst I shrugged my heavy burgundy coat on and buttoned it up. My mother had tailored her own coat for me and it felt wonderful, so grown-up.

Mother tightened the ribbon in my hair to pull it back a little more, then sent me on my way. As soon as we stepped outside onto the pavement, Harry offered me his arm and I held it carefully.

'Right then, what do you want to do first?' he asked as we stepped out across the road and headed towards the pleasure beach.

'I don't know,' I giggled a little, 'I've not done this on my own before, only with my family.'

'Well,' Harry replied, glancing at me before he looked ahead, 'you're not on your own, you're with me.'

'That's true.' I held his words in my heart, priding myself on not swooning. 'In that case we can decide on a whim when we get there – no plans needed.' I extricated myself from him and spun around. 'We're free.' He looked at me and laughed, then offered me his arm again. I took it and we began to walk in companionable silence.

Except. The thing is, I'm not good with silences. I find there's so much to see or talk about, that it's odd when people go quiet. With every pace I began to tell myself companionable silence was less favourable than silly chat. And eventually I had to give in.

'So, tell me, Harry, why haven't you been swimming lately?' It had been preying on my mind for a while, he swum beautifully, everyone said he did. But his look made me regret breaking the silence. He looked uncomfortable and his arm that mine was looped through shifted a little as though he was looking to shed me. Not wanting to pry further I refrained from saying anything else and we walked along North Shore in silence. It wasn't until we reached the promenade with the beach to the left of us that he spoke.

'Mother's baby died three days ago.' He looked at me for a reaction and I was torn. If we'd been behind closed doors I'd have considered embracing him as he looked so disconsolate but I couldn't in public.

'Oh, Harry, I'm so sorry,' I replied lamely, knowing it wasn't enough but unsure what else I could offer. We had wandered onto the pebbles and stood facing the sea. The scent of the iron-rich water filled my nostrils.

'Just wasn't a strong infant, was sick from the day it came into the world.' Harry delivered the information in staccato points as though it was being dictated. 'Only lived for ten days. Mother is distraught. Father says they should have another to take her mind off of it.' Harry threw a stone and we both watched it skim across the surface in front of us before disappearing beneath, to continue its perpetual journey.

'And what does she think to that?' I asked carefully. Mother had been telling me how campaigners were talking about women having options and I'd wondered how Mrs Heaton had taken the news. Being encouraged to have alternatives other than motherhood. According to Mother we could consider roles in teaching, or working in a hospital or something else. We didn't need to be at home all the time.

Harry skimmed two other pebbles before replying.

'I don't think she wants any more children. Besides me, Edward and Agatha, she's had three other pregnancies. Two didn't go to term. The third was this one.'

The mood was turning gloomy and I wanted to remind Harry of the joy of our day so I stopped him.

33

'Come on, I challenge you to a sandcastle competition,' I made my way down on to the sandy patch the sea had uncovered, with Harry following closely behind.

'Lucy – I mean, Miss Morton,' he caught himself as a family looked up at us, 'it's the middle of October, autumn is almost upon us and we don't have anything to make sandcastles with.' He reached me and grinned. 'How are we to make anything?'

'We only need to use our imagination. See here.' I picked up an enormous flat piece of driftwood, 'I shall dig mine with this, and,' I looked around for inspiration, 'I shall decorate it with these tiny shells.' I looked up and saw him smiling indulgently at me. 'What is it? Come on, let's make one at least – it doesn't have to be a competition if you're afraid I'll beat you.' I smiled. He shook his head.

'No, you won't beat me. I'll build mine over there. Let's give it ten minutes and afterwards whoever's the best gets to choose what we do next. Fair?' I nodded but he'd already knelt on the sand and was shaping it.

The next few minutes passed with just the sounds of gulls shrieking overhead and young children squabbling nearby, breaking up the suck and roar of the sea as it rolled in and out to the shore.

'Right, I'm finished,' he called and I looked over. As soon as I saw his I laughed out loud.

'What?' He was put out. 'I think it's pretty good.' He grinned and stood back to admire his work. I walked over to take a proper look.

'Well, I thought I'd said we were having a sandcastle competition – emphasis on the castle bit.' I laughed, looking at the extraordinary sand octopus he had fashioned. The tentacles wound out a yard or so each and its head was impressively globular. It looked like the ones I'd seen in books.

Harry rubbed his hands together to knock the sand off, then rubbed his hands on the tops of his trousers to get rid of the last grains, leaving a light dusting.

'Ah, but you also said to use your imagination. My imagination told me to make an octopus-shaped house. That way you could live in it, in the sea. And no one would know you were in there.'

I took in the smooth shape of the head and thought how carefully precise he'd been in making it.

'Ingenious,' I grinned. I think Harry liked the idea of disappearing and no one knowing where he was. He had a far-away look in his eyes, but when he blinked his demeanour changed as he looked at me.

'Let's see yours then.'

When we walked over to mine, the two couldn't have been more different if we'd tried.

'What is it?' He was incredulous, but then, on kneeling to inspect my mini sculpture, he realised.

'You've made a swimming bath.' He laughed hard. 'There's nowhere to live, but I like the detail.' We both looked at the oblong shape I'd created, decorated around the sides with tiny shells to reflect the tiled area. I'd even managed to dig deep enough so as to make my way to the dark, wet sand, where a natural pool filled the space.

'It's beautifully done Lucky but I don't think anyone could live there.' Harry raised his right eyebrow at me. I shrugged a little.

'I don't know. I often feel like I do. I'm there enough.' A gull yelled at a fish in the water before diving in. The way it entered the water reminded me of the numerous times I'd gone under whilst continuing with backstroke.

'Hey, look. If you want to be brilliant, you have to practise or there won't be any more of those certificates. Who knows, maybe one day you'll be competing nationally.' He laughed at the disbelieving face I was pulling.

'Ah, fine, maybe a little too optimistic.' He looked at our sand creations. 'I think we declare a draw. Neither of us created a sandcastle, but both created something impressive – I suggest we head to the ice-cream shop.'

'That sounds like a marvellous plan,' I said casually as he caught my hand in his and walked me off to the shop, though my heart was hammering in my ribcage. I wanted the world to see us.

'I think I may have a little sand in my shoe,' I said, walking uncomfortably. 'Hold on.' Harry stopped and offered his arm out to me as I wiggled the black polished shoe off my foot, shook it and replaced it, all whilst trying not to lean too heavily on him. As I put both feet on the ground I realised I was clasping both of Harry's hands in mine and for a brief sweet moment he and I locked eyes and I realised I couldn't breathe.

He broke the glance first.

'Well, I think we should be getting that ice cream, don't you?' I nodded, relieved I wouldn't have to talk and took

his offered arm, watching the little children running bare-
foot on the sand despite the chill in the air. I remembered
doing the same with Alice in a time not so long ago and it
dawned on me I may not do it again. My childhood had
disappeared when I wasn't looking.

The peace of the promenade was broken by a young
boy yelling.

'Extra, extra, Doctor Crippen found guilty of murder,
read all about it.'

Harry visibly shivered.

'Terrible, all that. Absolutely terrible. Fancy killing
your wife like that.'

'I know, Mother says the poor woman was poisoned
and hacked to pieces. How can someone be so in love with
someone else then do that to them?' We shared another
intimate look with each other and I felt heady with it.

Harry shook his head.

'That's because not all love stays Lucky. Sometimes
people are fortunate and get to savour and enjoy it for
years – look at your parents, they're clearly in love. They
care for each other. Others tolerate each other – like mine,
whereas some make the wrong choice and end up...' He
raised his hand in the direction of the newspaper seller.

'Yes, well. I'd rather never be in love then,' I replied
quickly, trying to cover my feelings of embarrassment at
discussing love with Harry and the butterflies telling me
it might be how I felt for him.

Harry laughed and I blushed.

'Not sure it's that simple. Ah, here we are,' he stopped
at the ice parlour. 'What'll it be?'

'I'll have whatever you have.' I grinned, enchanted with the day and filled to the brim with happiness. I tried to commit all the sights to memory so I could tell Alice all about it when I returned home. He chose us both a strawberry ice and when I licked it, the shock of cold caused my head to ache almost instantly. Absent-mindedly I rubbed my left temple.

'You need to eat it slower – let your body become accustomed to the chill.' Harry looked fondly in my direction. 'I think we should go on a ride – don't you?'

We began walking again and hovered in front of the House of Nonsense – it looked fun but I was worried it might be frightening.

'Tell you what, how about a go on The Flying Machine?' Harry looked so handsome, I decided not to reply that I'd been on it a few times with my family and had of late felt a little like I was growing out of it.

'I would love to.' I squeezed his arm as we queued in the warmth of the late-autumn sunshine and enjoyed the feeling of his scratchy woollen suit beneath my hand.

When it was our turn to step into our carriage he held the door open for me and helped me sit on the wooden bench, my skirts and coat seemingly trying to take over most of the room that was available. Soon though, as the machine started, we began to twirl lightly in the air as we lifted from the ground and the sounds of the pleasure beach seemed to drift away from us. It occurred to me this was the first time we'd ever truly been alone.

'Hold tight, don't want you falling out.' He hung onto a bar to give himself some stability and I did the same as the machine began to tilt and send us up to the heavens before rotating and soaring down towards the floor. Onlookers fleetingly became a little larger as we got closer, like fleas under a magnifying glass, before disappearing from view as we began our journey higher once more.

When we were at the very top the machine stopped and our carriage swung in the breeze, the two of us hanging on as it swept gently from side to side.

'It doesn't do this usually,' I said, then quickly allowed a short gasp of recognition at admitting I'd been on it before, but Harry didn't seem to mind.

'No, it doesn't.'

He looked over the side making the carriage swing a little, causing me to shriek.

'Stay still, it'll keep swinging otherwise.'

Harry sat back, his body pressing into mine.

'They'll get us down shortly – anyway,' he brightened, 'I'm with Lucky, the girl who didn't drown.' He winked. 'So I'm sure we'll both be fine.'

'I didn't drown because you were there.' I looked at him, and realised how very, very far away the rest of the world seemed.

'I'm here now, too, aren't I?' His voice was deep in his reply and he coughed to clear his throat. 'Lucy, I— would you, I mean...' He stuttered over every word and I looked at him, concerned.

'What?'

'Kiss you?'

The carriage was swinging lightly in the breeze and it felt dizzying. Though whether it was the movement, the height, or the fact I was sure I could hear Harry's heartbeat matching mine, I couldn't be sure.

I nodded, my heart in my throat and fireworks in my head. Harry leant in and very lightly brushed my lips with his.

Chapter Seven

NOVEMBER 1910, BLACKPOOL

The next few weeks blurred wonderfully into one. I spent the majority of it either with Harry, swimming with Mr Swarbrick, or thinking of Harry. School suffered but it was indulged because myself and the other Christ Church girls were entering and winning our swimming competitions.

Harry's mother had taken more work with the lady with the big house, Lady Dupont, and was spending more and more time out of her own home. For Harry and I that meant we had somewhere we could spend hours together in our own cocoon. We would make picnics and eat them on the floor of his living room, he would read to me or me to him, and we'd kiss. A lot. He would work in the shop when I was at school and swimming so we could share the spare hours together.

In November the baths were closed for the winter and my parents would expect me home directly from school which gave us less time together. We only had the Thursdays when I told them I had extra tuition – giving me the opportunity to spend two blissful hours with Harry. We knew it would be frowned upon to talk of our relationship just yet, I was still twelve and he fourteen, but we were in love. We knew we were. We did, however, speak of our dear friendship – a white lie which both mothers at least seemed happy with.

The time away from her own home meant Mrs Heaton wasn't at the whim of her husband and had begun to speak of things she'd learnt at her employer's. I'd noticed a change in her. One day when I was at Harry's, I was huddled by the fire in his kitchen, attempting to warm up. It was a bitter day, so cold my breath made great white gusts whenever I stepped away from the direct heat, and his mother came in, her face glowing with life.

'Lucy, oh Lucy, it's all so terrifically exciting.' She came over and stoked the fire, pushing the logs around to give extra bursts of heat across the kitchen. Harry came in straight after, snowflakes caught in his hair falling to the ground as he held an armful of wood he'd brought from the log store next to the kitchen.

'What's exciting?' he asked as he set the wood down neatly by the fire in a stack. His mother looked at him.

'Lady Dupont says tomorrow she and the other million or so women in the country who own their own home could get closer to getting the vote.' She beamed at us and I smiled, a little uncomprehendingly at what she was telling me.

'I thought you said you didn't think a vote was all that important,' I reminded her, thinking of the conversation we'd had just a few months before in this very kitchen.

She looked sad. 'I didn't understand then. I do now. We will have a voice. A small one, but it'll be a voice nonetheless.' She hugged me tightly.

'So is it agreed?' Harry asked from the fire where he was stacking up the logs and embers flew as they sparked out of the flames.

Mrs Heaton was unpinning her hat and allowing her hair to unfurl down her back like a thick rope.

'Well, no, what I understand is there's a bill going through parliament,' she replied, a hairgrip in her teeth, 'and tomorrow some of the women Lady Dupont knows are going to London for a meeting, followed by a peaceful visit to the Houses of Parliament.'

'Mrs Heaton?' I had warmed up and could see the enthusiasm shining in her eyes. I didn't fully understand but I knew something exciting was happening. 'Is Lady Dupont going tomorrow?'

Mrs Heaton had turned to the sink, tying an apron around her waist and busying herself by washing some dishes. I saw her back stiffen as I asked.

'She might be, I'm not sure.'

Harry and I exchanged a glance.

'Mother, are you working tomorrow?' he pressed. She stood taut at the sink and then turned around with a big smile spreading across her whole face, but it didn't seem convincing.

'Yes of course Harry, what else would I be doing?'

Harry looked mollified as she began toasting some bread in the fire in readiness for his father's tea. I watched them both and decided I needed to get back to my family, where I felt I could understand people a little better. Their glances. The body language.

'I think I need to get home. Harry will you walk me back?'

We bundled up and attacked the route home. It was ice cold so I had to wrap my scarf over my face just under my eyes, so that all I could do was peek out of the top. Harry did the same so conversation was nigh on impossible. When we parted at my door he leant in to kiss me gently on the nose.

'Keep an eye on your mother Harry,' I urged. I had a sense of foreboding I couldn't place but he smiled and patted my head.

'Don't worry, she's just going to work. She said didn't she?'

I watched as he turned and walked away through the cold night. A slight figure wrapped in a thick coat, his flat cap squashed tightly down to his ears, his boots making marks in the snow. I watched until he disappeared into the darkness.

***

I went to school that Friday. I learnt about geography. I was told I should write more neatly. I sang with the choir, surrounding the piano that Mr Mason played. I ate my jam sandwiches Mother had made. I laughed with Lorna. I was reprimanded for not paying attention in mathematics.

I returned home.

Harry woke up, went to work in the shop for the morning. Returned home for lunch. His mother was at work so he reheated the stew for himself and his father. He went back to work for the afternoon. Dealt with orders. Read a smutty magazine with his friend. Returned home for his tea. His mother wasn't there.

His father and he waited until eight o'clock before they began to be concerned. His mother was always home by six o'clock.

At nine o'clock they went to Lady Dupont's house. They stood on the doorstep of the magnificent house and knocked. It took three solid knocks at the door for the maid to answer. When she did, she at first said she'd not seen his mother that day. When his father asked again the maid told him Lady Dupont had brought his mother to London for the meeting of suffragettes.

She told him he should be proud.

The maid didn't know when to expect them back. Yes, they could wait in the kitchen. No, they couldn't wait in the parlour.

It wasn't until Saturday afternoon that Lady Dupont arrived in a carriage with Harry's mother. He told me later she was carried into the house by a footman, and was unrecognisable. Her face was puffed up with navy bruises that bloomed across her face. Her lip was badly split, dried blood congealed around her left ear and her ankle appeared to be broken.

When she looked at him it was with such horror in her eyes that Harry told me after he was certain he frightened her. But he wasn't sure why. Lady Dupont insisted his mother was taken upstairs and looked after by two of her maids and allowed to rest in the house for a couple of days to aid recuperation.

Harry's father had disagreed, vehemently, according to Harry, but Lady Dupont had stood firm. She too looked as though she'd been in a scuffle, her dress torn, scratches and welts across her face, but she spoke carefully to the two of them whilst she drank a generous brandy.

'Your mother was incredibly brave yesterday. She had asked to be at the meeting and I'd said yes – she'd been so interested in the suffrage meetings we'd held here I thought it would be a good experience for her. And it would have been if Asquith hadn't decided to call another election and stop our bill going through.'

The women had planned to walk on Westminster as a peaceful group after the meeting but when news broke that the potential partial victory towards women gaining the vote had been stopped by the Prime Minister, the air had turned dangerous and the ladies marched on Westminster in a furious mood.

Lady Dupont told Harry it was as though a storm had burst.

'All the clouds that had been gathering for weeks suddenly broke and the downpour was terrific. There was not one of us who would not have gone to our death at that moment. Had it been willed.'

She went on to tell Harry and his father that the police fought with the three hundred women. That the women were beaten and assaulted and their personal areas interfered with – at this statement Harry told me his father uttered an expletive and Lady Dupont moved the story on quickly. Many were arrested. After they'd been beaten by police officers they were thrown to the crowd where further hostilities ensued.

'It felt as though the whole world were men at that point,' Lady Dupont said. 'They tore at us, they hit us mercilessly, ceaselessly. And your mother was there beside me until two police brutes grabbed her, held her skirt up high and then threw her into the crowd. I didn't see her for a long time after that.'

The women who were injured and avoided arrest were taken to the suffragette's base at Caxton Hall which acted as a makeshift hospital. When Lady Dupont had returned to the building, injured and in need of treatment, she had found Harry's mother there. But it was too late to make the long journey home so they had stayed the night with Lady Dupont tending to Harry's mother's injuries.

LISA BRACE

She told Harry's father he could take his wife home in a few days but she needed to be treated with care.

Harry relayed all this with grave concern in his eyes, adding that Lady Dupont had cautioned whilst his mother's external injuries would heal quickly, the ones they couldn't see, and the memories, could take a long time to recover.

Black Friday had made its mark on Harry's mother and would be a turning point for all of us, I was sure.

Chapter Eight

MAY 1911, BLACKPOOL

Although I continued to swim, honing my strokes and lengths, even competing a few times, there was something in the air, something which leant a sense of tension to all aspects of life that made everything feel like it was on a knife edge.

Swimming began to lose its appeal the more time I'd spend with Harry and I'd find excuses to not go. My competition results reflected my interest but I didn't care. I was thirteen and in love.

Besides, Harry needed me.

Ever since her part in Black Friday, Harry's mother was spending more and more time at Miss Dupont's house, something which his father was struggling to understand. Or endorse. He was finding the lack of food, the un-darned socks and the cold bed an embarrassment. He just wanted his wife back and for his house and life to go back to normal. Harry also wanted his mother back and we spent many hours discussing what she did at the big house which meant she didn't want to return to her own.

And I? What did I want?

I didn't know.

I read the newspapers that my father left out for kindling. I saw the headlines. Strikes at a factory in Scotland where 11,000 people walked out. Suffragette protests, Emily Davison hiding in a cupboard in Westminster so she could be counted in the census as a resident there.

And then in May even the weather seemed to think it was time to ratchet things up a bit, the heat beginning to increase little by little.

To begin with, the warmth was welcome. I'd become fed up leaving the pool with wet hair, goose-bumps prickling all over my skin as I made my way home. I'd grown tired of having a constantly runny nose, I assumed from swimming and competing in outdoor pools where the water was rarely any warmer than the air.

Whilst May had been joyful and warm, it soon became clear there'd be no let-up in the weather and as we moved into July life became far harder. The heat of the day would begin to climb from ten o'clock, reaching its most unbearable at five o'clock in the afternoon, when the sun's rays would feel as though they were reaching inside you and heating up your internal organs.

If I had to leave the house I'd try to go early in the morning, but on one occasion I had to visit the corner shop to collect some bits for Mother that she'd forgotten. I think the heat was affecting her memory and I'd said yes to get away from the niggly arguments my sister and I were having over everything.

As I walked along to the shop I allowed my thoughts to drift to those of cool drinks, long shadows and lying submerged in the swimming pool. It had become almost impossible to visit the baths as so many other people had had the same idea and I'd stayed away for the last week.

I was just dreaming of the ice creams on the pleasure beach as I pushed open the door to the shop, the bell tinkling on my entering, when I walked straight into a woman some ten years older than me who was, until that moment, carrying two bags of shopping. One of which fell to the floor, causing half a dozen eggs to spill from the bag onto the brick steps and crack in front of me.

'Oh gosh, I'm ever so sorry.' I picked up the lady's bag and began to collect items from the floor and considered how best to clean up the eggs. Lorna had told me that if you cracked an egg on the pavement when it was this hot that it would fry, but all I could see was an uncooked globular mess.

'You most definitely should be sorry – how dare you barge into me like that,' the woman cried, and when she spoke I recognised her as one of the Christ Church teachers.

'It was an accident, I didn't see you, I'm really sorry,' I added again, flustered at the anger spitting out of this woman so ferociously.

'Oh, it's you, Morton. I should have known. Just get out of my way.' She grabbed the bag I was clutching. 'And give me that.'

After she'd shoved past me I re-entered the shop and tried to calm my breathing, my heart hammering hard.

'Pay no mind to her, a lot of people are quick to temper at the moment,' Mr Axewell, who owned the shop, explained. 'It'll be the heat.'

I felt truly shaken. No adult had ever spoken to me like that, not even my parents. Mr Axewell took pity on me and sat me down on a stack of newspapers.

'Here you go, have one of these – on the house.' He smiled and handed me a Fry's chocolate bar.

'Thank you, she was just so mean.' I nibbled on some of the chocolate, enjoying the sensation of it melting.

'I've seen a bit of that lately, I'm sure it's because it's getting warmer. The other day two men had a fist fight outside the shop for no reason other than one bumped into another, as far as I could work out,' Mr Axewell explained. 'Don't you feel it though?'

I swallowed another mouthful of chocolate.

'Feel what?'

Mr Axewell put his head to one side as though to assess whether I'd understand or not.

'I feel it. I see the headlines. People are striking. There's a lot of anger. And then those women, they're angry,' he added.

'The suffragettes do you mean?' I checked as I polished off the bar, licking the remnants off my fingers.

'Yes, exactly. Them. They're angry. It feels like the country is coming apart at the seams and it's only getting worse as it gets warmer.' Mr Axewell spoke confidently in his view. I nodded, but didn't feel I understood any of it enough to say anything.

'I should get the shopping. Mother will be furious if I don't come back soon.' I grimaced. Mr Axewell nodded in understanding.

'Another angry woman, I'm not surprised.'

As he busied himself, grumbling about women and strikes, I threw what groceries I needed on the counter in a bid to get out of the shop as quickly as I could. I felt as though the blood was rushing into my head as I put the money down and impatiently waited on my change. I couldn't bear his puce face, full of anger.

Throughout the following weeks it got increasingly hotter. And tempers much, much shorter. There were days in July when I was convinced my blood would boil I was so hot, and I'd dream of those downpour days where the rain would hit the pavements and there'd be that fresh smell in the air.

Instead, it was so hot the weather broke records. And that wasn't the only thing which was broken. There was more unrest with strikes around the country. Miners were walking out, factory workers were downing tools, there were even pupils striking from schools – boys, mainly, who were fed up with receiving the cane.

Food spoiled so quickly we had to buy what we were going to eat that day, otherwise there would be the awful scent of gone-off meat in the air.

My mother and father, usually so placid with each other, were argumentative and snappy. It even reached Harry and me.

'Come and walk with me.' He'd swung round on his bike ostensibly to say 'hi', though mother had taken one look at his face full of longing and suggested he had a bucket of ice-cold water thrown over him to calm his ardour.

'Have you told her?' he asked, concerned, and I shook my head.

'Of course not but she has eyes,' I grinned, then my face dropped at the look he gave me.

'We can't be caught, Lucy. Father will kill me – he's told me I shouldn't be hanging around you, it would be much worse if he knew we were courting.' He faltered on the final word.

I shook my head.

'It's barely anything Harry. It's not like we're getting to see much of each other is it? What with you in the shop.'

He was stood on the doorstep of Brighton Cottage. I couldn't let him in, Mother had already said I needed to come for tea down in the kitchen at the bottom of the house. Whilst the ground floor was reserved for our front parlour, we always ate our meals together at the table in the kitchen. Harry looked at me with sadness in his eyes. 'You're one to talk.'

I was confused.

'What do you mean?'

Harry shook his head in disbelief.

'You really don't see it do you? You're obsessed with swimming. You go what, four, five times a week? You're competing at least once a month. You say you never see me, well I never see you – because you're always in that bloody pool.'

I opened and closed my mouth, though nothing would come.

'That's. Not. True,' I managed.

Harry laughed.

'No? Then tell me where you were last weekend? Or maybe the one before that? How about the shelf above your bed with the small collections of medals and awards? Or are they someone else's? I hear you telling people you don't swim much but you do. You swim a lot.'

With that he parted and I watched him go, not keen to have an argument on my front step, but equally not prepared to admit he was right. He wasn't. Sure, I swam a little, but I needed to keep up my strokes for the competitions. And of course I competed, I was part of the Christ Church team. But it wasn't as often as he said. I used swimming to plug the gaps around Harry when he was busy. I didn't squeeze Harry in around the competitions.

Or did I? Reluctant to think about it any longer, I headed in for tea.

However, the next day it was still hot and I was still angry with Harry, so I did the one thing I could which would calm me.

I decided to go swimming. I barely allowed myself to note the irony, I was too hot and frustrated to care.

The baths were too busy and I didn't enjoy rubbing skin to skin with others. It was warm enough as it was so I decided to go swimming in the sea. To begin with my mother wasn't happy about me going there on my own so

I'd encourage her to walk to the promenade with me. And when I went into the sea, shivering with the first bite of the water she would sit on a folded newspaper and watch me. We'd go first thing in the morning, or late in the afternoon – or sometimes both – and I think it brought her a similar sense of calm that it did to me.

Although there was one thing we definitely disagreed on.

'Mother, I need to dry off a little,' I complained one day on the beach as she tried to force a dress on me as soon as I'd walked out of the water.

'You are in public and you are a young lady. We can't have people get the wrong idea about you,' my mother replied, briskly rubbing the towelling blanket I'd brought, over my shoulders. It felt as though she were trying to detach my collarbone from the rest of my upper half.

I shook her off.

'I don't know what idea you think people will have. I'm standing in a swimsuit which has CHCH on, and a load of badges sewn into it. I couldn't look any more like I'm a swimmer and,' I paused, irritated, 'I'm dripping wet, so one would assume I had been... swimming.' I shook myself at her so droplets would fall off. 'There's nothing else to deduce about what or who I am. No wrong ideas to be had.'

'Lucy, you are growing into a young woman.' Her voice softened a little. 'You may not be aware of it but I am. I can see your hips rounding out, even if you are as slim as one of my runner beans in the garden, and your bust is coming in.'

I crossed my arms over my chest to cover myself.

She smiled, a hint of melancholy surrounding her. 'If I can see that, you can be guaranteed other people – men – will see it too, and when you stand there in very little, you will invite an audience. It's different in the baths but out here on the beach,' she threw her arms out expansively, 'you need to be aware that there are different rules. And one of them is to cover up,' she said, pushing my white cotton dress over my head so hard my ears burnt with the friction.

I looked at her, at the beauty I still saw even if she didn't, and decided she needed to win this one.

'Yes, Mother. I'm sorry.' I smiled at her and she grinned.

'See, Mother knows best – at least for now.' She took the towelling blanket from me and carefully dried off my hair as best she could, then forced it into two plaits on either side of my head. I hated it when she plaited it like that.

'Tell you what, how about we get one of those ices you were telling me about? We could split it, so it doesn't affect our figures?' she asked, and for a brief moment she looked like a young girl, so I nodded.

'Excellent.' She grabbed the newspaper she'd been sitting on and placed it into her bag, rolled my towel and placed it on top, pausing as I shuffled my feet into my sandals. 'Come along, slowcoach.' I loved my mother when she was like this. Free. She'd be spontaneous and mischievous.

She'd glow.

LISA BRACE

Then, it was as though she remembered her world. Her life. And she'd close down. Her face would turn back to the older woman she was. Her eyes would lose their spark and there'd be no way for me to reclaim it.

It was never, I realised, when my father was around. He was a kind man, but I'd begun to realise that sometimes kindness wasn't everything you needed in a relationship. My mother was shaped by him and her father to be the woman she needed to be. To fit into where she should for society to accept her. But that meant hiding away anything that was her. The essence of her.

When she was free with me I liked to think it was because she felt comfortable enough to be herself. I was accepting of all she could be.

Chapter Nine

SEPTEMBER 1911, BLACKPOOL

In September when the weather was still unceasing in its heat, Harry, who had become a weekly fixture in our household disappeared for a month.

I'd become so used to him being in my life it felt like I was missing a part of my own body. An arm maybe. Or my lungs. I'd thought of him as a permanent piece but he'd gone.

'Thank goodness, it's like you two are married or something,' my friend Lorna exhaled and stretched as part of our warm-up before hockey.

'What?' I was shocked at her mocking tone. 'You've always been so encouraging of him – you kept telling me he was handsome.' I stretched my hands down to my feet.

'Yes,' she puffed as we began our star jumps, 'but it's so predictable. He comes around, you have dinner, you talk or whatever and then he goes again. If you told me you'd taken to darning his socks, I think I'd believe you.' She wiped some sweat off her brow. 'Blast, it's hot already. I hope they don't expect us to play a full game.'

School had moved physical education to our first lesson of the day in a bid to avoid the hottest part, but already by ten o'clock it was becoming uncomfortable with beads of sweat running down my back.

'What if I did darn something of his? It's only because his mother isn't there to do it,' I retorted and Lorna stifled a giggle. We'd got in trouble with Ms Chambers, our hockey coach, last week after a particular outbreak of laughter as she'd heaved and squatted so hard we were convinced she was going to split the men's shorts she always wore, so I gave Lorna a filthy look to keep quiet.

'Oh Lucy, you haven't. Well, you may as well give up now. Become Mrs Heaton Jnr. You'll need to get better at housekeeping though, your pie was jolly awful yesterday.'

'Right, girls, now a quick lap around the field before we start,' Ms Chambers bellowed.

'I swear she only tells us to do this because she is an actual sadist,' puffed Lorna, attempting to cross her arms over her ample chest. The poor girl already wore two brassieres to stop her breasts from bouncing too much whilst running, something I had absolutely no problem with. I was almost as flat as an ironing board. With my broad shoulders from swimming and the height I'd acquired from Father, I was also not too bad at physical education, though it did make me stand out from the petite girls who all swooned and ran away from anything too difficult.

'Come on, Lorn, you'll be fine. Keep going,' I cajoled as I came to the end, barely out of breath, and clapped her in.

'Right then, ladies – teams,' Ms Chambers bawled at us and Lorna and I trailed up the field in the direction she'd pointed.

'So you really think it's a good thing I've not seen Harry for a while? I don't like it very much,' I admitted and Lorna grimaced.

'Look, you're thirteen, he's fifteen? It's a big gap.' She held her finger up for me to be quiet. 'It is, and I know he's a nice lad but he doesn't want to be hanging around with a kid anymore. He's probably, and I'm sorry to say this, but he's probably found someone closer to his age to spend time with.' She could see the look of hurt on my face. 'But yours was good whilst it lasted, right?'

'I suppose we have become more like friends of late, but I assumed that was because we're getting older and we've known each other for a year,' I suggested tentatively.

'Look, I don't want to be indelicate here,' Lorna looked around discreetly, 'but has it not occurred to you that maybe he'd be after more than some hand-holding and kisses? He's practically a grown man Luce. It's probably for the best if you two drift apart for a little while, eh?' She smiled and hugged me and we began to run forward for the ball as the whistle was blown to start our game.

***

'Hey, as you're free now, why don't you come and sleep on the beach with me this evening? The whole family is going to do it. It's bloody boiling and it's a great way to cool off,' Lorna suggested as we changed for our next lesson. I was so warm from running around and the incessant heat, I felt as though I would burn up if I put any clothes on. A dip in the sea followed by sleeping in the outdoors would be perfect, it might stop me from thinking about Harry too.

That evening as I reached the beach with Lorna I couldn't help but giggle at the sight. I'd steered clear of the beach during the day for the last few weeks as so many people had flocked to the seaside to cool down. The problem with that was there was nowhere for us locals to go. On the way I watched as yet another car got stuck in the asphalt of the road and a group of men worked to free it.

'Odd how this has become so normal for us now, isn't it?' Lorna asked, looking in the direction of the car. 'Not that long ago I'd have said seeing anything stuck in the road was out of the question, but now the heat's melting the roads, anything's possible.'

I nodded.

'How's your mother faring?' I looked in her family's direction who were walking ahead of us, dropping my voice a little so as not to draw attention.

'Struggling. Between the crop shortages making food more expensive, and the speed the food is spoiling at home, it's a wonder she can find anything for us.'

We went quiet. I could see the picnic basket Mrs Smith was carrying and prayed she had enough for me. Mother had been glad I was out of the house that evening as she was to sleep in my bed to cool down instead of sharing a bed with Father. But she had little else other than a hunk of bread and a small lump of cheese to give me for the night. The rest had spoiled that day.

'We just need it to rain. It's going to have to happen at some point,' Lorna panted as we sat down on the beach, allowing the light cool air from the sea to wrap around our shoulders.

Later, as we settled on the beach, having scoffed the little she had in Mrs Smith's wicker basket, I lay next to Lorna and looked up at the stars.

'They're so clear, aren't they?' She held her arms up as though to catch one.

'One day we'll be stars Luce. I'm sure of it.' She hugged me and we lay holding hands until we fell asleep – even the pebbles pushing through the blanket into my back couldn't stop me, I was so tired.

In the middle of the night I awoke to an uncomfortable feeling on my face. Wiping my hand over my cheek I realised it was wet.

'Lorna, Lorna.' I shoved her until she awoke. 'It's raining. It's actually raining.' The rain began to pour down as we helped her family collect up all their belongings and we rushed as quickly as we could home, squealing with joy as the large droplets hit the parched road.

'It's glorious.'

The water splashed onto the cars and the roads and washed everything clean. When I woke later and looked outside, everywhere sparkled. I'd forgotten how beautiful even our most mundane of roads could look when it was washed of the dirt and debris which had accumulated over the past three months. And the air. I stuck my head out of my window, sucking down the oxygen, and realised the temperature had dropped some ten degrees, giving the air that crisp September feel.

When I drew in the fresh air, I realised how stale my lungs had felt. How stifling it had been. Sitting on my bed in our room I looked around and wondered why, with the air lifting as it had, I still felt like I was stifled. Still suffocating.

Lying on my chest was the heaviest of weights. It was as though Mother had taken the irons out of the fire and had laid them on me. I didn't want to acknowledge it but maybe I needed to admit Harry and I were over.

Why else would he disappear for weeks and not get any word to me?

Chapter Ten

OCTOBER 1911, BLACKPOOL

T wo weeks later I had my answer.

Walking out of the swimming baths and thinking of the turns I'd learned that morning, I walked straight into a solid body. And when I looked up, there he was.

'H-Harry,' I faltered.

'Lucy. You must think me such a dreadful person, do you hate me? You must,' he said, his eyes so sincere my irritation was quickly fading.

'I was... um... I was surprised,' I tried, 'that you disappeared. Anyway, glad you're all right.' I began to walk away, unprepared for the emotions that had taken root in my stomach.

Harry grabbed my arm.

'No, Lucy, stop,' he pleaded. 'Please.'

I turned on him, full of fury.

'Why, Harry? Why should I? You can't disappear for weeks on end and just expect to reappear and for everything to be all right. How would I know if you were fine? That you weren't dead? It wasn't funny. It wasn't fair.' The fire in me was burning out quickly. 'If you'd changed your mind you could have just said. You could have told me you wanted to go with someone else.' I choked a little. I didn't want to cry but my throat hurt so much at holding it in, I hoped he'd let me go so I could go and sob somewhere alone.

Now it was Harry's turn to look hurt.

'Someone else? You thought I'd gone off with someone else?' He watched me nod slowly. 'Lucy, I know you're younger than me but I don't care. There's no one else I'd wait for – you know that.' He grabbed both of my shoulders. 'You do know that don't you?'

My head hurt. I wasn't sure of anything anymore.

'No. I don't know. It wouldn't be difficult to let me know where you were.'

Harry looked at me.

'She was arrested.'

I looked at him, unsure.

'Your mother? Why?' We had come upon a bench in a small park area and I indicated for him to sit. As he got closer to the bench it was as though he crumpled into it and all of a sudden he looked like a young boy. He leant forward and put his head in his hands. I could barely hear him as he spoke through his fingers.

'They force-fed her whilst she was there. She was arrested over a disturbance – lots of suffragettes were – they'd been campaigning outside of Parliament, then a few tried to get in. Mother was one of them and when she was arrested they left her in a cell for days.' He looked up at me. 'Days, Lucy.'

'Lady Dupont told Father she couldn't find out where Mother had been taken to – or any of the other women who were arrested. Every time she went to a police station she'd been expressly told was where the women had been kept, she was told something else. Eventually she found them at one of the women's prisons – they were being held there instead of a police station despite their cases not being heard yet.'

I held Harry's hand and stroked it. I didn't know how to apologise for my reaction when Harry had clearly had a nightmarish few weeks.

'When Lady Dupont found Mother, she got word to Father and he went to London to finally appeal on her behalf, which left me—'

'On your own with the children to look after, and the shop,' I finished for him. 'Oh, Harry, why didn't you say?'

He shook his head sadly.

'Father didn't want anyone to know. He was embarrassed about what people might say.'

I moved closer to him on the bench and held his hand.

'I'm so sorry, Harry. What's happening now?'

'She's home. But she's...' I could see him trying to find the phrase which would suit what he wanted to say. 'She's broken I think.'

'Do you mean injured?' I prompted.

Harry looked away, focusing his attention on the laurel hedge that edged the park area. I watched the back of his head and tried to summon up the support I thought he might need. When he spoke it was as though it was from very far away.

'I think, maybe, her mind has shut down. She just looks blank most of the time. When I talk to her it's as though she isn't there Lucy.' He exhaled slowly. 'When she came back from London the first time, I saw an element of it. But over the last few months she's shed the layers of fear she had.' He shrugged. 'Until she thought she was ready to go back, and when she did...' He threw his hands up in despair then turned to face Lucy.

'Why couldn't she just stay with us? Why did she have to go off and be so, so, stupid?' he asked loudly, spitting his sadness as he spoke. I slowly shook my head, I didn't know what to say. I didn't know why Harry's mother would leave her family but I understood why women were angry at their lot in life. My own mother seemed chained to the kitchen sink and although I was encouraged to swim I was constantly being reminded it wasn't a vocation. Despite the boys and men who trained at the same baths being encouraged to compete in ever more punishing competitions. Even discussions of them taking part in future Olympics.

I didn't have those discussions. Though I did dream of them. But to be a woman achieving those dreams, I had to be allowed to have a choice over my own education and whether or not I wished to marry. And since that wasn't a choice I was allowed to have, I could see the value in women having the same rights as men and being able to vote. To vote over one's lot in life seemed to be an incredibly straightforward decision.

One that I couldn't understand why it was taking so long for others to reach the same conclusion.

Despite all of that, I remained conflicted. I still didn't agree with Harry's mother leaving her own family to fight in London. Even though if it weren't for those women, I and others may never receive a voice. I felt to leave one's own children behind was forgetting a part of you.

Harry looked at me for comfort and I did the only thing I could think of, I put my arm around this man-child and held him, stroking his head, murmuring platitudes I couldn't be certain I could guarantee.

Chapter Eleven

DECEMBER 1911, BLACKPOOL

When it came to Christmas that year, I helped Mother as much as I could, whilst trying to help Harry whose mother had taken to her bed. I took my sister to help me gather the mistletoe and swathes of ivy we enjoyed decorating the house with and brought Harry's siblings along as well.

They were very sweet. I enjoyed spending time with them as we made paper chains to decorate our front parlour and kitchen. They were all swept up in the joy of the season and I enjoyed seeing Christmas through their eyes; it was glittery and sparkly with the prospect of a jolly man delivering presents on Christmas morning. It was in stark contrast to the bleakness Harry's mother brought with her wherever she went. If I spent too long in her company I would worry the darkness that seemed to have overcome her would cover me like coal dust and I'd somehow become infected with it.

She made it much harder to visit Harry's house. Not because I wasn't invited but I couldn't bear to be around so much despair. I felt for the little ones too, especially as Harry's father was out much of the time. I suspected he was using work as a way of keeping himself away from the house and its sadness. Still, I did what I could. I helped make paper decorations with the children and hung them over their fireplace, the bright colours attempting to warm up the chill that had settled on their house. I looked out old long socks of Harry's father's and encouraged the children to tie bright red and green ribbons on them so we could hang them over the fireplace, ready to be filled.

Mother made them a Christmas cake and I took the children to our house to help decorate it with ice-skating figures that brought a smile to their faces. Maybe the cake was a reminder of happier times in their home life. Maybe it was just because they were out of the house, but that afternoon a few days before Christmas Day was the happiest I'd seen the children in a long time.

We fed them chestnuts we'd roasted over our fire and when I returned the children to Harry's house, warm, fed and happy, he was thankful. Tired from working and sourcing the things his mother would have done in previous years such as a turkey, but he was smiling.

A week after Christmas Day Harry returned home early from the shop to check in on his mother. She'd been in good spirits that morning, singing in the kitchen and kissing all of them goodbye as they left, but he wanted to be sure she was eating.

When he got to the house, he told me he knew. He knew as soon as he stepped over the door-frame because his home didn't feel the same anymore.

He found his mother's body slumped in front of the fire in the kitchen, her eyes glazed as the sleeping tablets she'd been hoarding for months had done their fatal job. She was surrounded by mementoes – ribbons awarded for prizes at school, her dried wedding bouquet and the Christmas cake decorations.

She died holding a photograph of all of them standing stiffly on Blackpool beach, their smiles frozen forever.

Chapter Twelve

JANUARY 1912, BLACKPOOL

M y life changed after that. I went from thirteen with few consequences, to understanding that sometimes the world can be horrendous. I couldn't believe someone would leave their family behind but I think I also somehow understood that sometimes a nugget of something so hard and sad can take hold so that the person disappears. I think that's what happened to Harry's mother.

She'd campaigned for something she believed strongly in, only to be met with constant opposition. She and the suffragettes were trying to do something for all of us but they were met with so much misunderstanding. Even I knew. I could read the headlines, I could see the way the papers pitted the readers against the campaign.

My beloved father believed the nonsense in the papers. He would read out actions of the Women's Defence League and tut and shake his head.

'But Father, shouldn't we have the vote? Shouldn't we have a say about the future?' I challenged one day as we sat in front of the fire. Mother was darning, I was practising my stitches on a scrap of material. Father laughed a little.

'If you got the vote, what would you vote for? Who would you vote for? No, we don't need the thoughts of the weaker sex diluting the political process, surely you can see that. The men make the decisions, it's the best way.'

'But...' I began and Mother caught my wrist and gave it a light squeeze so that I would look in her direction, where she shook her head a little.

'Speaking of men making decisions, I bumped into Mr Swarbrick yesterday and he was asking after you. He seemed to think you weren't going to swim anymore.' My father looked over his newspaper at me keenly.

'I just— I thought maybe I was getting too old for it. Some of the girls have left school already, they're not swimming anymore. I thought I wouldn't be returning when lessons restarted,' I replied quietly.

Father shook his head, his seat creaking a little as he moved.

'Nonsense. We'll continue to send you to school for as long as we can. I may not agree with women getting a vote, but I do think it's important for you to get as much of an education as you can. That way, I hope, you'll have an interest in the world around you. So when you marry, you can travel, or at least be able to speak with intellect on subjects to your husband and your friends.' He cleared his throat to indicate he'd finished.

'I see. Of course, and the swimming?'

'Well, I thought I made it perfectly clear. Mr Swarbrick thinks you have talent, so we want you to continue. Maybe now Harry is out of the picture you'll focus more.'

My mother made a stifled noise and I looked up from my haphazard darning, confused.

'Harry's out of the picture? How?'

'Ah,' he looked a little uncomfortable, 'Mother, haven't you told her?' Father watched her as she looked off to the fire, lost for a moment. I watched her too.

'I saw Harry yesterday, we're going to the pictures on Sunday.' I was adamant. I wanted to be with Harry and help him, it's all I'd been doing since his mother had passed.

Mother put her sewing to the side and took my hands. My needle was caught in the middle. It pressed into my hand, lending a slight painful pressure to her hold.

'Lucy. Harry's father has decided they, the whole family, should move. He's taking them to his sister's in York.'

My stomach felt as though it had been sliced in two.

'But Harry, he doesn't have to go with them.'

Mother looked at Father. In the silence a log cracked and popped in the fire, sending glowing shards across the fireplace.

'No, he's decided he's going to join them. He wants to help his family.' The way she was holding my hands was putting pressure on the needle. I could feel it begin to slowly pierce my skin and I held onto the pain. It made sense, at least this pain had a physical reason, rather than what was happening to my heart.

'But he didn't mention that. I saw him yesterday,' I stammered and tried not to cry, instead clenching my hand into the needle, urging it in.

'I'm sorry but it's for the best.' Mother released her grasp and I opened my hand. The needle had only lightly penetrated my palm so that when I withdrew it there was barely a scratch, or droplet of blood to show for the pain it had caused.

She explained how Harry had left yesterday not long after seeing me. He hadn't wanted to say goodbye and thought it best to disappear.

I heard all this. I heard all the explanations. But all I kept returning to was one question – best for who?

***

For a few weeks I was in despair. I'd go to school where the teacher's words would float over me, not making any sense. I'd stare at my notebooks and chalkboards blankly, unable to correlate what had been said to what I needed to write.

It felt like words, actions, everything was too difficult for my body to recall. I would sit listlessly during our short breaks between lessons, ignoring my friends and their entreaties to join them and discuss the boys they had their eyes on.

Even Lorna became infuriated with me. She'd sit with me as often as she could, in some misplaced belief that by being with me I'd somehow be made better. Whole again. As though the last few weeks hadn't happened. My boyfriend's mother hadn't killed herself. My boyfriend hadn't upped and left, choosing a life with his family over any more time with me.

'You'll be better when you can swim again,' she told me, lightly patting my arm. 'When they reopen the baths you can power up and down with these ridiculously long arms and then you can tire out all the thoughts you have in your head.'

I looked at her and blinked slowly, painfully.

'But I don't want to tire out the thoughts. I miss him Lorna.'

She smiled and hugged me, the straggly loose ends of her hair tickling my cheek in the process.

'Well, at least we have you talking again. For a while back there I was beginning to think you'd forgotten how.' She smiled again and I nodded. Talking was difficult. Mother wanted to talk but I couldn't do it. I wanted to go to my bed when I returned home so that I could cover my face with my blankets and make the world disappear from view.

'Look Lucy, I know you miss him. But he's gone, you need to realise that. No amount of you sitting here and pining will bring him back,' she said wisely. 'You would do best to try and just get on with things. Take up another hobby, keep yourself busy before swimming starts again or, I don't know, read. Do something to take your mind off him.' She hugged me again. 'Don't lose yourself too.'

As she walked away, leaving me in the silence I had craved for weeks, I sat there on the bench and watched her laughing with the other girls. Friends of mine. There was so much light and warmth between the four of them. They radiated happiness like sunshine and, like a lizard which needed heat to refuel, I realised I needed their light too.

Standing up, I dusted off my skirt and walked slowly to them. As I got there they smiled.

'Here she is,' Elsie grinned, 'ready to have a laugh?'

Chapter Thirteen

FEBRUARY 1912, BLACKPOOL

'Oh, Mother,' I looked at the kitchen table piled high with teatime treats, 'this is delightful.' I ran to her and hugged her.

'I was particularly pleased with the cake,' she smiled shyly. 'I had hoped it would be just right for a fourteen-year-old.' She shook her head. 'How can you be fourteen already? You're becoming a lady now.' Her smile was tinged with sadness. 'You won't be looking up to me for much longer, will you?' I hugged her again.

'I think that's tricky Mother. I'm already the same height as you.' I moved quickly to avoid the sting from the tea towel as she attempted to whip my legs.

'I can find someone else to eat it if you like?'

She laughed as I immediately shook my head. 'No, it's mine. I'll share of course,' I added.

'We should leave some for Father.' As head groomsman at the house down the road, Father was out many hours of the day, but I knew when he returned it would be with some sort of treat he'd secured for me.

'Your sister should be along any time soon,' Mother smoothed my hair down, 'but before she is, I have a little gift for you.' She brought out a small package from her apron. It was loosely wrapped in a piece of fabric I recognised as an offcut from the curtains she'd made for our bedroom a week or so previously. It was covered in tiny cherries, each popping with crimson.

'What is it?' I held the small package between my hands.

'You have to open it,' she smiled. Her smile was always a quiet one, never big and flashing teeth, but ever present and bringing wrinkles to her eyes. I unfolded the cotton and gasped.

'But these are yours,' I said, taking the tiny blue-stoned earrings out of the material and holding them up to the light.

'My mother gave me these when I turned fourteen, I felt it made sense to give them to you on your birthday. I'll pierce your ears so you can wear them.'

'Oh, they're just beautiful. Thank you, really.' I held onto the earrings as though they were precious diamonds.

'As beautiful as you,' she said, before her words were drowned out by the din made by Alice's return home from school. She never entered a room quietly, there was always a sense of hubris and chaos in her midst – a dropped bag, a scuffed shoe, an exclamation at some misplaced thought she had about her looks. Selfishly I enjoyed the time I'd have at home when it was peaceful without her, but when she came through, planting big kisses on my cheeks and exclaiming at the tea, I decided she wasn't all that bad.

'Can we have cake?' Alice asked, looking pointedly at the Victoria sponge cake my mother had piped with cream. She'd filled it with her own strawberry jam too, and the smell was making my mouth water.

'Let's have these first,' I suggested, leaning in and popping a sandwich in my mouth. 'Delicious.' The three of us tucked in, and Mother held back a plate for Father. Then I remembered something.

'Today, in school, Miss Pollard was telling us about someone who swam across the English Channel last year.' I shook my head and looked my mother. 'Can you imagine that? Swimming that far? They went to *France.*' The feat. It was incredible. 'Can you imagine swimming that far? It took the chap almost twenty-four hours to get there.' I finished my cake. 'He must have been exhausted.'

'He's a man, he's strong – he's bound to have been brilliant. No women have done it,' my sister chimed in whilst cramming cake and sandwiches in her mouth between sips of hot tea.

'No women have done it – yet,' I replied. 'But there's no reason why they couldn't, is there, Mother?' I interrupted her pouring of tea.

'Well, no,' she frowned, 'but women have other duties which men don't, which get in the way of making an exhibition of themselves and swimming silly distances. It's not very necessary. Is it?'

My sister asked the question I didn't want to. 'What duties?'

'Well,' my mother came over and wiped a little cream from Alice's nose with the side of a napkin, 'having and bringing up children for one.' She smiled at the two of us. 'Then there's looking after the house and looking after your husband. He's out all day working. The least we can do is make ourselves and our home presentable,' she added.

'Mother, there are other options too,' I chided lightly. 'We don't have to have babies and create a house for a husband.'

She turned away from me and began folding and re-folding the tea towel in her hands, looking away from us and fussing with something on the dresser. When she spoke it was quietly authoritative.

'If you want any kind of life in the future you'll find a husband and settle down and have children with him. We can't guarantee you security Lucy. A marriage will do that for you.'

There was a silence at the table as I wrestled with what she was saying and what Lorna had learnt from her moth-er, something she'd told me about earlier that day. Lorna's mother worked at the Dupont house, like Harry's mother had. She'd heard at a recent suffragette meeting a speaker inciting other women to remain single and in control of their own estate. She'd been talking of attending another demonstration, this one involving damage to windows in

London and she'd been speaking of never allowing a man to control her.

'Have you given it to her?' I heard Mother ask my sister who shook her head. 'She chose you something.'

Alice produced a paper-covered gift from a bag. 'I hope you like it.'

When I opened it I had my second gasp of the day, a beautiful wooden jewellery box.

'Mother and I spotted it in one of the little shops on the front,' she explained happily and I leapt from the table to hug her dearly.

'Thank you, thank you, this is lovely.'

A few hours later when Father arrived, he called me into the snug where he was sat, warming up after a long day outside dealing with the horses.

'Happy birthday, Lucy.' He smiled and held up a box wrapped in gold paper which reflected the flames, casting the light behind Father in an orange hue. I peeled open the paper and a waft of the most heavenly scent reached its way out.

'Yardley's April Violets,' I read from the box which was decorated with delicate purple blooms.

'Well, put it on then – you're becoming a young lady Lucy and I've been told by some of the girls at the house that it is all anyone's wearing.' My father sipped on a small brandy as I opened the box carefully and withdrew the bottle.

I unstoppered it and dashed a little on both sides of my neck as I'd seen my mother do and inhaled the scent.

'Delicious, you smell like a summer's day,' Father enthused and raised his glass to me. 'Happy birthday.'

Chapter Fourteen
April 1912, Blackpool

M y birthday disappeared into a distant memory as the months of 1912 flipped over on my teacher's desk calendar. Soon the weather was beginning to warm again, meaning that the swimming baths were to reopen.

On the way to the pool I overheard a newspaper boy yelling about the *Titanic*, a ship we'd all been daydreaming about since it had left Liverpool docks. Interested in all things nautical and aquatic and wondering what marvels we would hear about this time, I moved closer to hear what he was saying. It was truly a beautiful ship and one I had secret hopes to travel on one day.

However as I neared the paperboy I saw the headline he was brandishing. '*Titanic Sinks, 1500 dead*'. The sentence sent shivers down my spine. Imagining what those final hours for those passengers must have been like. How so many may not have known how to swim. How many children would have died? I knew then that whatever happened with my competitive swimming, I would make it my life's mission to teach others. Even if there was never another '*Titanic*', it would help save some lives, I was sure of it.

Knowing this made my re-entry to the pool a little easier, even if when I entered the water it was a shock at first to be back. The water felt cold and my muscles complained. But once I'd eased out my body in the water with a relaxed few lengths, the muscle memory kicked in and I began to feel at home once again.

Mr Swarbrick was keen to push me. When I'd been back swimming for a few weeks, he came to the pool with a gleam in his eye.

'Miss Morton, fancy a challenge?' He waggled his pocket-watch at me.

'Yes, of course. What is it?'

'I would like you to swim as quickly as you can, doing either breaststroke or backstroke. I found out the men's Olympic times and thought it would be fun to see where you compared,' he grinned.

The Olympics was taking place in Stockholm and for the first time women had been allowed to compete, but only in the freestyle categories, which was interesting but not something I could compare myself with as I swam backstroke and breaststroke. Still, it was so exciting to think there was even the smallest of chances that one day I might even get to enter it – all they needed to do was add the categories I wanted to compete in.

Then all I'd have to do was get accepted on to the team, although I had a feeling it wouldn't be as straightforward as that.

'Oh yes, that sounds like terrific fun. Shall we get some of the other girls to have a go too?' I asked, looking over at Greta and Lorna, currently doing backstroke lengths.

Mr Swarbrick smiled. 'Yes, of course, the more the merrier.' He looked over to the collection of Christ Church girls. 'I say, girls, fancy a quick race?' There were shrieks of excitement as they all made their way over to the side where I was.

'You must all hold the side of the pool then listen out for my whistle. As soon as I blow it you can swim. You need to complete four lengths and I'll see how you do against the Olympians according to *The Telegraph* results. Winner gets a bar of chocolate.' He smiled again as the incentive got the girls chatting amongst each other again.

'This is the two hundred yards breaststroke, so none of that Australian crawl nonsense,' he reminded us all. 'Now hang on to the side. And...' He blew sharply on his whistle and I went off as though I was being chased. My fastest stroke was breaststroke and I pulled myself quickly through the water. I was deafened to the rest of the girls and ignored them and what they were doing. All I focused on was pulling myself through the water.

On the second turn I narrowly avoided crashing into Greta who was on my left but continued powering down the lane. My breathing was coming in huge gulps and I felt like my lungs were going to explode. I knew I'd left some of the girls behind but I was well aware some were in front of me. As I entered the final length I could feel the beginning of a horrendous headache begin to form at the front of my eyes and I tried to keep it at bay. I kept looking ahead, counting the dips I needed to do to just get to the end.

I could feel my whole body tiring as the end seemed to be moving out further and further away, the heat in my shoulders was pulsating and my legs were screaming in defiance of being kicked anymore, but still I pushed on. As I broke through to the end I slammed my hands on to the side, my lungs heaving so hard I was convinced they, and I, were going to pop.

'Nice one, Lucy. Not bad.' Greta smiled beside me, astonishingly serene despite swimming as hard as me.

'Th-thanks.' I looked around as I saw the rest of the girls making their way in. 'Who was first?'

'Me, of course. You've still got a bit of a way to go before you beat this old pro,' Greta laughed gaily. 'I've got two years' more experience than you – but don't worry, you're not far off. I'm sure I'll be stepping aside soon,' she comforted me.

It didn't help, though, as I realised I had been desperate to win. The urge inside me felt like a hot hunger. I was terribly upset with myself for not making it to the end first.

'Greta, well done. You did it in,' Mr Swarbrick consulted his pocket-watch, 'five minutes and twenty-three seconds. Not bad. The men did it in about four minutes – but they're going to be stronger than you.' He looked at me, my breathing still a little jagged.

'Lucy, you were five seconds behind her.' He paused and looked at me. 'Not bad.'

Not bad wasn't good enough.

The next day I returned to the baths and attempted to do it again. This time I tried to pace myself, but still on the final length I found my breathing feeling as though it was going to make me pop, like a balloon. And when I reached the side and looked at the clock on the wall I was closer to five minutes thirty. Slower than the day before.

I repeated this for the next three days, so that by Friday I was taking over six minutes to complete the lengths and when I saw Lorna on the Saturday she laughed at my despondency.

'What did you expect? That you'd somehow out-pace Greta? She's got more experience than you,' she chided as we walked to the picture house, our arms looped into each other. We had decided to see one of the moving pictures that day, *Dr Jekyll and Mr Hyde*.

I felt irritable towards her, she had no idea.

'No, I didn't think I'd outswim her, but I did think I'd improve this week,' I admitted glumly and she softened towards me.

'Look, you're probably just tired – it's not a good idea to train every day, you need a break occasionally and allow your body to, I don't know, prepare itself for the next time you need to use it like that?'

We went to pay for our tickets and I thought on what she said. I did need to give myself time. I'd certainly felt tired all week, and my headaches had come and gone. I'd even considered staying in bed today as I had such terrible back pain, but I'd ignored it.

All these symptoms made sense when I returned home from the pictures and visited the bathroom where, I discovered in the late-evening light, I had begun my monthlies. I was quite a late starter according to my mother, but she thought as I was so slim it might have had an impact. When I came in and told her in hushed tones that I was in need of some things, she came with me and showed me how to use the sanitary napkins and hold them in place with the unwieldy belt.

'Welcome to womanhood,' she whispered, and held me close for a hug in the doorway of our kitchen, whilst the smell of roast pork came through from the oven.

My monthlies were not a welcome addition to my life. They meant that for a week every month, I couldn't swim. And for a week before it, I was convinced they affected how I swam. I was slower, more sluggish. But the week after they had ended I could swim faster and harder. I was frustrated by my own body and decided to train for longer distances, but still as quickly as I could.

I focused on breaststroke and made it a goal to swim a mile every day in the pool, pushing through the water as rhythmically as I could. Some days my sister would come along with me, she had begun swimming the year before and was already showing some promise. She and I would power up and down the lanes, encouraging each other to keep going, to push through the pain. More often than not, though, she would stop a few lengths before me and practise her dives into the water. She would yell encouragement to me between disappearing below the water and appearing back out on the side.

'Come on, Luce, you can do it. Come on, push,' she yelled one day as I was beginning to slow up. She was stretching on the side, lean and catlike, her swimming hat on the floor and her hair dishevelled.

'Can't, I think I've got a stitch,' I shouted, as much as I could to be heard over the echoing din of the baths.

Mr Swarbrick arrived behind Alice and shook his head.

'No such thing. Come on, Miss Morton, get it done – I've something to tell you.'

I continued to push through my lengths, knocking them down with just three to go. One of the reasons I enjoyed swimming was because it made sense to me. As soon as I got in the water I understood the mechanics of it, my body could feel the momentum it needed to propel me forward, and my body worked in spite of me. It was as though I was born into water. All my body asked was that I remained alive, something I was happy to agree to. The payoff for me was that I didn't have to think about anything until I got back out of the pool.

Life *felt* complicated at the moment. School didn't make sense all of the time, I still missed Harry, though I didn't talk about him to anyone now. And I felt like women were within a grasping distance of something which they couldn't quite access. I didn't fully understand what it was, but I did know I wanted to reach it. Whatever *it* was. But without the disastrous results that Harry's mother encountered.

Finishing the final length I focused ahead, watching Mr Swarbrick near the edge in his heavy woollen suit, all dark and thick. I never could understand how he didn't overheat and swoon like those women of Mother's age who still retained their corsets.

As I reached the edge of the pool, Mr Swarbrick extended his hand and helped to pull me, heaving for breath, out onto the side.

'Looking good, Miss Morton, you've shaved another four seconds or so off your time.' He smiled at me as I tried to catch my breath.

He recovered himself and blushed a little.

'Sorry, better get to the news before you up and leave for the changing rooms,' he nodded at me. 'Right, straight to it. You've managed to get a few second places at the BES swimming galas.' He looked at me and I smiled in agreement, I'd been pleased and irritated in equal measures at coming second. 'Well,' he continued, 'there's a few more of those coming up but what's interested me is there's an open event coming up soon – which means anyone can take part – and I think you've got a very good chance of winning it. Even though you'll be up against a mixture of people of different ages and experience.'

'What is it?' I asked, my interest piqued.

'The Northern Counties Amateur Swimming Association's breaststroke championship.' He paused for a moment. 'It's in a fortnight – I've already signed you up.'

I grinned. 'Good. I want to do it.'

'I thought that would be the case, I think you'll be great.' Mr Swarbrick smiled back and Alice clapped her hands together.

'You're going to be brilliant.'

Chapter Fifteen

APRIL 1912, WIGAN

For the next fortnight I trained even harder than before, pushing myself just as I knew the girls I'd be
competing against would be from all different swimming
clubs, and I didn't know how good they'd be. I did know
that some of the best swimmers in the region would be
there though.

On the day, Father came with Mr Swarbrick. The
championships were taking place at one of the swimming
baths in Wigan.

'Bit busy isn't it?' Father commented on our arrival,
when a taxicab motorcar almost caught us on our way in.

'It's the biggest meet for the season, we won't be back
here for another year now. All the best swimmers are here
Alfred,' he told my father as he motioned me towards a
changing area. 'You need to go over there. Here's your
number.' He gave me a piece of fabric with my number
to pin to my swimming costume. 'You're up in half an

hour. Go and do a few practice lengths, but don't show what you're really made of. We'll go in the stands and find a spot.'

He stopped and looked at me, sincerity in his eyes.

'You're ready for this, Lucy. I assure you.'

I left the two behind and pushed open the heavy wooden door which led to a series of changing rooms. Many girls were already preparing but I eventually found a space where I could change into my swimming uniform. It wasn't all that cold in the room but I could feel goose-bumps beginning to prickle under my skin.

'Nervous?' a tall girl with blonde hair she was tying into an elaborate knot on top of her head asked.

'Not really. You?' I mustered as much confidence as possible. I wasn't nervous but there was definitely a feeling of trepidation or excitement starting to leach through me.

'I'm fine, see you at the end,' she called out and walked off full of swagger.

'Ignore her, best of luck and all that,' a shorter redhead told me before disappearing through the same door the blonde had gone through.

Swallowing down the bile which had peaked at the back of my throat, I took a deep breath and followed them both.

***

The noise hit me first.

Shouts echoing around the walls. Screams of excitement from spectators as events took place. The smell was the second. A mixture of fuggy dampness akin to my own baths, but mixed with a hint of something chemically enhanced that left a tang in the air. It felt muggy too. Not warm, not dry. Somewhere in-between. The warmth of many people pressed into one room and a stickiness created by sweaty, soggy clothes and the water being splashed onto the side by competing swimmers.

Although I'd taken part in a couple of competitions last year, they were much less professional than this one was. I could see umpires, respectably dressed men all in tweed, sat on chairs behind a desk watching the competitions. There were other people who seemed to have a role too, including men and women at the end of the pool, marking their lanes and declaring winners.

I looked around and spotted Father and Mr Swarbrick in the stands. They had relatively good seats, four rows from the front where they appeared to be enjoying a cup of tea. When they spotted me they both nodded and smiled and I grinned back.

My nerves, which I'd rarely been bothered with in the past, seemed to have arrived in the form of a variety of different-sized butterflies in my stomach and every time I looked at the water they fluttered a little.

'Miss Morton?' an official in his requisite tweed asked me. I nodded and he ticked me off his list. 'Over there.' He pointed to the end of the pool where some of the others I recognised from the changing room were warming up by stretching their legs and arms. I hesitated as I realised I'd not be able to practise in the water, but looked at what the others were doing.

Mr Swarbrick had run me through a warm-up on the side of the pool before, but I hadn't paid that much attention as I could always leap into the water. Mimicking the redhead I'd seen in the changing room who stood a few feet from me, I stretched my arms to my feet and touched my toes, then swung out from side to side to stretch my back. Peeling myself upwards I leant my arms over to the left, then to the right, and felt a stretch down my side. I pummelled my thighs with my fists a little to warm up the muscles. Finally I stretched my arms out in front, to the left, to the right and down again to warm them up.

'Ladies, if we're ready.' Another tweed had come over, this one bespectacled, and we all dutifully followed him. He indicated the places we needed to stand for our lanes. I was in the second lane. I tried not to be disappointed or distracted as I didn't much like that position. It meant I wouldn't be as aware of the other swimmers or where they were.

Unnerved, I looked for Mr Swarbrick and Father and giggled as they both waved. They believed in me. I needed to believe too. Just because I was competing against a few people I hadn't met before, it shouldn't be an issue. I refocused and looked towards the end of the pool. I imagined getting there, turning and coming back. I imagined being at the end. I saw gold. I needed to believe that.

'Ladies, take your positions,' a voice came from a megaphone and excited shouts came from the sides.

The butterflies had stopped, replaced with excitement. I crouched down and held the side as Mr Swarbrick had taught me and listened for the whistle which marked the start.

When I heard it everything else disappeared. I dove into the water and kicked hard, then rose to the surface and began powering down the lane. I felt as though I were floating above myself as the strokes came easily to me. The water felt like velvet as it flowed over my shoulders. Whenever I pushed through it was as though I was gliding. I barely even noticed the other two swimmers beside me as I kept pushing.

I turned, repeated the length, pushed away, the third stretch of four and powered to the end of the lane, then turned for the final time. I couldn't hear anything above the blood pulsing in my ears and my heart thumping. I was sure I was breathing but couldn't hear or feel it.

All I could see was the end.

I kept pushing, kept swimming. Kept gliding. Kept floating. My shoulders ached, my legs felt as though they were on fire.

And then I reached the side and threw my hand out.

To be beaten by the blonde from the changing room.

I had second place.

Chapter Sixteen

'Well done, well done,' Mr Swarbrick said, 'such a good time, well done.' He turned to my father. 'Didn't she do well? Marvellous. I say we have a competitor on our hands.' He disappeared amongst the crowd mentioning something about my certificate, and left me standing with my father as other swimmers and their entourages pressed in around us. The space was tight and there were too many bodies. I felt hot and overwhelmed.

And really sad.

'Lucy, you did so, so well.' Father placed a hand on my shoulder. 'I've never seen you swim so fast. You were motoring down that lane like a fox after a chicken,' he placated. 'The other girl, the one who won, it was by just a second, I believe.'

'A second too long then, wasn't I?' I didn't want to admit to myself that I'd not won, I kept replaying the swim. Surely I'd had it?

'I hear she's a very good competitor that one.' Father nudged me a little in the ribs. 'She's taken gold in every race she's entered for the past eighteen months.' He softened his voice a little so I had to lean in and listen with so much else going on around us. 'You did incredibly well to get as close to her as that. You're younger than her. You'll have your day. I know you will.'

'Ah, not moved then.' Mr Swarbrick had reappeared. 'Got them.' He brandished a certificate embellished with black cursive lettering, which I could see contained my name and in his other hand he held up something else. 'This one is beautiful, Lucy, nicest one you've had so far, I reckon.' He smiled and held out my medal.

As I accepted it, noting its weight, I turned it over in my hand. On one side the gold-metalled medal was embellished with a picture of what appeared to be a Greek goddess, bestowing a victor with a crown of leaves whilst shaking their left hand. I turned it over, feeling the raised embellishments of the words '*Northern Counties Amateur Swimming Association*' on the back. A golden-leaved wreath where the words '*Ladies Breaststroke Championship 1912, Second Prize, won by*' had been neatly engraved, whereas my name had been hastily added, slightly off-centre to the left.

'That sums it up I think. Slightly off-centre,' I mumbled, 'not quite at my best.'

Mr Swarbrick and Father looked at each other and shrugged their shoulders in a 'not a clue what she's on about' kind of a way, but I knew. To win next year I'd have to do better. Be better.

On the way home, as the two men discussed the prospects for Blackpool in the next round of the FA Cup,

I thumbed the medal, considering ways I could shave off time.

The next day, being a Sunday, I couldn't swim, but on the Monday I was back in the pool, with Mr Swarbrick poolside and he looked serious.

'I've been thinking about your times, Miss Morton,' his moustache twitched as he spoke. 'You were very, very close to winning it on Saturday and, although I'm still very proud of what you achieved I was thinking on it – and you.' He paused and looked at me as I threw water over myself in a bid to make the impact from the pool water less cold when I got in. 'But you're right, you could have done it. So we need to look at where we can save time. I think I've spotted three weaknesses, three areas for you to focus on.'

'And they are?' I was relieved he wasn't going to disagree with me and keep telling me everything I'd done was perfect. It wasn't and I was going to do better. I couldn't improve if I was told I did everything I could.

'One,' he began counting them off with his fingers, 'your turns. They could be smoother. I think you've got clumsy with them and could be more precise. We need to drill those as much as possible.' I nodded. He was right.

'Two, you're spending too much time up,' he craned his neck to demonstrate, 'out of the water between pushing through strokes. You need to come down quicker and spend more time in the water than out of it.'

'Well, hang on, I was only doing it how you showed me,' I remonstrated. All this honesty was beginning to have a slight effect on me.

Mr Swarbrick nodded.

'Yes, and I thought we were right.' He stopped. 'I thought *I* was right. But I watched the other girls who were swimming too, and your head was coming out higher than a lot of them. The one who won practically glided through the water, barely coming out for air. I think that's what we need to do with you.'

I nodded, put like that it sounded reasonable.

'Right, head closer to the water, quicker turns, and the last thing?'

'Ah,' Mr Swarbrick looked a little uncomfortable. 'I think maybe your costume might be affecting you a touch too.' He tried not to look at my body as he spoke about it. 'That material is heavy. I think some of your competitors were wearing different materials to you. Not that I looked closely you understand,' he rushed to explain to me. Even though the idea of moustachioed and ancient Mr Swarbrick would have done anything else was ridiculous, I nodded to make sure he knew I was listening. 'But I know that in the Olympics, for instance, some of the competitors are wearing silk. We can't afford that, but I feel there must be a middle ground between your woollen garment and the silken ones at the Olympics.'

I tried not to go red as I didn't want Mr Swarbrick to be embarrassed at embarrassing me with this talk of silk garments. As far as I was concerned a silk item was usually what rich ladies wore for undergarments. I'd heard of brassieres from Paris being made of silk.

'Right. So I'll focus on my turns and my tendency to come out of the water and you focus on, erm,' I giggled a little, 'swimwear.' Mr Swarbrick reddened and took a handkerchief out of the breast pocket of his jacket, pressing it lightly to his forehead.

'We'll have enough of that, thank you. In the pool.' He raised his heavy eyebrows at me and I did as I was told. 'Now, let's see those turns.'

Chapter Seventeen

MAY 1912, BLACKPOOL

'You're back, at last,' Mother sighed. 'Lucy, you've been at that pool every night this week after school. It's too much,' she shook her head. 'You look exhausted.'

I decided that I wouldn't let her know I'd been going before school on some days too, as the pool was much quieter then and I just nodded a little.

'I am a little tired and famished,' I admitted.

'I can do something about that, sit down.' She indicated the seat near to the kitchen door. The early summer warmth was beginning to creep over the threshold, lending the room heat and a honeyed late-afternoon light.

'Mutton, cabbage and potatoes.' Mother placed a plate of food in front of me and my stomach growled in reply. 'Go on then, tuck in.' She sat to watch as I forked each mouthful in.

'It's good,' I managed between inhalations.

'I know, I made it – it was lunch, which you weren't back for. Once that's gone I've got a crumble and some custard, which should hit the spot.' She smiled as I carried on wolfing the food down and gulping the glass of milk she'd set by my side.

'You need to keep your strength up. I may not know much about swimming, but I know you're beginning to disappear. You need lots of fuel to keep that engine going,' she indulged, watching for when I'd had the last mouthful of mutton and had pushed the plate away, to be replaced with a generous portion of crumble in a bowl.

'Thank you,' I managed once I'd finished off the pudding, the combination of the food and a lot of exercise beginning to catch up with me. I tried stifling a yawn, but she caught me.

'Bed.'

'But, Mother, it's not even seven o'clock,' I replied, though even I could hear the catches of exhaustion in my voice.

'No. Bed. No discussion – and tomorrow, you need a break. Your body isn't going to like being forced to swim every day, it'll do you good to have a day off.' She spoke so forcefully, I decided there wasn't much I could do to dissuade her. And if I was honest with myself, it felt like every part of my body was beginning to ache constantly.

Mother softened as she saw me straighten up and begin to make my way out of the kitchen.

'You and Lorna should go along to see if you can catch a glimpse of that princess tomorrow, the one that's coming to open some of the promenade. It could be fun. I've heard the council have some sort of surprise up their sleeve for it,' she grinned. 'Might be worth popping along to see, eh?' I nodded, as much because I couldn't find words but also because it wasn't worth arguing with her.

'Good girl.'

The next morning I was somehow allowed to sleep in. Father had already gone to the manor house to work, Alice had gone to work in the bank for the morning. I wasn't needed for my weekend job at the small dress shop on the high street as it was closed due to the royal visit and the opportunity of the quiet in the house and the peace of knowing I didn't have to go anywhere until midday was truly joyous.

I spent the morning enjoying a leisurely pot of tea and reading some of the newspapers Father had left behind. The May sunshine was keen to put its time in and I sat bathed in a pool of summer light. I must have nodded off, however, because I was awoken by Lorna standing over me, repeatedly telling me something. I tried to tune her in like a radio.

'Come on Lucy, you were meant to meet me half an hour ago. I've been waiting forever for you, come on,' she repeated, pulling on my hand. I was befuddled with sleep and warm from the sunlight.

'I think I want to go back to bed,' I grumbled.

Lorna looked sternly at me.

'Not a chance, come on. How often will we see a princess in real life? Come on, I want to see her dress.'

I allowed Lorna to pull and prod me into some kind of acceptable state to be seen in public. She brushed my hair and pulled it back, placed a hat on my head and retied my dress so I looked neater. She stepped back and assessed her efforts.

'Not bad, it could be better but to be honest we don't have all day. Come along.'

I hurried after her through the front door and out into the street. As we walked down towards the more central area of the town I noticed it was getting busier.

'Gosh, look. All those people have flags – I feel so underprepared,' I grimaced and Lorna laughed then tutted.

'Don't worry about that – they're giving them out on the promenade. We'll get a few, then what I want to do is get there soon so we can find a decent spot to watch from. I don't want her walking past and us only seeing her shoes. Or hat.'

I was much taller than Lorna and didn't have the issue with crowds that she did. Still, I knew how much it meant to her, so followed after her swiftly.

As we walked along I enjoyed the carnival feel to the day. When the King's coronation had been held, we'd had a street party where there'd been bunting and flags draped from all the windows in the road. Everyone had dragged a table out into the street and when they were all covered with white flapping table cloths, it looked as though it was one long table. Then all the mothers had brought out plate after plate of food, the fathers produced beer and everyone had a jolly day toasting the King.

Today felt similarly cheerful. Small children bumped into my legs, waving flags and shrieking with joy. Some were swept up onto the shoulders of their fathers or brothers and were pointing at the things they could see as they were carried.

'This way,' Lorna grabbed my hand and we left the sea of people making their way to the promenade to dive down a smaller side alley where it was much less busy. 'Short cut,' she explained breathlessly and I grinned, taking longer strides to keep up. After a few more twists and turns down backstreets I hardly recalled taking in the past, we burst out onto the promenade into a sea of noise.

'It has to be at least five people deep,' Lorna complained as she pointed at the crowd. 'Bother, now what will we do?' She looked up and down the promenade as though looking for inspiration. I looked too, taking in the wealth of flags being waved, the scent of cigarettes and illicit spirits wafting from a nearby public house and the scent of roses coming from somewhere above.

I looked up.

'Lorna, look. There – let's go there.' I pointed at a balcony that overlooked the promenade. It was bedecked in bunting and decorated with a collection of scented roses.

Lorna was incredulous.

'We can't just turn up at someone's flat and demand to be let in. No, we need to think of something else.' She carried on looking up and down the road.

'No, Lorn. Lorna,' I repeated to get her attention, 'I'm sure it's where our swimming teacher lives – he'll let us stand there, I'm sure of it.'

'Old Swarbrick?' Lorna didn't look convinced, but I caught her hand and looked in her deep-blue eyes. 'Trust me.' She nodded and we turned our back on the crowd.

Pushing through, we found a set of stairs leading up to the Sea View Apartments, and stood outside reading the names by the bells.

'Here, I knew it.' I pushed the bell which was marked '*Swarbrick*' and waited for an answer. Nervous and not wanting to miss out, Lorna was beginning to shift from foot to foot. If she had a watch she'd have been looking at it.

'Maybe they're not...' she began but was interrupted by the sound of the door opening and a tiny, white-haired woman standing in the doorway, a large blue blanket wrapped around the majority of her body. I looked behind her to see if I could spot Mr Swarbrick but there was no one else there.

'Yes?' The old lady squinted in the sunshine.

'I'm ever so sorry to trouble you, my name is Lucy, Lucy Morton,' I began and the wizened lady clapped her hands together.

'Oh my dear, my son has told me so much about you. Do come in,' she beckoned, 'but be quick, I want to see Her Highness,' she told us.

'Is that all right, Mrs Swarbrick? I'm sorry – we thought Mr Swarbrick lived here, we were hoping to get a good glimpse of the princess from your balcony as we can't see anything on the pavement,' I explained as we followed the tiny lady up a set of stairs, holding onto a dark ash bannister.

She laughed, a wonderful tinkling sound and stopped on the first floor, turning left to a front door. 'Of course it's fine. I was watching on my own and would be grateful of the company. My son doesn't live with me, though he is here very often.' She smiled and opened the door to a light and airy living room. The ceilings were high and the windows took up one side of the sizeable room. A door to the balcony was ajar and from outside we could hear a lot of cheers.

'Oh, that's why you thought he lived here,' Lorna whispered as we followed Mrs Swarbrick, 'you must have seen him when he was visiting his mother.' I nodded. I'd made the wrong assumption but at least we'd still be able to see properly.

'Come out here,' Mrs Swarbrick beckoned us on to the balcony. As we stepped out we were met with a wonderful roar from the crowd. Some way down the line we could see the princess on the back of a coach, being pulled by a horse. She was waving at the crowd.

'Excellent, plenty of time,' the older lady smiled widely and picked up a flag. 'Want one?' We both took a flag and started waving them. As the princess drew closer some of the crowd began singing the national anthem. The three of us stood on the balcony, waving our flags and singing. With so many people singing at the same time it felt like the world was full of joy. I felt so proud to be British and allowed myself a moment to daydream of a day when I'd have the opportunity to sing the same song whilst being awarded an Olympic medal.

This sensation, of pride in my country and love for the people in it, caused me to stop waving for a brief second and acknowledge how much I wanted success in swimming. I didn't care how many lengths I'd need to swim over the next few years, when the opportunity came I'd take each one and work so hard that one day, I promised myself, I would be the best in the world.

Lorna and I smiled with delight.

'Cake?' Mrs Swarbrick held up a plate of sliced fruit-cake and we both licked our lips.

'Yes please, Mrs Swarbrick,' I replied, taking a large slice of cake and enjoying every mouthful, bathing in the sunshine, the roars of the crowd and the happiness in my heart.

'She looks beautiful doesn't she?' The princess was still waving and, just as she passed us, the lanterns which had been hung along the promenade were lit with electricity.

The whole crowd stopped singing and began to clap.

'It's like artificial sunshine isn't it?' the old lady said, grinning. 'Amazing what they can do these days. Apparently these will be on tonight – can you imagine that? Sunshine in the evening.'

'Imagine.' I grinned.

Chapter Eighteen

OCTOBER 1912, BLACKPOOL

'There's no pressure on today, you just need to enjoy it,' Mr Swarbrick said to me over the noise of the rain pelting on our umbrellas as we made our way to the swimming baths. Our pool was playing host to an inner county championship. My sister and I were competing in different categories but we'd been looking forward to it, and with what had turned into one of the wettest Augusts on record, we'd had plenty of opportunities to practise over the summer.

'Pardon?' I asked of Mr Swarbrick, whose voice had disappeared behind a wall of noise as a horse and cart clattered past us, throwing up huge splashes of dirty water over my bare legs.

'I said, mind out for that cart,' his voice came and went as I giggled and moved a little closer so he could hear me.

'A touch more notice would have been gratefully received Mr Swarbrick.' I grinned as he looked morose, then, on seeing my good humour smiled too.

'Come now, Miss Morton, we're here. Now, remember what I told you,' he began and I held my finger up to shush him.

'Be calm, be in the moment, be relaxed, be joyful and be winning?' I added, watching as his nodding paused with my own last comment.

'Ah, very good. Just give it your best shot. We won't be going for any records today – it's just a local meet-up,' he reiterated.

'With some nice medals to win,' I smiled and then shook my head. 'It's fine Mr Swarbrick. I know you and Mother have been talking, I know you think I've been overdoing it, but I understand this is about enjoyment. I will enjoy it. I promise,' I appeased him. 'Now, don't you need to be judging somewhere?' I reminded him and he smacked his hand to his forehead after checking the time on his fob.

'Gosh, yes. Sorry I can't be on the side-lines cheering you on today, but you know, must do my bit.' He smiled, in a bid to cover up just how much he was looking forward to umpiring some of the competitions today. As we pushed through the double doors, shaking off our umbrellas and stamping our feet to get the droplets to fall from our coats, he leant down to whisper to me.

'I can't be seen as biased to anyone. But best of luck today. I know you'll do brilliantly.' His moustache tickled my ear a little as he spoke and then he'd disappeared, swallowed up into the crowd of familiar and unfamiliar swimming faces.

'Luce, Lucy Goosey,' my sister's voice rang out and I waved as she came running over. 'All the sheets are up, your races aren't until the end. You get a bit of a break – there's one race between them.' She shook her head. 'You'd have barely caught your breath by then.' She looked concerned but I batted it away.

'It's fine. All I can do is give it my best shot. What's the first one?' I kept my fingers crossed she'd say backstroke, I was better at breaststroke and hoped I could make up any losses if my better stroke was second.

'Breaststroke.' Alice pulled a face again. 'Sorry. I've got to go that way,' she explained, pointing to the '*under 12s*' poster that had been scrawled in messy handwriting – writing I was certain Miss Pollard wouldn't have been happy with if I'd produced it at school.

I looked for the '*under 14s*' sign and spotted it a little distance away. 'Right. Good luck, sis, I'll be cheering you on – Mother and Father will be along soon.' I hugged my sister, noting how tall she'd become. I was certain Alice would reach my height soon – and I was, I'd come to realise lately, quite tall for a girl. Still, the height helped in the pool. After watching Alice disappear through the door, I spotted Lorna and yelled over the mass of female heads all making their way towards various age-marked doors.

My friend looked around and I waved frantically to get her attention.

'Lorn – over here,' I cried, laughing and apologising as I accidentally caught someone on the head in my excitement. Lorna turned and waved, and made her way over.

'Have you seen the timings? Bit rubbish for you – but plays to my strengths,' she laughed. 'Still, I reckon you'll give me a run for my money, won't you?' She hooked her arm in mine as we made our way to our door. 'Are you feeling good today?' she pressed. It was part of the pre-race build-up – we always asked each other the same question before a race. If it was a yes, it meant we were ready to give it everything. If it was no, the other had to offer words of encouragement and advice to get them thinking positively.

'Yes, you?'

Lorna scoffed. 'When do I ever not feel ready?' She stuck a hand on her hip and posed like the starlets we saw on movie posters. 'I'm ready as I'll ever be.'

The two of us made our way through to the pool and were noted as being present by an official who looked familiar, though I couldn't place her.

'Who's that?' I whispered to Lorna as we walked away.

'Lucy, you are terrible,' my friend laughed. 'It's Penny's mother.' I must have looked blank because Lora sighed and offered an explanation. 'Penny was the blonde who beat you last season? Kept pipping you to the post in almost every race.'

'Oh, *Penny*. Funny, I've not seen her around.' I searched around for my foe.

'Of course not, she's training with the British team now – made the Olympic squad to compete in the 1916 event in four years' time, lucky so and so,' Lorna grumbled.

'Olympics. But she's so young, isn't she our age?' I couldn't believe something like the Olympics could be open to someone like me, but just as I was daydreaming my way to gold, Lorna interrupted my thoughts with a bubble of laughter.

'No, she's not our age. We're in the over fourteens category aren't we?' I nodded and Lorna, looking satisfied, continued. 'That means anyone aged fourteen to eighteen could compete. There aren't many female competitors over sixteen, what with so few of us being taught how to swim that the competition is quite open at our age group.' She looked at my mouth opening and closing like a fish. 'What? What have I said?'

I shook my head. 'I just had no idea. I thought we were all similar, roughly the same age, you know?'

Lorna scrunched her face up in confusion.

'But don't you see, Lorn? I've been beating myself up for consistently coming second – to a peer,' I emphasised. 'But I haven't. I've been losing to someone with four more years' experience than I have. Four more years' growing, of strength. It was never a fair match.'

Understanding dawned on Lorna's face. 'Oh gosh, yes. I suppose I hadn't thought of it like that. Plus I knew about the age thing, I rather thought everyone did.'

I shrugged. 'There's a chance old Swarbrick told me, maybe I wasn't listening,' I admitted. 'It is the sort of thing that upsets the teachers most terribly about me.'

'Could the competitors in the two-hundred metre breaststroke, please make their way to the pool,' a familiar voice bellowed through a megaphone and I smiled in recognition.

'Speaking of old Swarbrick...' I nudged Lorna and indicated our swimming coach holding the loudspeaker, discussing something with a fellow umpire. He was nodding and in deep conversation as we passed, but still smiled quickly in our direction.

'Lane four, Miss Morton, Miss Smith you're in lane six,' he said to us and we nodded our thanks.

'Right, I best go and do a few stretches,' Lorna told me as she walked off to her lane. 'Prepare yourself for a loss, Luce,' she yelled.

I couldn't think of a smart reply. I never could in the moment, so I let it pass and just shook my head as I made my way to lane four. I shrugged off the large towelling robe which was keeping me warm and laid it on the bench behind me, much like the rest of the swimmers were doing. Bending down to touch my toes, I felt a slight pull in my right hamstring and eased it out with a long stretch. I stood up, taking in deep breaths and stretched side to side, swinging my arms around to get the blood to them and to warm myself up. Hearing my name being shouted, I looked to the stands and saw my father and mother sitting and waving in my direction. I grinned, then refocused on the pool in front of me.

As was usual, the stands realised when a race was due to start before anyone announced it via the megaphone, and a hush fell over the spectators, punctuated solely by a few individual shouts from younger children in the crowd. Too excited to stay silent.

'Ladies. Are you ready?' I crouched by the poolside, as did my competitors and prepared myself to dive in as soon as I heard the whistle.

I dove deep into the cool, familiar waters of my own pool and hammered the lane as hard as I could. Each length went by in a blur and I realised I could hear nothing except for the pulse of blood in my ears and Mr Swarbrick's voice in my head telling me to push. Then, coming into the final length, I felt like the world rushed in again. I could hear screams of excitement, cheering from the stands and a roar from all sides. The water frothed furiously as we all attacked it with vigour.

From the constant stream of blue I'd focused on with every stroke as I'd gone through the pool, suddenly the world was in glorious technicolour. The bricks that held the building up were bright red, the water the most cyan of blues, the glass in the roof the most vivid of greens. All colours were colliding into a rainbow of sound and space.

And then I was at the end.

And being pulled out of the water.

And the crowds were crowing for their home champion. I had done it. Me. First. First. First. First. First.

'I did it?' I asked of the man who had stuck his hand up in the air to say I'd hit the side.

'You did it. You did it very, very well. You did it in four minutes, thirty-two seconds. Very impressive.' He grinned and slapped me on the back. 'You could have heard Mr

Swarbrick from the other side of town, he didn't do well as an unbiased umpire.'

'You did it, Luce, well done.' Lorna had come over, breathing deeply, water dripping off her like a seal that hadn't shaken itself properly. 'I knew you would.' She pulled me in for a hug. 'I'm so proud of you. So you know what comes next don't you?'

'Backstroke?' I replied, equally as tired as Lorna. My lungs felt like they'd never get enough oxygen into them and I had to lean onto my knees to try and get more in, but I felt good. I'd won.

'Yep, we've got thirty minutes, I believe, then we're back in. Cup of tea and a biscuit?' Lorna checked. I nodded and the two of us dripped our way to the table where a matriarchal woman that reminded me of all the dinner ladies in my life poured out a weak brown tea for the two of us in mint-green thick ceramic cups, and placed a biscuit on our saucers. Nodding gratefully, we made our way to a bench poolside.

'Let's watch the next race from here,' Lorna suggested and I nodded. The tea was too hot to drink so I balanced the saucer on my knees as I nibbled on the biscuit.

'I could do with ten of these,' I admitted and Lorna nodded, her mouth full of the biscuit she'd crammed in.

'I know,' she replied, little crumbs escaping her mouth as she spoke, 'they're missing a trick here. I could eat two bacon sandwiches right now.'

We ate our biscuits in silence as we watched the next round of competitors take to the pool.

'She's good, that one,' I pointed out a diminutive red-head. 'Very quick. Watch her,' I advised, 'that's the one I'd bet on.'

A little later in a spew of white foam, Phyllis, the red-headed speedy swimmer, had reached the end to wild applause from the crowd.

Lorna grinned.

'Good guess. Well done, looks like you're back in,' she pointed out.

'Look after these,' I said as I left my robe and teacup next to Lorna. I strode back over to the pool feeling as though my legs weren't good enough for walking, let alone kicking as hard as they'd need for the backstroke. My suit was damp and my skin felt cold, but I could feel the sense of anticipation from people in the crowds again, and I couldn't help it, the butterflies in my stomach came, giving me a surge of excitement at what lay ahead.

'Ready to go again?' Mr Swarbrick stood a little way from me in a bid, I thought, to appear non-biased but smiled broadly when I looked at him.

'As I'll ever be,' I admitted, doing my best to ignore the jittery feelings in my legs.

'Lane two, Miss Morton,' a steward told me. I nodded to show I'd heard, then I stretched, and entered the pool. The water felt colder this time and my tea sloshed in my stomach, along with the undigested remains of my biscuit.

'Ready.' I held the side, my feet pressing the edge as my knees bent, ready to push off as quickly as possible.

'Get set.' I arched my back in anticipation.

The whistle blew and I threw myself back as quickly as I could just as Mr Swarbrick had taught me, kicking hard and throwing my arms behind. I focused on the ceiling above and counted my strokes. I knew it took forty to get from one end to the other and I powered down. This time, unlike the last, my body felt more fluid, not less. I'd thought it was going to be tougher swimming hard with barely a gap between races, but it hadn't, if anything it was as though my body was in tune with the water. It felt like I was gliding.

In no time at all I was on the last length and I kept up the momentum, pushing through the water and kicking my legs as though my life depended on it. Within a matter of minutes I was at the end and being pulled out of the water by a jubilant Mr Swarbrick.

'You've done it. Another bloody win, well done,' he hugged me fiercely. 'And a record for the club. Well done, Miss Morton, a smashing afternoon.' He beamed at his fellow umpires who appeared to be deciding his future as an impartial judge.

'Lucy.' Mother and Father appeared through the crowd and I turned away from the situation Mr Swarbrick seemed to be getting himself in.

'Two wins, poppet, well done.' My father grabbed me for a hug. 'I'm so proud of you.' He pulled away suddenly, his face changing to a look of slight disgust. 'You're all damp.'

I couldn't help but laugh, and when my mother took one look at him with an imprint of my wet body on his light-grey suit, she laughed too. 'Sorry, Father, I am. But...'

I left the implication of the hilarity of the situation and he shook his head, his face beginning to crack into a little smile.

'Yes, well, it's probably time for all of us to get on. We have a little surprise for you if you hurry up.' He winked at my mother who smiled at me.

'Oh yes, go and get changed. We've got somewhere to go,' she hinted.

'All right, but I'm starving and feel like my legs may never work again,' I reminded them both.

Mother tutted. 'Don't be silly, we're not going far – Alice is coming too – and you'll both be tired and hungry, but we've had an idea we think you'll enjoy,' my mother organised me. 'We'll see you out the front as soon as you can.'

Intrigued, I returned to the changing room and climbed into my clothes. My dress stuck a little to my back as I couldn't get dry enough, and my undergarments all decided to knot themselves together. I took a deep breath and untangled myself, trying to slow down so I could get things done.

Eventually, after vigorously rubbing my hair dry and thanking the decision I made a week ago to have it chopped to the ear into a severe bob, I tied up my shoes and carried out my coat. When I arrived in the entrance of the baths, Alice and my parents were there, waiting.

'Here she is. Took your time.' My sister mimicked checking her watch and I poked her in the ribs.

'Tell you what, *you* win two races and gain a record for the club, then try and get yourself dressed in five minutes whilst boiling hot and soaked to the bone.' I poked her again and she squealed, laughing.

'Fine, I'll let you off,' she smiled. 'Can we go now, please?' she asked of our parents who smiled in turn at the two of us bickering.

'Any idea where we're going?' I asked Alice as we walked behind our parents on the pavement, the late-September afternoon sunshine filling Blackpool with a golden glow.

She shook her head. 'No, they're being very mysterious. I hope it involves food though. I'm starving.' She rubbed her stomach and mine grumbled in sympathy.

'This way, ladies,' Father called to us as we made our way to the promenade. We exchanged a look and Alice shrugged. 'Not a clue.'

'Right, this is part one of the surprise.' Father stood by the fish and chip shop, the smell of vinegar scenting the air. 'Whatever you two want, our treat.' He placed an arm around Mother who beamed. We both chose battered haddock and chips and when Father handed us our packets that had been open-wrapped in newspaper, a wooden fork speared into the top, the two of us fell on the food with gusto.

'Thank you,' I managed, before shovelling chip after chip into my mouth, stuffing myself with the vinegary food.

'Don't eat it all in one go, there's a second part,' Mother smiled mysteriously. 'Why don't we sit here?' she asked, indicating a bench on the promenade, looking out onto the sea. Alice and I were still too interested in the food, so we shrugged as one, then sat down.

Sated after a few minutes of silent scoffing, I looked around.

'It's going to get pretty dark down here in a bit,' I noted, seeing the sky turning evening blue, and some early rising stars already trying to push through. 'We may want to get back before we can't see where we're going,' I suggested.

'Oh, I don't think that'll be a problem.' Father winked, and as he did, behind him the promenade became daylight again.

'What?'

'How?' Alice and I spoke at the same time, our surprise causing Mother and Father to laugh a little.

'Don't you recognise it, Lucy?' Father asked, moving his head a little so I could see better and then I realised what it was.

'These are the lights we saw the princess switch on a few months ago,' I guessed. Mother nodded.

'That's right, they've decided to switch them on this autumn – they're calling it the *Illuminations*. Stunning isn't it? The perfect end to a perfect day for our girls.'

I looked at the beaming faces of my parents, the happiness radiating from them to my sister, her mouth stuffed with chips, a look of satisfaction as she licked her lips, and I nodded.

'Definitely.'

Chapter Nineteen

MARCH 1913, BLACKPOOL

'Do you feel good? Ready?' Mr Swarbrick, for the first time since I'd known him, actually looked the slightest bit concerned.

'Of course.' I looked him straight in the eye. 'Of course I'm ready. Why would I compete if I didn't think I could win?'

My father laughed and ruffled my hair – a trait he knew I found incredibly irritating, but he continued to do.

'That's the spirit, girl.'

Looking around at my fellow competitors, the memories of last year's Northern Counties Amateur Swimming Association's Championship came flooding back. The embarrassment at my second place. I'd worked so hard this past year to be better. I'd won other breaststroke competitions but this one had kept the fire burning all year.

I wanted this more than anything else.

'I say, Lucy,' Mr Swarbrick said, 'they're calling for the competitors – they're going up in age categories, you'll be in about half an hour.' He looked at me, concern filling his eyes. 'You've done everything you can. You know that?'

I nodded, but he mistook my lack of words for nerves, and grabbed me by the tops of both of my arms so I'd look at him.

'You are a brilliant swimmer. Fine, you came second last year – but you were up against stiff competition. This year, Lucy,' he breathed deeply, a fire in his eyes, 'this year, *you're* the stiff competition. Look around you, girl.' He nodded at me and I glanced over my shoulders. Everywhere I looked were swimmers of different ages, with family, coaches and others. Some were stretching, others watching warm-ups in the pool. It was a typical sight at a swim meet.

'What? What am I meant to be looking at?'

Mr Swarbrick grinned.

'They're the ones afraid of you – look at the glances you're getting. You're the one they all want to beat. That means you're going to have to give everything, leave nothing behind. You hear?' He looked sternly at me and I nodded.

'I mean it. You can win this, but you're going to have to swim like the bricky girl I know you are.'

He looked so serious I was surprised by his emotion. 'I promise.'

As he walked away with my parents, I began to make my way to the poolside in readiness for my competition, when I heard Mr Swarbrick yell. 'Turns, don't forget the turns.'

'How could I forget?' I replied, smiling. We'd spent so many hours in the freezing water with me practising my turns. In fact, I felt like I'd turned more than swum this past year.

When I'd lost last year – which is how I saw it, second place is first loser really – when I lost, we agreed to work on three things. I'd persisted in keeping my head lower in the water, I'd practised my turns and Mr Swarbrick had discovered a new swimsuit for me, to replace my woollen one. It wasn't silk, like the Olympians were said to have, but it was cotton, which didn't drag so much in the water. It also gave me very little privacy, so we made sure I was in the darkest material possible. Still, it was a lot sheerer than what some of the other girls were wearing, and I decided to keep my robe wrapped around me until the last moment.

I smiled at the story Mr Swarbrick had told me a while ago. That the British women who'd competed in the Olympics last year had worn such sheer costumes they had a matron who accompanied them everywhere they went, in case they were of too much interest to the male competitors.

'I'll be wiping the smile off your face,' a slight brunette whispered in my direction as she waltzed past me, her ponytail swishing.

'I like to keep my energy for winning in competitions, so I have no interest in petty bickering,' I replied, undaunted. With not even a glance at the brunette, I held my head high and took a seat on the side of the pool to watch the younger swimmers competing. Alice was in there somewhere, but I couldn't spot her. Even though she had a dark swimming hat on, so did many of the other competitors. I had to guess which one was her. One, though, looked like she was roaring up the outside lane.

I looked over to the stands to see my parents jumping up and down and pointing and I nodded. So that was Alice then.

'Go on, you can do it,' I yelled from the side, attracting looks from some of my own competitors. I smiled and explained, 'My sister,' to varying nods of understanding and disinterest, then continued watching her. She was really going at a terrific lick.

'Go on, Alice, go on,' I yelled, excited for her. She was so close. She was going to win. I realised I was holding my breath, watching her race down the last length. Her breaststroke was good, but she needed to stop bobbing out of the water so often. I'd have to remind her of that later. Cheers were erupting from the stands from Alice's teammates and our family. I walked over and helped her out to the side. She was panting hard.

'Did I?'

'You did,' I clapped as she got closer, I was so proud of her.

'Yes. I knew it. Yes,' she leapt with glee whilst I grabbed and hugged her, then moved aside to let her have her moment.

'Good work,' I shouted after her just as the announcer's voice came over the speaker that it was my race. A bolt of butterflies shot through my stomach, but then I saw my sister's elation and I decided to just go out and enjoy myself.

'Ladies, make your way to the pool please,' the announcer stated. Dutifully I left my robe on the side, rearranged my swimming cap and walked to the water's edge, stretching out my arms. I found my lane, number four, in the middle of the pool, and felt calm yet focused. Determined.

Standing on the edge of the pool I could feel the water rippling over my feet. I buckled my cap and stood, waiting for the next set of instructions.

Inhale.

'Right, ladies. Keep to your lanes, let's have a fair fight,' the announcer said with a laugh, but I didn't look around to see if anyone else joined in. I continued to focus ahead on the end of the pool.

Exhale.

'Ready, set.'

Inhale.

The whistle blew and I dove in beautifully breaking the surface far from the side. Keeping the end of the pool in sight I continued to keep my motions fluid. I could hear Swarbrick's voice in my head to keep below the water, breaking only for a gulp of air.

The stroke was a part of me now. Like breathing. I didn't have to fight it or ask my body to do as it was told. Instinctively I could feel my way through the water.

I turned.

Carried on down to the other end. I needed to keep up this pace. Not chancing a look to either side I motored down the lane.

Turn. Inhale.

Somewhere I could hear bubbles of noise whenever I broke the surface, but they'd be quickly muted as I went back under the water. My lungs were starting to hurt.

Turn. Final length.

To the left of me I could feel someone else nearby but other than that, I wasn't sure where the rest of the swimmers were. They could be well in front of me, but I didn't think so.

Now all my body wanted to do was explode. My limbs were burning, I felt like my lungs were going to be torn out of me, my vision was blurry through a combination of the water and the exertion.

Every time I went below the surface I could hear an odd drumbeat which followed me. I was certain there was no music but I could hear this rhythm, then I realised. It was my heart. So loud it was thumping in my ears below the water.

I could see the end. I could see the side.

Inhale.

Two more big pushes.

I touched the wall and looked around hastily, was it like last year? Had I come second again? Or worse?

Trying to catch my breath whilst hanging on to the side of the pool I spotted Mr Swarbrick bearing down on me with a huge grin.

'You did it. I knew it. Well done, girl. Well bloody done.' He grinned and laughed.

'Did I?' I gasped, trying to get my breathing under control.

'You won. No one was even near to you, Lucy. You were... incredible.' He beamed. 'You swam like I've never seen you swim before. So graceful, so fast. So complete. You were just, well, wonderful,' he extolled, whilst helping me out of the water as I had done for Alice just a few minutes before.

He flung my robe round my shoulders to protect my modesty and I continued to breathe deeply, but I was grinning. A movement out of the corner of my eye made me look round, it was the brunette with the ponytail. She wasn't smiling like before. She was gasping too. When she saw me staring I thought she was going to have something to say.

'Good show, Morton. Nice one,' she told me, nodding.

I nodded back, too tired to show any kind of one-up-manship. And anyway, I'd won. There was no need to rub it in.

'You get a prize.' Mr Swarbrick had walked over to me again, after speaking to the umpire. 'There's a medal and you need to stand over there whilst they give them out – remember last year?' he said. Though to be honest, I didn't need reminding. Last year I'd barely got through the medal ceremony as I'd wanted the ground to swallow me whole. A small part of me cringed at that childish response to losing, but the other part, the one which had just powered to win, was pleased.

That hunger to win had driven me on.

A little later, as I stood to receive my medal, my sister whooping from the stalls, it felt nice to be good at something. To be proud of oneself.

'Well done,' said a smartly dressed woman who I suspected was the wife of someone important and who was handing out the medals. She smiled at me as she placed the medal in my palm. Turning it over in my hand I noted it was inscribed already, *Ladies Breast Stroke Championship 1913, Won By Lucy Morton.* The weight of it was comforting and I beamed at her.

Later, as Mr Swarbrick and my family came over with words of joy and more warm clothes, I held my hand up, in charge.

'Before anyone makes a fuss, I'm very hungry and could do with a steak. And maybe some ice cream,' I began, causing Mother to laugh.

Chapter Twenty

MAY 1913, BLACKPOOL

T raining was all well and good, but even Mr Swarbrick had to accept a royal visit would put paid to me spending time in the pool when the King and Queen made a trip to Blackpool as part of their motoring tour of Lancashire that summer.

'It was terribly kind of you to welcome us back into your home, Mrs Swarbrick.' I leant into the old woman who was carefully pouring tea for my mother. 'And to let me bring the family too. Thank you.'

The old lady gave me a wide smile. 'I've heard so much about your success, and your sister, of course.' She looked in Alice's direction who was demolishing a slice of Victorian sponge cake. 'I simply insisted to George that he bring you all.'

I looked over to Mr Swarbrick, it was amusing hearing his first name.

'It's a super view from here, Mrs Swarbrick.' My father walked back into the airy flat, from his spot on the balcony, sipping some tea. 'Thank you for inviting us all.'

'Of course – you're all practically family anyway. The amount of time your daughter and my son are spending at that pool, they may as well be family,' the older woman refreshed my father's cup then turned to me, 'by all accounts you'll be winning the Olympics in a few years.'

My stomach suddenly felt as though it were going to drop at the thought of the Olympics. The next event was due in 1916 – just three years away. I'd be eighteen by then and just the right age to compete, Mr Swarbrick had said as much, but I wasn't convinced I'd be fast enough to make the heats. Let alone get the chance to compete with the world's best.

'Let's not rush things Mother?' Mr Swarbrick had seen the panic in my eyes and was steering the conversation away to other things. 'I think we should be getting out onto the balcony.'

'Oh yes, let's.' Alice had jumped up from her seat and had me by the elbow. 'Let's go right to the edge, it'll be as though we're soaring above everyone.'

'Good plan.' We walked onto the balcony and I was suddenly hit by the noise of the crowd below. Since we'd made our way into Mrs Swarbrick's an hour or so ago, the amount of people on the pavements had seemingly doubled. Alice and I walked to the right of the balcony and stood, holding tight to the side, leaning as far over as we dared.

'Gosh, isn't it glorious?' I breathed in the salty, crisp air of the sea that was rumbling its way across the shore, just across the road from us. But below the balcony and opposite were hundreds of people. Schoolchildren all in white smocks were lined along the road. Flanked by their schoolmasters and teachers, they had shiny, freshly washed faces, their hair brushed so it looked like flaxen and they all held small Union flags, waving them excitedly in the light summer breeze.

The crowds were four people deep all along the promenade as far as the eye could see, the route of the royal visit marked out in bright bunting, held up by the lights that that been switched on the last time I'd been in Mrs Swarbrick's flat. Music was being played by a brass band that had set up on a raised dais, giving them a perfect view of the special visitors, whilst giving us a soundtrack to watch them by.

'Tea?' Mother was pouring a cup for us both indoors. 'Why don't you sit here for a bit, girls? We can watch everything when they arrive.'

'Oh.' Alice looked as disappointed as I felt. I wanted to soak up every last minute of the fun below us. When suddenly, there was a ripple of excitement through the crowd.

'I see a car, I think,' I shouted, a little louder than I'd intended, at Father, Mr Swarbrick and Mother, who all stood from their table and made their way to the edge of the balcony, shading their eyes from the sun to see if I was right.

I was.

'Yes, look, there's a car. And another.' Alice whooped with joy. 'Oh my, we're going to see the King and the Queen. I wonder what she's wearing.' She hung over the balcony again as we began to see a parade of cars breaking from the horizon, moving slowly towards us.

The cars coming down the road were quite a sight. Ten of them in a cavalcade came towards us at a leisurely pace, their slow entrance marked by cheers as they went past different sections of the crowd. Policemen who were posted at intervals down the length of the crowd stood proudly, their helmets and white gloves gleaming in the sunshine. They were clearly keeping a close watch on the crowd, but it seemed everyone was in good spirits. Though maybe since the death of the suffragette under the King's horse, there was a need to step up security around the royal family.

'The first car, Lucy. Look.' Alice pointed at it, being driven by a white-suited naval officer. He was smiling at the crowd, enjoying the role he was playing.

'No sign of royalty though.' I looked at her, then looked back. 'Maybe they're in that one.' We leaned over the balcony, looking through the opera glasses Mrs Swarbrick had lent us.

'Yes, look, there,' I squealed, 'it's the King.'

We began waving frantically and were heartened when one of the cars hooted its horn – whether it was in our direction or not, we took it to be and cheered loudly, along with the rest of the crowd. The King was waving in all directions. He looked smart, and very handsome.

'The Queen – look.' She was waving to the crowds on either side of her too, beaming at everyone.

'Lovely, so lovely,' Alice breathed as she looked through the opera glasses. 'She's wearing a beautiful dress, lovely colour on her. I think lilac can be difficult, but she looks wonderful. What a fine pair they make.' She smiled and looked at me. 'How lucky we are to see them. And to see a parade such as this,' she said laughing with joy.

'It's wonderful, isn't it?'

The brass band had begun again as other cars that were part of the royal entourage passed us by. The flags were still being flown, giving me an enormous sense of patriotism. For King and country.

I could understand the sense behind that phrase.

'Mrs Swarbrick, any chance you've got any more of that delicious sponge cake going still?' Alice was rubbing her stomach. 'All that cheering has left me quite famished.'

Mrs Swarbrick shook her head. 'I don't know, girl. It's lucky you swim so much.' Alice pouted at the suggestion she was a glutton. 'But it might as well get eaten. Lord knows there's not much room in here,' Mrs Swarbrick continued, whilst patting her own tiny stomach on her sparrow-like frame.

I was still looking over the balcony, watching as some of the crowd began to disperse now the excitement of the cavalcade was over. I'd stepped back into my daydreams, giving myself permission to consider the Olympics in three years. Maybe I'd even return to a welcome such as this. With cheering. And flags. And a brass band.

'A penny for them.' Father had appeared at my side.

'Oh,' I laughed and blushed a little, 'I wasn't really thinking of much.'

Chapter Twenty-One
JUNE 1913, BLACKPOOL

In a funny way I think it was seeing the crowds for the King and Queen which lit a spark, because from then on I had the bit between my teeth, so to speak, and all I wanted to do was win.

Whereas before I had spent time with Lorna and Alice, accompanying them on trips to the seaside, or attending the pictures, I spent every bit of free time I could in the pool.

I finally finished school, and whilst my parents were convinced I should work in the big house, I chose to continue at the haberdashers. My boss there, Mr Thompson, was a kind and understanding man. He made it clear as long as I arrived on time and completed the sewing projects which were required of me, then I could leave on time – unlike many of the women who wasted time chatting and catching up, I would keep my head down.

If the other women noticed me, they did a good job of ignoring my existence and that suited me just fine. I would swim after work most days, which meant I rarely joined in with the office chats, which led to shopping trips, bonding time. Friends.

The only problem I had was my bag containing my swimming costume and towelling robe and the like, which I took everywhere with me.

'What have you got in there?' asked one of the ladies, Mrs Elder, one day. She was slight and dark-haired, but she'd already made it clear that as the youngest apprentice in the shop, and the oddest one, she wasn't going to waste time talking to me. My obvious disinterest in her affected this dynamic though. She seemed keen to either befriend me or hold me up as an oddity.

'Just my swimming bits,' I replied, stowing the bag under my table and reaching for the dress I was taking up for one of our regular clients.

'It's got an unpleasant smell,' Mrs Elder replied, wrinkling her nose up so that a few of the other women laughed and I reddened a touch.

'Sorry, it's the water. It's salty and my clothes aren't fully dry,' I explained with a smile, hoping that would end the conversation but our interaction had attracted the attention of some of the other seamstresses in the room.

'Why do you bring it in with you every day?' another asked, she couldn't be much older than me, yet she had a way which suggested she was ten years my senior.

I smiled again, looking up from threading the needle.

'I swim every day. I'm training,' I explained, surprised at the tittering of laughter which filled the room.

'Training? For what?' Mrs Elder asked.

'I bet she thinks she could be in the Olympics,' said another with a laugh.

I chose to stay quiet. There was no need to explain that as much as I'd like to compete in the next Olympics, due to take place in 1916, the swim strokes I excelled in weren't due to feature.

'No,' the younger woman said, looking at me with a haughty glare, 'I know why she does it. Those women, the swimmers, they're known to be a bit... you know, free. Haven't you seen the size of their costumes? Doesn't leave much to the imagination, I can tell you.'

They all began to laugh and chat amongst each other as I tried to still my mind. I knew I was quick to temper, quicker still to say what was on my mind before thinking it through, but I needed this job and I didn't want to ruin the chance I had to get to training. I had a two-mile swim I was due to compete in one month's time. I needed to remain focused.

'She probably needs the smallest costume she can find, goodness knows no man would look twice at her right now,' whispered one of the women, though loud enough for me to hear. 'Fancy walking around with hair as scruffy as a dog's, spending all your time in a swimming pool. Sounds like she needs her head examined if you ask me.'

I was just beginning to wonder if I could take my sewing into another room far enough away that I didn't have to listen to their nonsense, when an older lady, similar in age to my mother spoke for the first time.

'Maybe it's time we allowed women a choice in their lives? If Lucy is a keen swimmer, shouldn't we encourage her, rather than mock her? Can't any of you women read?' There was a muted silence in the room as a I realised there was a high chance many of the women didn't read much, or what they did was what was permitted by their fathers or husbands.

The older lady shook her head, putting her sewing down on the table in front of her for a moment.

'If you'd been reading the papers over the last few months you'd know now's the time to support your fellow woman, not tear her down. Those suffragettes are dying for us so we can have the vote. So we can have freedom.' She went quiet for a moment. 'Life shouldn't be about whether Lucy can attract a husband. It should be whether she's got a talent which is worth nurturing.'

'Absolute nonsense,' replied Mrs Elder irritably, 'the only thing those women are doing is causing a nuisance for the rest of us. I haven't asked for the vote, I'm happy for my husband to choose for me.'

The older woman muttered in the corner.

'Personally, I'd rather see the tenacity in a young girl like Lucy, choosing to push herself day in, day out, for even a modicum of achievement, than a woman doing as her husband bids. The best day of my life was when my husband died, freedom at last.'

There was a sharp intake of breath in the room, interrupted by Mr Thompson's arrival. He glanced around and saw little work taking place.

'I don't pay you to sit around chatting,' he barked. 'Well, get on with it then. There's plenty more jobs to do before the weekend.' He nodded, pleased, as he saw us all resume our sewing. The women waited until he left the room before any more discussions took place, and I held my breath, intrigued by what the older woman was saying.

'If you're so keen to live a life free from men, why are you working for one?' hissed Mrs Elder to the widow, who smiled naughtily in response.

'I don't plan to work for him after the weekend. I've got my lucky ticket out of here.' She waved a slip of paper, which attracted my attention.

'What is it?' the younger woman asked.

'My betting slip, it's the Derby tomorrow. I've got my money on the King's horse, he's bound to win,' she grinned. 'I've put a lot on, but I have a feeling it's going to be an exciting race.'

The rest of the women groaned.

'Waste of money, that,' said Mrs Elder, and some of the others nodded.

For the rest of the day I carried on with my head down, working hard. I found a sense of peace in the rhythm of sewing, a little like swimming. Plus, with sewing it allowed my mind to wander to my swimming technique.

***

The following day, as we were returning from our swim – we'd gone later than planned owing to Alice being a terrible riser in the morning – we were congratulating ourselves on how far we'd managed and decided we would take the scenic route home, along the promenade. Alice was infatuated with the newspaper lad who worked on the parade, so insisted we stop by his stand.

'Derby tragedy,' I could hear him hollering, 'suffragette dies under the King's horse.'

Alice and I looked at each other in horror.

'That can't be true,' I stuttered, whilst we made our way to the newspaper stand. I'd had my reservations about the suffragettes, recalling what Harry's mother experienced, but I had, in the last few months, begun to question my own place in the world. The more I read about what the suffragettes were willing to go through so women could get the vote. Have a voice. Be heard. The more it made me realise maybe I wasn't cut out for the *married with children* life. Maybe I was made with something else in mind.

I knew swimming wouldn't change the world, not in the way the suffragettes wanted. But whilst they campaigned I felt entitled to pursue swimming. It wasn't a mere hobby. I wanted to make a success of it, whatever that looked like. When I'd read about the swimming in the Olympics last year it made me burst with excitement. What if I could be there? I could dream. Right?

But now a suffragette had died for the cause. She'd seemingly committed an act of suicide. And with the King's horse. It was too much to bear.

'They'll never be taken seriously now if they throw themselves under a horse to get attention,' Alice whispered, then smiled at Alfie the paper boy.

'Hello, Alfie.'

'Alice.' He nodded, the tips of his ears reddening. 'Seen the news? Shocking innit? Bleedin' wimmin, trying to get themselves killed. And for what? Nothing. That's what my dad says anyway. They won't get the vote, so why die trying?'

'It's that kind of thinking that will keep us in caves, without electric light,' I replied curtly. 'Come on, Alice, let's go.'

I walked away shaking my head, so angry I could feel my heartbeat everywhere, from my fingers to my neck.

'What an absolutely foolish boy,' I heard myself say to Alice, who looked shocked at my outburst. 'What? You're not going to defend him. Are you?' She shrank a little under my gaze and I focused on controlling my breathing and bringing my pulse back to normal.

She caught my arm, to slow me down.

'Lucy, what was that all about?'

I pulled up, causing a few other pedestrians to have to go around us, cursing as they did so.

'Don't you see? If she died in vain, then they all did. Everything they've fought for is for nought if people like

Alfie's father have anything to do with our future.' I looked keenly at Alice. 'It is *our* future you know. Not theirs. Not Mother's, not Father's. *Our* future. We should be in charge of our own minds, our own votes, our own money. Our own...' I broke off, trying to explain what I knew I couldn't, 'our own paths. Why should it be down to old men in Westminster to make decisions on behalf of us?'

Chapter Twenty-Two

JUNE 1913, BLACKPOOL

'What's a pilgrimage?' Lorna caught up with me outside school. At fifteen I knew I was lucky to still be going, but I was beginning to feel it was almost impossible to work without daydreaming. I'd often stare out of the window in class and think of competitions coming up at the weekend, or the results of races I'd had and what I could have done to better myself.

Still, there was only a matter of a few weeks left and I'd soon be leaving. I'd agreed with Mother and Father to carry on until the summer and intended to extend my job at the seamstress's to four days a week, giving me three to train.

'A pilgrimage? It's what religious people go on, I think,' I replied, searching my brain for a response and screwing up my face in thought.

Lorna was a touch out of breath as she'd ran to catch up with me, her cheeks flushed.

'That's what I thought, but I didn't think Miss Pollard was altogether that religious,' my friend replied, confused. 'I mean, she's quite earnest and pious, but I don't think she's devout.'

'Erm, no. I don't either.' I felt irritated with the conversation. 'Lorna, where's this going? What are you talking about?' We began walking away from the school, heading home. Lorna clapped her hand to her mouth and laughed.

'Sorry, you must think me a mad old thing.' She widened her eyes in a mock mad way, making me laugh. 'I just overheard her saying to one of the other teachers how she was joining "the pilgrimage",' Lorna pulled a face, 'and I didn't know what she was referring to. I thought you might.'

I pulled a crumpled paper bag out of my coat pocket pleased to find two sweets left, and popped a barley sugar in my mouth. Seeing Lorna's pained expression I sighed and offered her my last one, which she took with alacrity.

'I don't know what the pilgrimage means,' I admitted, 'though it does sound interesting.' We both walked along in deep thought, sucking on our sweets.

'Maybe it's a way of getting a husband?' Lorna offered. We both shook our heads.

'No – she'll never get a husband.'

'Maybe it's a religious holiday and we didn't know she's actually very keen on it all?' I suggested, but neither of us agreed with that.

'Maybe it's code, and she's actually a spy... for the government.' Lorna's eyes widened with the thought, then we both laughed at the idea. We stopped to let a cart pass us, then continued to the road where we'd say our goodbyes and head off in separate directions to home. All of a sudden, Lorna grabbed my arm, then released it, laughing.

'What?'

Lorna shook her head. 'No, it's silly. For a second I thought that was your, I mean, Harry, up ahead.' She nodded to a lonely figure walking along the road. My heart thumped so hard in my chest I considered what it would be like to have it outside of my body.

'I don't think it's him,' I said, uncertain, as from this distance it could be anyone. But at the same time, the man did look kind of familiar.

'I think it is, Luce, I really think it is,' Lorna mumbled to me as we got nearer to the figure. As the shadowy man turned around I gulped. It *was* Harry. It had been over a year since we'd seen each other and I'd learnt to ignore the part of me that missed him. This time it was my turn to grab Lorna's arm.

'What do I say?'

She shook her head, sucking her sweet to give her respite from offering an answer. But just as I was about to say something to her, Harry appeared in front of us. His shoulders were broader, his hair looked thicker as it bristled out from under his flat cap. He looked like a grown-up. Until he took the cap off his head and folded it into his hands, looking every bit the boy I'd known.

'Oh, hello, Lorna.' He nodded at her. 'Lucy,' he murmured and I couldn't think of anything. Not one thing to say. What do you say to the boy you were in love with?

Who you were there for in his darkest of days, but who just left without a word?

Sensing I needed help, Lorna came to my aid.

'Hi, Harry, tell you what. Lucy and I were just trying to work something out. We overheard some people talking today and we were trying to work out what they were on about. Bet you know. What's this "pilgrimage" people are discussing?' She fluttered her hands in the air in a vague sense of unknowing.

If I was expecting any response from Harry, the colour draining from his face was not it.

'What's the matter, Harry?' I pressed, concerned Lorna had done something terrible by overhearing. Maybe our teacher really was a spy.

He shook his head.

'Sorry, ah, took me unawares didn't you, Lorn. Erm, it's just a walk, by loads of suffragettes. They're walking different routes and meeting in London to have their voices heard,' he swallowed, 'again.'

Realisation dawned for the two of us and I was first to apologise, grabbing his arm so he knew how sincere I was.

'We're so sorry, Harry, we had no idea otherwise we'd never have asked you. Ever. Obviously,' I added, aware of the warmth of his arm under my hand. He seemed aware too as he removed his arm slowly from me and took a step back.

Replacing his hat on his head, he coughed.

'It's fine. Just caught me by surprise. Anyway, I was only here on errands for my father, I'm finishing off a few things for him before I go,' he added.

'Go? Go where?' Lorna asked the question I couldn't. Harry smiled slightly.

'Ah, well, I've enlisted. I hear the Army is the place to be – hopefully get a chance to travel a bit, plus they pay you well and I get free bed and board.' He nodded at me. 'It's all right, it's better than anything my father can offer. He's...' he looked to the sky as though it would give him inspiration, 'it's not good there,' he concluded.

Before I could say anything, he touched his cap, looked at me – a little sadly I felt – then walked in the direction we'd come.

'Well,' breathed Lorna, 'at least we know what this pilgrimage is, I suppose.' She paused and looked at my hands. 'Any more of those sweets left?'

'Mmm,' I replied, my thoughts elsewhere completely.

Chapter Twenty-Three

JULY 1913, BLACKPOOL

'Lucy, I think you might find two miles to be too far,' Mr Swarbrick commented as I pulled myself out onto the side of the pool, my breaths so heavy it felt as though they were pure fire. We had three days until a two-mile competition and I still couldn't get past one and a half miles without feeling utterly exhausted.

I tried to reply, but kept coughing so hard I felt as though bits of my lungs might turn up on the cold, stone tiles of the pool, so I concentrated on getting my breathing under control, shaking my head at Mr Swarbrick.

'Look,' he pulled up a wooden chair next to me and settled down on it, groaning as he sat, 'you're good, Lucy. You are, but you're young and I'm not sure you're ready for this – so many of the other competitors will be older than you, with experience in swimming longer distances.' He smiled at me. 'I will always be in your corner, you know that. I'm on your side. But, no one will mind if you decide to pull out of this competition and concentrate on the next one?'

'No.' I breathed deeply, my throat rasping. 'I'll be fine. I just need a couple of days' rest, and then I'll be fine.'

Mr Swarbrick shook his head.

'You're under my care when we're here and I owe it to your parents to make sure you're making the right decisions. I'm not letting you swim yourself to death in a bid to prove something.'

'And I don't think anyone should be allowed to make decisions on my behalf, when it's my body, and therefore my choice to swim or not.' I glared at him.

'Don't forget your place, Miss Morton. I'm your coach and your father's friend. You only swim because I teach you and because I pull enough strings to make sure you have access to the pool as much as you can.'

I breathed out irritably, aware he was right but still frustrated.

'I know how much you support me, I do,' I implored, 'and I do appreciate it, but you need to understand I do know my body. I know I can do this. I can.' I looked at him squarely.

Mr Swarbrick sighed and rubbed his moustache.

'I knew you'd say that.' He looked up at the ceiling of the baths, as though the answer were up there, along with the pigeons that always roosted in the gaps. 'Fine, if you're insistent upon it—'

'I am.' I stretched my arms overhead to distract myself from grinning at getting my own way. My biceps were aching and I rubbed my left one absent-mindedly, then laughed as my stomach growled loudly. Mr Swarbrick smiled and reached his hand out to pull me up as he stood too.

'I've decided, you have two options.'

I stood and wrapped my robe around me. I was cooling down and goose-bumps were forming on my skin. 'Right, and they are?'

'Option one, today you call it a day. Rest up the next few days, eat well and then just attack the swim on Saturday. Hopefully the time to recover and rest will help you go further.'

'All right, and what's the second option?' I wanted him to say I could swim at least once between now and Saturday. Three days seemed a long time to keep away from training.

'Don't compete.' Mr Swarbrick raised an eyebrow at me. 'That's it. And if you go against my recommendations I'll no longer coach you, Lucy.'

'Fine. I'll do as I'm told. But after this competition, if I do well, you and I need to discuss a training schedule we both agree on.'

He smiled. 'Deal.'

***

Three days later, Mr Swarbrick and I made our way to Hoylake Lido for the two-mile competition. He'd met me from my house and we'd made our way from Blackpool Central Station to Hoylake via a series of train journeys.

It had taken three hours and we'd left shortly after breakfast that morning. The journey had been long and between the early morning wake-up and the intense training regime I'd put myself through, I'd been lulled to sleep by the rocking motion, waking only when Mr Swarbrick had bought us tea and cake from the food trolley.

When we arrived at Hoylake, I felt jaded. We had two hours before the race began but I had other, more pressing concerns as we made our way from the train station.

'I'm famished,' I told Mr Swarbrick, and he grinned.

'You always are. Lucky for you I've booked us a table over there.' He indicated a small hotel with a restaurant attached overlooking the promenade. I allowed myself to be steered down the road and up the front steps of the Hotel Sunshine. The name made me smile, I liked their optimism. And they were right, the sun was shining down on us today as Mr Swarbrick checked our name with the maître d and we were settled at a small, white cloth-covered table with views overlooking the promenade and out towards the Irish Sea. However, I was too hungry to appreciate any such view, and instead consulted the menu quickly.

'Ready to order?'

'I'll take the soup, the fish, and then...' I paused, looking longingly at the other dishes on the menu, 'steak and chips for main. That's it. Oh, and a pot of tea.'

The waiter nodded, and looked at Mr Swarbrick.

'I'll have the same. May as well, eh?' He chuckled a little jovially. 'Though make sure to bring me a glass of wine, there's a good lad.' He looked at me. 'We need to make sure you're well fed ahead of this race, can't have you fainting a mile in.'

'Have you seen the pool? If I do that I'm on my own,' I laughed, 'it's so long, by the time anyone would have reached me to give any kind of rescue I'd have drowned.'

'Even more of a reason to keep you full.' Mr Swarbrick smiled at the waiter as he placed our steaming bowls of mushroom soup in front of us, accompanied by a plate of bread and butter. 'Thank you.'

As we tucked in I snuck a look around me at the other diners.

'I can't see anyone else who looks like a competitor,' I whispered, placing the spoon in my bowl just as the fish course arrived. Mr Swarbrick dabbed at his moustache with a thick white napkin, which bore a few loose threads, and he looked casually about the room.

'No, I can't. But then there are quite a few places to eat around here, and there's not that many of you competing. I think there's twelve,' he started cutting up his fish, 'I should think it's pretty easy for us to not bump into anyone just yet.'

The fish was a little dry, but the sauce was delicious and I enjoyed polishing it off, along with the handful of small potatoes and peas on the plate. I leant back in my chair, the heavy wooden back dug in a little but I needed to make a little room for my main course.

'So this is the first time they've held this competition then?'

Mr Swarbrick nodded as he too finished his food and leant back, sipping on some of his wine. His face looked a little flushed and I felt relieved that all I needed to wear was a light summer dress. He was in his suit. I was certain I'd have overheated if I was wearing as many layers as he was. But then, as I thought about it, it occurred to me I'd never seen Mr Swarbrick dressed in any other way other than immaculately turned out in his three-piece suits. Come rain or shine. Or snow. Or in this case, summer heat.

'The baths only opened a month ago in June. The competition is a way of announcing it's open. Celebrating it a bit. It'll be good for you though – if you win you'll definitely seem like a force to be reckoned with. You'll be like that Emily whatshername.' He whispered the last bit, as though embarrassed, but the wine had loosened his tongue a little and he smiled.

'Emmeline Pankhurst?' I prompted.

'Yes. She's a force to be reckoned with when it comes to parliament – if you can be half like her in the pool, no one will know what to do.'

I frowned at the steak and chips placed in front of me.

'I don't think what we're doing is the same, Mr Swarbrick.' I began carefully slicing the meat in front of me. 'She goes on hunger strike to be heard. I... don't.' I nodded in the direction of my food.

Mr Swarbrick smiled, this time a little apologetically.

'Forgive me. I don't think the things you're both striving for are the same, how can they be? But you need to believe what you're doing is more than just swimming, Lucy. You and the other women who are swimming are proving that both sexes have a place in the pool. The Olympians have helped, of course. And the Americans in particular have made huge strides to make things easier for you. But let's face it, five years ago when you first learnt to swim, children and women had to bathe separately from men.'

'That hasn't changed,' I replied glumly.

'True, but now you're allowed to compete. Five years ago there were far fewer opportunities for women swimmers. The more you push, Lucy, the further the women below you will go too.' He carried on eating his food as I chewed on my chips thoughtfully. I'd never really paid much consideration to how I could affect others, but maybe Mr Swarbrick was right.

'Dessert?' The waiter had returned and Mr Swarbrick nodded at me.

'She definitely needs something, what'll it be, Lucy?'

I scanned the menu. 'Definitely the peaches and cream, and don't skimp on the cream,' I pleaded, causing the waiter to smile.

'Peaches with lots of cream, and for you, sir?'

Mr Swarbrick looked at me and smiled broadly, his moustache moving with the gesture. 'I'll have the same.'

Chapter Twenty-Four

JULY 1913, HOYLAKE

L ater, as we left the restaurant replete and patting our full bellies, we made our way slowly towards the lido.

'Feeling confident?' Mr Swarbrick peered at me as we walked side by side as Hoylake Lido came into view.

'I feel ready – is that the same as confident?' I broke off as I looked up at the building. Mr Swarbrick doing the same. The entrance was flanked on either side by sleek yet grand white domes and white stone walls stretched down the road as far as I could see. For a second I felt a little sick.

'This is incredible,' I breathed, 'nothing like ours in Blackpool Mr Swarbrick is it?' My coach was still gazing up at the smart-looking entrance, the brand-new gates, the unchipped tiles and the overall magnitude.

'It really is pretty impressive. How about we make our way in to get a little familiar with the place?' I nodded, watching at what appeared to be hundreds of people streaming through the entrance.

Mr Swarbrick announced me to the competition official in the ticket booth who checked me in and pointed me in the direction of the changing rooms. As I walked to the changing area I considered my surroundings. The pool was enormous, easily twice the size of the one I practised in – over sixty metres in length. It was a beautiful sunny day and the light bounced off the water, causing glittering slices of light to cut through the pool. It was enchanting. And daunting.

A length looked a very long way.

And I was going to have to do fifty of them.

'The sea is just over that wall,' Mr Swarbrick explained. 'If there was less noise in here you'd probably hear the waves.' He was right, the place was noisy. Currently the boys' competition was taking place and cheering on the twelve young men in the water was a crowd of hundreds around the edge of the pool in the stands. Families had come with their picnics and couples sat with their arms around each other. A group of bored younger boys had begun a game of football off to the side, and were kicking it with such ferocity it made me wonder how quickly it would take for the ball to land in the pool.

'This way.' Mr Swarbrick led me to a quieter area where there was a cluster of young women, though the majority all looked a touch older than me. Most were stood or sat with a parent or governess, a couple with what looked like their coach.

I dashed away to the changing rooms and did the quickest change into my swimming kit and robe before returning to Mr Swarbrick who looked surprised at my return.

'You were quick.'

'I know, I didn't want to miss anything, this place is incredible,' I gabbled, the excitement at the upcoming race mixing with the anticipation of it.

Mr Swarbrick smiled. 'Good plan. The men are on their final length.'

We watched as a battle took place between two very strong swimmers. I watched with interest. Even with all the swimming I did now, I was still segregated from the men when I was in the pool but I was keen to see if they did anything differently to me. I watched the ferocity of the two swimmers competing for first place. Granted, they were doing the crawl but it wasn't until that point that I realised what a difference in strength there was between the sexes.

'They're so fast.' I watched with my mouth open, shocked. Mr Swarbrick looked at me with an odd expression, then nodded.

'Yes, they are – but they're almost fully grown men, they're going to be quicker than women.'

I scowled at him. 'I know there are some physical differences, but their technique is different too – look how often they breathe compared to how often I do.' I'd noticed they only came up to the side on every sixth breath, whereas I was every fourth. 'That will make a difference to their times too,' I pointed out.

161

'We can try that for you, but I think you'll find it harder. You're built differently to them,' Mr Swarbrick smiled. 'That's no bad thing. We use your own size in your favour, that's why you're quick.'

The shouts from the stands were getting louder and I watched as the winner touched the side, then immediately hung onto it looking every bit as though he were going to pass out.

'He looks exhausted.'

'I should think so too. He's given it everything. He needs to bring everything to the pool, leave nothing on the side, that's the motto.' Mr Swarbrick grinned. 'You should do the same. Give it everything. Leave nothing. I want you shattered.' His moustache wiggled with the merriment on his face. 'If I have to carry you home to your parents, even better.'

'Oh stop it, you couldn't lift me.' I watched as the rest of the male swimmers all pulled themselves out of the water, their chests heaving and I prepared myself for the pool.

'Right, off you go. Good luck.' Mr Swarbrick patted me on the shoulder and I nodded, removing my robe and giving it to him. 'Give them hell, Morton,' he advised and I grinned.

'Always do.'

The other women and I walked over to the pool to await our instructions. When we got to the edge of the pool I tried not to blanch as I realised just how far the other side was. I knew I could swim the distance and it would mean fewer turns to get to the two-mile mark. But it looked a bloody long way.

'All right. Ladies ready?' he looked to confirm we were in our places, then blew a short pip on his whistle.'

I dove in, allowing the shock of the cold water to wrap itself around me. Even though it was a warm day the heat hadn't worked its magic on the pool temperature and it felt freezing, but I ploughed on, knowing I'd become accustomed to it soon enough.

Quickly I got into a rhythm, pounding my way down to the end of my first length, ignoring the other swimmers around me and hoping I'd get used to the longer lengths as quickly as possible.

I touched the side and quickly turned to return down the pool.

Just forty-nine lengths to go.

Chapter Twenty-Five

'Damn and blast. Damn it, damn it, damn it, damn it.' I strode quickly down the road towards the train station, stomping my feet as Mr Swarbrick trailed behind me, attempting to keep up.

'Lucy, slow down. What do you think you'll achieve haring off? The train isn't due for another forty minutes, we have plenty of time,' he puffed, and I slowed my pace a little. The anger was fizzing inside me like an angry wasp that needed to escape. I'd hoped walking it off would help but to no avail.

'I don't know why you're so angry,' Mr Swarbrick began, and I stopped mid-stomp, turning on my heel to face him. I noted how much closer to him in height I was nowadays.

'I'm angry because I came second,' I spluttered. 'You of all people should understand that. I had it in the bag – I was in front for such a long time and if my stomach hadn't begun cramping up...'

'Stitch they call it, you had a stitch,' Mr Swarbrick supplied rather unhelpfully and I shot him a look to be quiet.

'Whatever it's called. I had it and the pain was so severe it's a wonder I got to the end. But to finish second after all that, it's just so damn frustrating.' I breathed out quickly, feeling like a bull who's been in one of those Spanish rings, my nostrils flaring.

'Have you quite finished?' my coach asked as we began a much slower-paced walk towards the station, my fight and fizz dissipating into irritation.

'I suppose,' I replied glumly, swinging the second-place medal in my hand. It had a satisfactory weight to it, I could see myself thwacking the winner with it quite successfully.

'You came second. You came second in a group of very talented female swimmers – not to mention, of course, that you were one of, if not *the* youngest there. You showed incredible promise and skill out there. You were just let down by your sportsmanship,' he chided and I grimaced.

'How do you mean?' I thought I'd behaved calmly.

Mr Swarbrick chuckled.

'You stood, arms crossed, with a pout and a face that clearly said you wanted to be anywhere but there. Yes, it was obvious. We need to work on that too.'

'I don't think it was just my sportsmanship that let me down.'

'Oh?'

Mr Swarbrick had an air of amusement and interest about him as we reached the station and were waved through by the ticket inspector to wait for the train on platform two. I settled on one of the wooden benches and Mr Swarbrick positioned himself next to me. He began to pack his pipe whilst we waited.

'With hindsight, I do wonder if I should have eaten as much as I did before the race,' I suggested and Mr Swarbrick laughed.

'What? Why? You needed the energy.'

'Yes, but soup, fish, steak and chips and to top it all, peaches and cream? I'm not so sure that was a good idea – I wonder if I should have had a little less,' I suggested, watching the pipe smoke curling upwards towards the heavens.

Mr Swarbrick shook his head.

'No, I shouldn't think so. Maybe it was just the timing. You need the food, we just need to work out a better time for you to eat it.'

'Or maybe I should think about dropping pudding if I have the other courses too,' I mooted, though I enjoyed dessert immensely, and it would be a shame to miss it. We both looked up as we heard a train whistle, and it came into the station.

'Ah, excellent, the train's early – we can take our seats and I plan on ordering some tea and cake. Watching you is hungry work, Lucy.' Mr Swarbrick gathered up the bags and opened the door to the carriage for me, allowing me to step on first. Having had the opportunity to sit on the bench for a little while, the swim and the anticipation of the race was catching up with me. Just stepping onto the train felt like an extreme effort.

'Come on, over here.' Mr Swarbrick guided me to my chair and sat me down.

'Are you joining me for tea and cake?' he prompted, as I made a pillow for myself with my light summer coat and put it under my head, against the window.

'Not yet. Maybe in a bit,' I managed, succumbing to sleep before the train had left the station.

When I awoke a few hours later we were pulling into Blackpool and Mr Swarbrick had moved from tea and cake to sandwiches and a glass of wine. He was tapping out his pipe and looked relieved to see me awake.

'I thought I was going to have to carry you.' He smiled. 'I'll get us a cab when we get out, I think you'll need to go home, eat some supper then head to bed.'

My mouth felt dry and my head was groggy.

'Are we training tomorrow?'

Mr Swarbrick smiled, chewing on his pipe.

'No, but we'll have you back in the pool on Monday, I've got another competition for you in a couple of months. It's not quite as far and I think you'll enjoy it.'

'Just as long as you don't expect me to smile.'

Chapter Twenty-Six

AUGUST 1913, BLACKPOOL

'Quite the collection you're building there.' Alice sat on the end of her bed as she watched me pin the gold medal for my latest breaststroke win to a cloth-covered board Mother had made. I was sat on my bed, the light-pink eiderdown scrunched under me a little, and as I held the board and looked at the variety of medals beginning to cluster on it, I felt proud of what I'd achieved so far.

Replacing it on the shelf above my bed, nudging a couple of other swimming certificates out of the way, I grinned at my sister.

'You're not doing too badly yourself.'

She smiled from her bed, but looked a little distant.

'What?'

She shook her head.

'My medal collection will never rival yours, but I don't mind,' she accepted. 'I'm proud of you, you know? Really proud. It's great to have a little taste of what you achieve, but you're special, Lucy. I hope you know that.'

I felt myself going red.

'What's going on? Are you after some money?' She was being unusually kind and, as we were sisters, this felt like something to be concerned about.

'Oh you, can't I just be happy for my sister?' She put her head to one side and went to pick up a book. She always had her head in one. 'Anyway, I do much better in all my classes than you – so we're pretty even,' she smirked.

I grabbed a pillow and threw it at her hard, taking her by surprise and leaving a cloud of feathers in the wake of the attack.

'Oi, I was unprepared,' Alice screamed, throwing her book to the side and grabbing her own feather-filled pillow. 'Time to take your medicine,' she laughed and propelled her pillow at me. It missed and fell on the floor but caught a pile of books, tumbling them everywhere.

'Oops,' she jumped down and picked up the pillow and books, 'quick, before Mother comes upstairs and tells us how irresponsible we are.'

She was right of course, Alice always did come across as the mature one out of the two of us. We jumped as we heard the familiar sound of Mother's footsteps coming up the stairs and quickly scrabbled to tidy up.

'How did she hear that?' I asked, trying to smooth my eiderdown and seeing, out of the corner of my eye, Alice rearrange her own bed and sit on it quickly holding her book. Just as I sat down, picking up a copy of my own book – *Pygmalion*, which I was finding terrifically good fun, Mother opened the door and looked at us both, then smiled.

'Well done, girls, good to see you're keeping yourselves busy.' She turned to me. 'Lucy, your father and I thought we should all come to the next competition. Mr Swarbrick thinks you're on the cusp of making a record.' She smiled at my embarrassment. 'He's downstairs by the way, said he'd walk you to training if you liked?' I nodded and picked up my bag following in Mother's wake, but catching Alice's eye as I left the room. She was barely able to stop herself from laughing.

I almost walked straight into Mother when she stopped suddenly, spun on her heels and returned to the bedroom. She looked around and frowned. Alice was shielding her face with her book, still.

'When you get back Lucy, you'll need to help Alice fix the pillows by the looks of it – unless you've been shooting birds in here?' She knelt down to scoop something off the floor, then turned to face me, opening her hand to show one tiny white feather.

'Ah,' I replied. Fortunately she smiled.

'Ah, indeed. Anyway, let's get you on your way.' She walked again in front of me, then stopped and looked at me, as though struggling with what she was to say next. Instead, she looked ahead to walk down the stairs, and as she walked she spoke to the air in front of her.

'There's a postcard for you. From Harry.'

I stopped mid-step as my stomach flipped. It had been a few months since bumping into Harry in the street, a meeting which had unsettled me because it had been so out of the blue. But I'd decided to leave it in the past. I'd been focusing on my swimming, I'd been improving. A lot. And I wasn't going to allow letters from a boy I'd once known ruin my future.

I swallowed. 'I don't want it. You can bin it.' We reached the bottom of the stairs and my mother turned to look at me. I was taller than her now, so she had to look up at me a little.

'Are you sure?' I felt her eyes on me, searching mine, but I nodded.

'Very sure.'

'Right,' she nodded back, 'if that's what you wish.'

I nodded again. 'It is.'

Chapter Twenty-Seven

SEPTEMBER 1913, BLACKPOOL

'Go, Lucy, go.'

I could hear Mr Swarbrick's voice from a long distance away and it did little to spur me on. I was going as fast as I bloody could. How about he got in and swam, rather than yelling from the side-lines – which, by the way, made next to no difference to my time.

I gritted my teeth and continued pushing my arms through the water.

I could hear other yells around me as I made my way down the pool and I studiously ignored those too, hoping I could focus on the task in hand. Two hundred yards of breaststroke.

One more length to go.

I tried to push down the excitement. Tried to focus it as strength as I pushed through the water. I couldn't see anyone in front of me and I felt good. Better than good. The hours I'd been putting in with Mr Swarbrick were definitely paying off.

As I made my way down the final few yards I pushed the hardest I'd ever gone, reaching my hand out to the side and gasping in exhaustion.

'And it's a new ladies record,' boomed the announcer, 'Morton has set the new national ladies record in the two hundred yards breaststroke, with a time of 3.48.'

I heaved in, trying to capture the oxygen I'd used up in pushing to my absolute edge, not sure I could believe what I was listening to. Quickly though, Mr Swarbrick was pulling me out of the water onto the side and someone else handed me my robe. A huge cheer from the sides roared in my ears as I stood up straight and I grinned at the spectators.

'Fantastic work, well done.' Mr Swarbrick pumped my arm up and down in his excitement to congratulate me and I laughed with relief, despite my shoulders burning from the previous efforts.

'All right, leave me intact – I've got another race in twenty minutes,' I reminded my coach, who beamed.

'I know, but you've got a record – at fifteen – it's brilliant, you're brilliant,' he told me, and I smiled again. It was good to hear.

'Are my parents here?' I looked around at the spectators, trying to find them, and Mr Swarbrick nodded.

'They're here, they were waving and cheering like mad for you over there somewhere.' He carelessly gestured in a certain direction of the indoor pool, the shouts of the crowd rolling over each other in a bubble of noise.

'Come on, medal ceremony and then you need to get ready for the next one.' Mr Swarbrick said happily. 'Just imagine if you can do it again for the one hundred and fifty yards.'

I shook my head.

'I'm not sure I have much more energy,' I protested and Mr Swarbrick smiled again.

'That's not the Lucy I know. Once you get in the water you'll want to motor up and down there like in training – and anyway, it's a shorter distance, it'll be even easier for you to win again.' He laughed at his own comment and walked away to talk to my parents in the stands.

After the medal ceremony I stood drinking a cup of tea, gripping the cup so as to press some warmth into my fingers. My robe was helping keep me warm but I was in need of another layer to stop the goose-bumps from forming. As I looked up at the large clock on the side of the pool building, I noted I only had a few minutes until the next race. I'd warm up once I was back in the water and moving, no doubt.

'Lucy – you were incredible.' I looked to my right and was thrilled when I saw who it was.

'Greta, how are you? It's been ages.' The two of us hugged and she held me at arm's distance, shaking her head slightly and smiling. She looked so grown-up now, her clothes were closer in similarity to my moth-er's outfits than my own light smocks.

'Yes, at least a year I think?' She cocked her head on one side. 'I can't believe you're still keeping the Christ Church girls in medals. Good for you.' I noted a slight tone in her voice and my lack of understanding must have made itself known across my face.

Greta put her hand to her face in horror. 'Sorry, Lucy, don't mind me. I'm just jealous, that's all – I've not swum in a few years, and now I'm getting married I wonder if I ever will again.'

'Wow, married. Congratulations, Greta,' I managed. It was odd, I'd looked up to Greta when I'd swum on her team a few years before, but our age gap of four years had barely registered with me. Now, I realised, she was almost nineteen, the world was very different for her. I was still at home with my parents. Still swimming. She was to be someone's wife.

'Lucy, over to the pool,' said Mr Swarbrick, at my side, and I'd lost the opportunity to ask Greta what she was doing at the pool if it wasn't for swimming. As I watched her walk away I noted she fell into step with one of the pool marshals, their heads bent together in a familiar way and I took that as an answer.

Ignoring the creeping thoughts that I would, inevitably, have to become like Greta and give up swimming one day when I became a wife, and presumably a mother because I'd have other things I'd be expected to concentrate on, I pulled myself back into the present.

'I'll take that, pet.' Mr Swarbrick took my robe and immediately the shock of the air chilled me. I slapped my thighs and arms to get some feeling in them again and stomped my feet.

'Right then, no pressure but you've already broken one record, fancy another? It's yours, Lucy. I can feel it.' My coach patted my shoulder.

'I'll just do what I can.'

He nodded.

'Right, see you in three lengths.' He nodded again and then took his place a few yards away, where the rest of the coaches stood. I briefly watched him make his way, then set my sights on the pool. It had barely been twenty minutes since I'd last been pulled out of it and I wasn't sure I had much strength left in my legs.

'Ladies, to the side please,' the announcer began and I shuffled my feet to the edge, rolled my head and worked two cricks out of my neck, shrugged my shoulders to remind them they'd be moving again soon and listened to the words which would send me back in the water.

'Ready, set...' I responded immediately to the short sharp chirrup of the whistle.

The next minute and a half disappeared in a flurry of arms pumping, legs aching, lungs burning, eyes streaming, eardrum bursting, crowds cheering and then finally, there was just a few yards between myself and the poolside. Between gulps of air and pushing through the water, I could see Mr Swarbrick yelling, encouraging me to the end.

When I reached the end, the pain in my ear was searing but I could see Mr Swarbrick punching the air, I'd never seen him so animated. He ran over to me, a huge smile on his face.

'You did it, Lucy, you did it.' He punched the air again and I shook my head. I was thrilled but completely done in. Mr Swarbrick spotted how tired I was and stooped down to pull me up on the side. I slumped onto the cold bricks, every part of my body felt like it had turned to jelly.

'Two national records. Two.' My mother and father had arrived by my side, my father shaking Mr Swarbrick's hand.

'Fantastic work, great coaching, George,' my father said jovially to him. My mother cautiously dropped to the ground, trying not to get her skirt wet, and failing. I watched as the moisture from the floor began to seep into the material, dark shapes chasing upwards.

'Lucy, what do you need?'

'Water, and food,' I replied quietly, unsurprised it was Mother who'd spotted I was flagging completely.

'Right you are.' Turning to the men as she stood, she spoke authoritatively to them. 'She needs her robe, Alfred. George, can you find her a glass of water and a biscuit?' I could see her holding his arm for attention. 'Try and get more than one.' She looked in my direction as I sat slumped on the ground, afraid of standing. Untrusting of my limbs.

They did as they were told and barely a minute later I had drunk the water down in three greedy gulps, coughing as the liquid cleared the taste of the swimming pool, and hastily cramming the biscuits into my mouth in the hope I'd begin to feel better. The pain in my ear had quietened a touch, but it was worrying. I'd heard of others having to give up swimming once they'd burst an eardrum. I tried not to think about it just then.

A few minutes later I was feeling a lot more like me.

'Can we get Miss Morton to the prize-giving yet?' An official had hovered next to my small group of supporters. 'We have the local press here to take her photograph – congratulations by the way. Two records, incredible.' He grinned then walked away.

Mr Swarbrick pulled me to my feet, allowing me to lean a little against him whilst I regained my trust in my legs.

'Ready to make a little local history?' he asked, a huge smile rippling his moustache.

Chapter Twenty-Eight

'Watch it,' Father exclaimed as he pulled me back onto the kerb, where seconds before a horse and its cart had been overtaken by a shiny black motorcar. It had veered so quickly around the corner of the bustling promenade, I'd been convinced it was going to balance on two wheels and it had frightened the horse. The motorist had barely noticed the commotion he'd caused as he disappeared off, up the road, smoke billowing out of the exhaust.

Father was shaking his head and talking animatedly to the coach driver.

'Happens most days now,' the driver was saying, 'frightens these half to death.' He was stroking the horse, calming it down and my father nodded.

'We have the same problem.' He spoke of the issues he'd been seeing with the horses he looked after at Knutsford House. But, I noticed, he neglected to mention that Sir Standon had his own deep-burgundy car. A car which I was pretty certain I'd seen my father look at longingly.

I waited as patiently as I could, then lightly pulled on his sleeve. 'Father, the show.'

'Of course,' he nodded at the coach driver and began to walk towards the tower. 'Come on don't want you missing this. Your mother and Alice should be inside, holding our seats.'

My family had booked tickets to the circus as a wonderful surprise for after my competition. They'd wanted to take me to something to either commiserate, or, thankfully, to celebrate my swimming success. Though the timing was getting a little short and I was beginning to worry we'd miss it.

We'd had just enough time to get back to the house, thanks to all the photos I'd had taken. I'd then swiftly changed into my neatest of dresses, noting that I'd need to take the hem down soon as it was getting a little short, ran a brush through my hair then dashed back downstairs to Father so we could walk to the tower. In the meantime, Alice and Mother had bagged our seats, and were waiting, I hoped, with some sort of food to watch the show. I was starving. And tired.

But as we crossed the road, avoiding another horse and cart, Blackpool Tower appeared in front of us in all her beauty. Lit up like a Christmas tree, she had lights all the way the eye could see and the huge sign on the front of the tower was emblazoned with the words '*Wonderland of the World*' and my tiredness lifted.

'Something isn't it?' Father sighed next to me and squeezed my hand. 'Never fails to take my breath away.'

'Makes you proud to be from here, doesn't it?' I replied, watching as families streamed into the front of the tower, presumably to go to the circus too.

My father's squeeze got tighter, and he looked at me with a silly grin on his face. 'You make me proud you know, you're only fifteen but I see big things for you.'

'Come on, let's go inside.' I pulled his hand. I wasn't one for public scenes, nice as the sentiment was.

We made our way to the tower and pushed our way through the crowds, eventually finding our way to the circus arena. Housed between the four giant legs at the base of the tower, the crowd of over one thousand ticketholders were already jostling to get the best position.

'There,' Father pointed out Mother and Alice, a few banks of seats away from us. I gripped his hand as tightly as I could as we pushed our way through the other last-minute audience members vying to get as good a seat. The smell of popcorn, mixed with the sawdust on the floor of the arena sparked memories of the other times Alice and I had been taken to the circus. It was something all four of us enjoyed.

'You made it, jolly good.' Alice stood and waved as we made our way down the aisles, forcing other people to move or stand up, so we could get to them.

'So sorry, so sorry,' I kept repeating, aware my height was incredibly annoying to people who had settled down already.

'Shhh, the show's about to start,' a man hissed in my ear as I edged passed.

I sank gratefully next to Alice as Father took his place on the other end, nearest to Mother and Alice took my hand, squeezing it in her gloved one.

'You're so clever, I'm so proud of you. If I could have a tenth of your speed,' Mother began, but before she could continue, the rumble of the drums began and the ringmaster's voice spoke out to the crowd through the darkness.

'Ladies and gentlemen, boys and girls, are you ready for the best circus in the world?' His voice vibrated amongst the stands and the audience cheered and clapped in response.

'Be prepared for wild beasts that will jump through hoops,' he continued, and Alice squeezed my hand. Her favourite had always been the lions who tore around the arena floor, snarling and growling, only to behave themselves and turn into good-natured kittens who'd jump through rings of fire, should the ringmaster tell them with a crack of his whip. I wasn't as keen. I couldn't help but think they looked a bit sad.

And I was frightened of the bear. Not that I'd tell Alice that – I was her big sister, I wasn't frightened of anything. But privately, the bear worried me. He was chained so heavily, the ankle weights dug into his legs. If he really wanted to be there, surely he wouldn't need to be chained with such force? The chains reminded me of the pictures of suffragettes still in the newspapers. They were chained to beds. Drugged. Force-fed.

I shook my head to rid myself of the images and stories I'd heard lately, focusing on the ringmaster. He was stood on a large red box, painted in gold stars. His red coat was decorated with gleaming gold buttons and he wore a black top hat. He looked immaculate.

'Look out for our stunning acrobats and be amazed as they perform the most extraordinary feats of balance and strength,' the ringmaster continued and I brightened up. They were my favourite – I loved watching them walking along the tightrope, so high in the air. I loved the elegance as they tumbled and threw themselves around the top of the arena. Always on the precipice of danger, but just in the nick of time, being caught.

'Without further ado, let's get on with the show,' the ringmaster's voice boomed out.

I settled in with the chips Mother had picked up for me and demolished them in their salty gloriousness in a matter of minutes, whilst watching the clown rolling out onto the arena. His face had been painted white, with black diamonds to mimic the ones on his collar and his shoes were so enormous they'd make him trip up. He wandered over to a bathtub and promptly fell into it – my father's booming laugh was the biggest in the arena.

The one clown was shortly joined by two others who began a skit of never-ceasing silliness, with one after another falling into the bathtub, then pulling each other out and throwing the third in. The crowd roared with laughter as two pushed the bath around with the third inside the tub, the smallest one, with a red nose, holding on. They pushed him faster and faster, his screams streaming out across the audience as he was wheeled around the entirety of the outside of the arena. He was gripping on as the other two pushed him at such a speed they seemed a blur. Tears of laughter were streaming down Alice's face.

'Do you think he's all right?' she gasped, pausing a little in her mirth to dab her eyes, as we watched the next part of the act. The smallest clown had got out of the bathtub gingerly, walking with a wobble to the back of the arena. He had disappeared and the other two clowns appeared concerned, unsure as to what he was doing.

'Look.' I pointed to the back, as the smallest clown walked back into the arena, followed by something on a lead.

'It's Wanda,' Alice beamed. Wanda was the most famous elephant in the circus. She was a beauty. The chain the small clown held went directly to the metal anklet which encircled her tree trunk of a leg.

'What's he doing?' Alice giggled, staring ahead.

'I'm not sure,' I replied. It had been well over a year since we'd last visited the circus, and the whole show had changed.

'Oh wait... look.' Alice was pointing in the direction of the elephant who was gently dipping her enormous grey head into a bucket the small clown was holding. Her trunk was immersed and she was sucking up something. The pair of clowns had realised what was happening at the same time as the audience and had begun to run for cover. But first they ran into each other, falling comically to the floor, enormous shoes swinging into the air.

'Go on,' I laughed, 'go on, Wanda, you can do it.' We all watched as the elephant lumbered her way carefully to the clowns, who stood, cowering, trapped between a cage where the lions paced, and the side of the arena. They had nowhere to go.

The smallest clown had walked slowly with his steed, he looked around the arena, and raised his arms to suggest, '*Should I*?' and the crowd cheered.

'Do it, do it, do it,' chanted the crowd, many of whom stood, including myself and Alice. We stomped our feet, cheered the smallest clown. He was going to win. He looked at the elephant, raised his arm and she did as she was bid. She sprayed the two clowns up and down, with a jet of water like firemen would use.

'Oh my, they're soaked, they must be so mad,' I applauded wildly, smiling broadly at Alice. 'Wait, look.' The elephant was reloading from the bucket the smallest clown was holding, and this time, all three clowns stood together.

Looking at the crowd.

They looked at one another as the front row realised what was to happen.

They raised their arms.

Wanda did as she was told.

And I grinned that it wasn't me getting soaked for once.

Chapter Twenty-Nine

FEBRUARY 1914, BLACKPOOL

'Happy birthday!' The cheer came from around the table in our kitchen. I blew out the candles on top of my cake, feeling optimistic for the year ahead.

'Well, did you make a wish?' Alice leaned in and whispered over my shoulder, the scent of violets which always accompanied her lightly enveloping me.

'Yes, I wished for a less irritating younger sister,' I grinned at her, then dodged as she tried to land a punch on my shoulder.

'Girls.' Mother had turned her back to us whilst slicing the cake. 'You are young women, behave like them. Honestly, we'll never find nice young men for you if you behave like this in company.'

I looked around the table.

'But we're not in company,' I reminded her, and Father laughed a little, coughing to cover it as Mother looked sternly in his direction.

'May I remind you that Mr Swarbrick counts as company,' she looked at my coach. I watched as Mr Swarbrick's facial expressions veered between wanting to agree with his friend, and me, his charge.

'I'm sure they behave wonderfully when outside the home,' he placated. 'Indeed, when Lucy and I are at the pool, or walking outside, her manners are impeccable.' He turned to my father. 'You should be very proud of her – of them both, Alfred.'

Mother handed around plates of cake.

Aiming to shift the conversation along from my inevitable future, I remembered something. 'Are we really going to the pictures today?' I kept my fingers crossed under the table in hope.

'Yes, a Charlie Chaplin picture – I've said Mr Swarbrick's daughter can act as your chaperone.' Mother nodded at Alice and me. We smiled back. Molly was marvellous. She had a sparkle in her eye and a brilliant sense of humour, but because she was twenty-two and unmarried, Mother was a little uncomfortable about what effect she would have on us. But she was Mr Swarbrick's daughter and Mother had to give in sometimes.

'Looks like it's still kicking off in Ireland,' Father said to Mr Swarbrick, rustling his copy of *The Telegraph*. 'Here, Jessie, there's a women's supplement for you and the girls.' Mother took the paper from him and placed it on the dresser to the left of the fireplace. I knew she'd pick it up later in the day when she stopped for a pot of tea.

'If we could just get those Irish to behave,' Mr Swarbrick replied, his moustache moving animatedly as he spoke.

'And the suffragettes – did you hear they've taken to defiling works of art now?'

'Everyone's a critic,' Alice giggled into my shoulder and I moved abruptly, surprising her.

'It's not a laughing matter,' I snapped. Had they all forgotten Harry? His mother?

My mother had looked up sharply, her last piece of cake left forgotten on her plate. 'Let's be civil. It is your birthday. Sixteen... When I was your age I'd met your father already.' She glanced over at Father, causing Alice and I to roll our eyes.

'It was different then,' I replied between mouthfuls of sponge cake. Deliberately eating in a way to irritate her. 'We have more opportunities now.'

Mother raised her eyebrows. 'Maybe we don't need as many opportunities.' I went to reply but before I could say anything, she continued. 'Don't get me wrong, I'm pleased you've both had a chance to go to school, I'm pleased you can both swim. Those are things I never did. But...' Mother looked away for a moment, recovered herself, looked at my father and then sighed. 'Nothing. Your world is very different to mine.'

'Change is a good thing, Jessie,' Mr Swarbrick interjected. 'Change is exciting. We're in an age of horses and motorcars, there's new medicines, technological break-throughs. It's an exciting time.'

'Hear-hear, and long may it continue.' Father raised his teacup to toast and we all did the same thing.

Chapter Thirty

MARCH 1914, BLACKPOOL

'I've met a boy,' Alice confided as she threw herself breathlessly onto her bed in our shared room.

'A boy, what kind of boy, how?' My head was full of questions. Alice, as far as I was aware, never went anywhere but swimming or to school, or to her job. Just like me. When did she have the opportunity to meet somebody?

'Do you remember?' Alice's eyes were gleaming, a picture of joy. 'When we were at the pictures to watch that Charlie Chaplin film for your birthday? He showed us to our seat.' I shook my head, I couldn't remember.

'James.' Alice hugged herself as she said his name. Then I remembered. At the time when he'd shown us to our seats there'd been a certain spark that flashed in his eye and I had fleetingly considered that he and Alice had somehow connected, but I didn't think much of it at the time. Instead, I enjoyed the jolly good picture and sharing a laugh with Molly.

'How have you been meeting up?' I couldn't believe she'd kept a secret from me. Of all people. We shared a room. We swam together. I felt cut out. 'Alice what's going on?'

From her bed, Alice laughed with joy.

'Hush now, sister, hush – all in good time. Lucy, he's just wonderful.' She sat back and held her hands over her heart. 'Honestly, it's like we're meant to be together.'

I scoffed a little.

'Alice, you're fourteen. You can't surely want to settle down with somebody as young as this.' I was caught a little off guard when Alice guffawed before answering.

'Don't be silly,' she said. 'I don't want to settle down. Not yet. But I do wonder if maybe Mother and Father wouldn't mind in a couple of years. He's seventeen – there's only a three-year gap. I do believe it'll be fine when we finally live together.'

It was difficult for me to try and work out a response. I wasn't certain that Mother and Father would be fine. But at the same time, she did seem happy.

'So, tell me more about James, who is he? Does he have any prospects?'

Alice laughed and ignored my question.

'Oh Lucy, I am really very happy. We've been meeting every day. I go to the picture house where he works. And he showed me how he runs the pictures and everything. It's fascinating.' Alice lay back happily on her bed. 'We chat. He makes me laugh, Lucy. I'm just so happy when I'm with him.' She was beaming.

'I'm really happy for you. So what's the plan now then?' I was a little bit jealous. After Harry, there hadn't been anybody else who made my heart flutter, not in the way that Alice was acting.

'Well,' Alice took a deep breath, 'he's asked me to go to the amusements with him today and I'd like to tell Mother and Father. But I was hoping that maybe you could be our escort – and you can be there when I tell them.'

'Ah, that's why you've told me, so you can have someone be there with you. So it's all seen as above board.' I shook my head, fondly yet sagely.

'Oh, Lucy, will you?' Alice looked at me with her eyes wide, imploring. 'Please, please, pretty please.' Alice jumped over onto my bed and was hugging and kissing me.

'Please.' She had her arms around my neck.

'Please, please, please, please, please.'

'Fine, anything to put a stop to this nonsense. But you have to tell Mother and Father now, and you have to agree with whatever time they tell you to get back by. I don't want to be responsible for anything going on.' I looked knowingly at her. 'You know what I'm saying, Alice, don't you?'

She nodded.

'I understand. You know, I'm not like Glenda.'

There had been a fair bit of hoo-ha in the neighbourhood lately with one of the girls that Alice had been at school with falling pregnant to some boy out of wedlock.

She'd gone to the countryside apparently to be married to a much older gentleman. Her parents hadn't admitted the truth, of course. They'd spoken of a marriage to a good family. How it had all been arranged for months but we all knew the truth. And knew about the boy she'd left behind.

'I'm going to be careful, Lucy, I promise. I just want to be with the man that I love.'

I was shocked. 'You love?'

I looked over at my younger sister and shook my head, a smile forming on my lips. 'Well, who am I to stand in the path of true love?'

'Does that mean you'll be our escort? We can begin courting?'

'If Mother and Father say it's all right.'

Later on, as we walked down the promenade with the lights twinkling, I saw Alice take James's hand and I smiled to myself. They really did seem very happy together. Mother and Father had understandably been concerned about him but he was lovely and kind. Being three years older, they did worry about what his intentions would be. But she had convinced them. Alice always managed to convince them.

I did feel rather like a third wheel walking behind the couple, just a few steps away all the time and, surprising myself at my reaction I found joy from seeing them so happy. Watching them as they enjoyed their ices reminded me of when Harry took me on our special walk along the promenade. I allowed them to go up on The Flying Machine together, on their own, because I hoped they'd have an opportunity to have that secret kiss – if that's what they were after. As long as nothing else was going to happen.

As I was waiting for them to come down, I stood, watching the people who passed by. All of them were unknown faces but then I recognised one of them.

'Greta,' I said loudly, surprising some of the other passers-by who looked flustered at my bellowing. Greta looked over her shoulder and when she recognised me made a dash to embrace me closely.

'Lucy, how the devil are you?' She was her usual exuberant self, dressed head to toe in burgundy. She struck quite an intriguing character on the waterfront. I noted that she looked a lot older than when I last saw her, but then she had to be around about twenty now, I realised. A couple of years older than Harry. The thought was in my head before I could prevent it, I needed to stop thinking about him. It was the trip down memory lane that was doing it.

Greta was talking and I tuned in to what she was saying.

'I'm very well, and how are you? I know everything about you,' she squealed. 'You're doing so well – winning those records last year. I tell everyone I know that I know you,' she said, grinning. 'Do you have any other swimming plans? What about the Olympics?' I realised her enthusiasm was infectious. I was smiling too.

'Oh, I don't know about the Olympics, obviously it'd be marvellous,' I said whilst, trying to keep an eye on Alice and James who had disembarked from the ride and looked as though they were going to walk off in the opposite direction to me. 'But I don't think it'll be possible,' I admitted, 'it looks like the strokes women can compete in aren't either of the ones I swim. It's mainly freestyle, so unless that changes it doesn't look likely.' I shrugged and waved at Alice to stop her disappearing. 'But we'll see.'

'Well, I think you're doing marvellously, I'm so proud of you.'

A warm glow of pride spread through me, and to spare my blushes, I covered them with a cough. 'And what about you? What about your swimming? You could compete?'

Greta laughed.

'Oh, I don't think so, I'm getting a little bit old to swim – I'm twenty, I've got things to do. There's too many younger people out there behind me, just like you, gunning for my record and anyway, you'll do better than I ever could,' she laughed happily. 'Plus, I'm not sure I could get by with this.' She opened a button on her coat and revealed a small bump.

I clapped my hand to my mouth with surprise.

'Well, no wonder you're not swimming – when are you due? You're not going to drop right now, are you, I'm not sure I'd know what to do.'

'No, no.' Greta stroked my arm fondly. 'Not anytime soon. A few more weeks, but I'll be pleased when it's all over – bloody ridiculous carrying this thing around all the time,' she whispered, aware we weren't expected to complain about being pregnant. Recovering herself, she stood straighter, and rubbed her back. 'Anyway, I love Bertie. We're very happy together and happy to have a baby. Well, that's a proper family isn't it? I'm a lucky woman.' To my sixteen-year-old ears I couldn't help but wonder if Greta was trying to convince herself more than me, but I didn't have long to think about it, as Alice walked over to me.

Ignoring Greta, she grabbed my hand.

'Lucy, come on, less chat, more walking with James and I.' I laughed at the pleading voice.

'You did promise,' Alice continued and I caught Greta's eye, trying not to laugh again. 'Come on, James is going to get bored and leave me behind.' She looked at Greta as if it was the first time she'd spotted her. 'Greta – nice to see you so well. You look as though you're fit to burst.'

I gasped.

'Alice, always a charmer.' I gave her a hard stare, hoping she'd understood she'd crossed a line, but Greta grinned.

'I think I probably am. Fit to burst. You're quite right, and my feet are starting to ache somewhat as well so I will have to make my goodbyes and head off. It was so lovely to bump into you, Lucy. Best of luck with the swimming. I do hope we'll see some more successes from you in the future.'

'Thank you, but who knows.'

Alice looked between us. 'You'll see all the successes, Greta. Just don't believe what she says, she's ever so quiet about it all but she is really very secretly ambitious.'

Greta smiled at us both.

'I think you've got a good cheerleader there, Lucy. You're a very lucky lady.'

I looked at Alice who was staring pensively at James, holding three ices.

'Oh, ever so lucky – now what was that about me having to follow behind you on your date?'

Chapter Thirty-One

AUGUST 1914, LIVERPOOL

At a time when men were considering how they approached hostilities around Europe like pieces in a complicated game of chess, I was stood with eleven other women on the shore of the western side of the Mersey.

We were to swim from Eastham bay, where we stood slapping our thighs to warm them in the mid-morning breeze and making last-minute adjustments to the chin straps of our swim caps, to the Conway training ship moored near Rock Ferry, then back. It would be one mile in total.

Looking at the Amazonic nature of my competitors I rolled my shoulders back. We were one and the same. All slim-framed, all distinctly angular of shoulder and relatively bulky of bicep. I recognised Phyllis, we'd bumped into each other at other swim meets, so I smiled at her, and she returned in kind. All the women, except one, were of a similar height – the exception being a swimmer a few along from me who appeared to be shorter than five foot.

The president of the Liverpool Ladies Swimming Club, dressed in a neat dark-blue outfit comprising of a skirt showing off dainty black court shoes, accompanied by a matching blue silk jacket and a cream blouse, stood on a podium, brought down to the shore for this very purpose, and held a megaphone to her lips. The action brought a hush to the chatter from the crowd drawn from the swimmers' supporters and interested passers-by.

'Ladies and gentlemen, especially these brilliant ladies who are to embark on the first ever Ladies One Mile Mersey Championship, it is a privilege to welcome you to our competition.' She took a deep breath, smoothing a blonde strand of hair behind her ear, which had escaped from under the wide-brimmed hat she was sporting, decorated with an ostentatious bow before continuing. I couldn't remember a time when Mother had worn anything so fashionable. I realised I was grinning broadly at the president looking at her shoes when I should have listened to the rules.

The rest of the swimmers began to walk to the shoreline and I followed suit. I blew out the excitement and fear I'd been holding in for the past hour or so with a deep breath. Just as I was walking to the shore to get the race started, the smallest swimmer made her way to me.

'No breathing like that in the water, remember.' I nodded but as she walked away I wasn't sure what she was talking about.

'Why?' I yelled after her, hoping she'd stop.

'Didn't you listen to the speech?'

'Yes,' I lied.

She shook her head. 'Just keep your mouth closed,' she advised.

I quickly realised what she was talking about as the race began.

'Shit,' one of the swimmers near me yelled, and I was mortified to realise she was right. The water was filthy and filled with all sorts of unimaginable things, including raw sewage but we were already at least a hundred metres out from the shoreline and I wasn't turning back. It wasn't the most attractive of propositions but I was going to do my best to win, that's why I was here.

Pushing forwards I kept up the usual breaststroke, but kept my face further out of the water in a bid to prevent anything unwanted getting into my mouth. Whether it was the potential encounter with excrement or that I was feeling strong and I'd got into a rhythm, I'm not sure, but I was getting closer to the ship, our turning point, and I could tell I was beginning to lead the others.

The nearer I got to the Conway, the more impressive it looked and I marvelled at its size. A black ship with enormous white lines painted around its entirety. All three sail masts stood tall, bedecked in flags of every colour and nation imaginable. The sight was one of gaiety and, I realised, all for us. As we swam closer I could hear the sounds of a brass band playing and a large group of naval students were stood cheering and hollering in our direction. It was a moment of pure joy, in what had been a month lacking in it. The way the newspapers were telling it, things were only going to escalate in Europe and whilst no-one knew what the future could hold, I had a pretty good feeling it would mean this was to be one of the last swimming competitions for a while.

Holding this thought, I pushed forward and touched the rough wooden side of the ship briefly, to huge cheers from the. I turned away from the frivolity and continued, back the way I came, passing the other swimmers – many still hot on my heels.

Going against the tide now, it was harder to push through the water, but I continued whilst keeping a fixed stare on the shoreline hundreds of yards away, the sounds of the band receding as I went forwards. Soon it was just me, the splash and slap of the sea against my body and the occasional squawk from the gulls that were watching the odd spectacle of eleven women swimming to a ship and back.

The sun was on my back and I was relieved whenever the water washed over me. Whatever muck it contained in its depths, it did at least cool the sunburn I was beginning to suffer from due to the past twenty minutes of my back being exposed. Soon though, I was in view of the crowd on the beach. I could feel the water beginning to warm as it grew shallower but I kept kicking out my legs, thrusting out my arms and hoping I wouldn't swallow any water.

'Go on, Lucy, you can do it,' my sister's voice came at me from the shore. She was jumping up and down, clapping her hands enthusiastically.

I used everything I had left and kicked and pushed for all that it was worth, then suddenly, my feet hit the ground and I stumbled and walked out of the water across the pebbles, the pain of them shooting into my bare feet but it was easy to ignore, knowing I was first.

'I won,' I yelled at Alice, who came running to me with a dressing robe, 'I won.' I jumped up and down with her.

'I know, you were brilliant – I kept telling everyone around me that you're my sister.' Alice laughed joyfully. 'Mother and Father were doing the same. Look.' I gazed in the direction she was pointing and grinned at my parents' huge smiles, then turned to watch the rest of the swimmers making their way in, battling their way across the waves and shoreline as I realised I'd been ahead by quite some way.

Alice returned to my parents as the others trudged up through the pebbles and soon all of us stood dripping and shivering on the shoreline, wrapped in robes, our caps removed from our heads, and smiles on at least three of our faces as we awaited the medal ceremony.

Once the press were in place and ready for us, we stood on the makeshift podium to show who was in first, second and third. From my prime spot I could see the happy smiles from Mother, Father, Mr Swarbrick and Alice and I smiled widely too. The hours of training had begun to pay off.

The sun was beating down, drying my body and warming me. I turned my face to the beams of light and felt lifted by them. As I smiled I heard the click of a camera and realised that would be the photo in the paper tomorrow.

'And in first place, Lucy Morton, who completed the challenge in twenty-four minutes and twenty-five seconds, with a lead of forty yards,' announced the swimming president, handing me a gold brooch with the mythical Liver Birds on it. 'Jolly well done,' she said loudly, then leant in to whisper, 'good show, Lucy.'

Chapter Thirty-Two

July 1915, Blackpool

S wimming rather pales into insignificance when you're faced with the death of men and boys you've known all your life. What's the point in immersing oneself in water when people you've grown up with are dying in manners so grotesque? Or men who you used to buy bread from coming back from the war with a far-away look in their eye and a tendency to look forever haunted?

I stopped swimming shortly after my mile race in Liverpool, though the draw of the water was strong. How could it not be when I walked past the sea on my daily journey to work? Past the waves that crashed and broke on the shore. The suck and draw of the water over the pebbles rattling with the upset of the movement. The memory of walking into the sea and diving into the waves, exerting power over nature.

The pool was closed, the focus was on other things. I accepted swimming was unimportant – anybody I spoke to would say as much – it couldn't help the war effort, it didn't put food on the table and it wouldn't bring anyone home.

Instead, I committed to helping those men fighting in any way I could. I signed up to work in the Post Office after a huge advertising campaign from the government to get women into jobs in the civil service, so men could serve on the front line. I worked in the sorting office with a jolly bunch of women, and we kept each other's spirits up.

I tried not to look back and remember life as it had been before. Life when we could make a birthday cake with all the ingredients, could blow out candles and make ridiculous wishes, when everything was possible. I didn't think back to a year before, when we had no idea that life would change in the way it did. When we still gaily bought dresses, traded gossip, went about our tiny lives making no impact on anyone.

It felt as though Blackpool had been invaded. It hadn't. But with the sheer volume of troops descending on the town – the *Lancashire Gazette* claimed fourteen thousand, though I didn't know if that was true – it felt like the height of summer with all the tourists who came to spread out across the promenade like a plague. But unlike the summer hordes who went home, this was unceasing. An unrelenting flow of young men coming to our town to prepare for war.

Between training sessions, the troops visited the entertainments on the seafront. I watched many of them walking past Brighton Cottage, beyond North Shore to get to the tower, which had so far remained open to 'keep spirits up'. In the summer that had almost passed, they'd be seen sunning themselves on the beach, or spending their money in the amusements, or visiting the pubs. Not that you could hold any of this merrymaking against them. I'd rather they came here and had a few laughs and a few pints, before heading to the war where so many of them would then lose their lives.

On one of his many regular trips to our home, Mr Swarbrick had settled into his favourite chair next to the fire in the kitchen and was stirring his teacup slowly. Lost in thought.

'Lucy, did you know there's a competition being organised?' He spoke quietly, gauging my reaction.

'What of it?' I replied, pouring out my tea, wiping up a spill on the kitchen table, purposefully not meeting his eye.

'I thought you'd like to take part.' His response was lightly muffled as he wiped his moustache with a napkin I'd left out for him. I used the opportunity to search for one of Mother's oat biscuits in the scullery, to hide my face, my emotions from him.

'And what would give you that impression?' I returned with three of the biscuits Mother had been able to conjure up with the paltry butter and sugar we were now allocated, arranged on a plate covered in a pattern of faded wild flowers.

Mr Swarbrick took a biscuit and held it as though he was weighing up what to say next.

'You're good at it, Lucy. You know you are.' He leant forward in his chair, resting one hand on his thigh, the other still holding his teacup. 'Why aren't you swimming? The pools have been open for two weeks and I thought you'd be the first through the door. The troops want to use them, so you've got the chance. Why aren't you training? Your father says he can't remember the last time you trained. What's going on?'

I sat heavily in front of him and took time stirring a little milk into my cup.

'I can't.'

Mr Swarbrick looked confused.

'Can't? Why, yes you can, of course you can swim. For God's sake, you've been given a gift – use it.'

I shook my head. How could I explain it? How could I say that I went to the pool, not a week ago, and that as soon I got into the water I enjoyed the rush the cold brought. My body felt entirely at home once again. Me again. Reminded me I was alive. But in an instant the guilt came. To do something frivolous like swimming seemed an indulgence, an affront to the men who were dying, or signing up to fight in a war that seemed endless. And mirthless. And senseless.

'It just doesn't seem... right.' I chose my reply carefully, and sipped my tea, looking solidly at Mr Swarbrick, whose face creased a little with sadness. As I replaced my cup in its saucer he reached a hand out to pat mine.

'It's for that exact reason, pet, you need to swim. All those men are dying. Their lives are being cut incredibly short – many of them are your age.' He broke off and shook his head. 'It's such a waste.'

'But that's why I shouldn't be—' I began, at the same time as Mr Swarbrick continued.

'You're not dead. Don't waste your life. Live it as best you can right now. And that includes using the gift you've been given, to swim. It may not help the war effort, but you never know – you may bring joy to someone who needs it.'

When I didn't say anything, he sighed, leaning back in his chair.

'We have no idea how long this war will be on for. You could be turning your back on something you're good at forever, Lucy. Don't do that. For me.'

I looked up when he said that. The clock above the fireplace ticked loudly and I counted thirty seconds before I spoke.

'For you.'

Mr Swarbrick's face lit up.

'But if it becomes obvious this is in bad taste, I'm dropping out. I don't want to do anything which could suggest I'm not supporting the war effort,' I said, and my coach nodded.

'It's a deal. Cheers.' He clinked his teacup against mine and smiled broadly, taking another biscuit and dunking it enthusiastically in his tea. 'There aren't many competitions, as I'm sure you'll know. But next week there's a short race, and at the end of September the five mile from Preston to Lytham.'

I almost spat my tea out.

'Five miles? But I've barely been in the water.'
Mr Swarbrick put his tea down.
'Best start practising then.'

Chapter Thirty-Three

SEPTEMBER 1915, PRESTON-LYTHAM

I came a pretty respectable second in the short race two months before, for which I grudgingly accepted. Truth be told – though I wouldn't tell this to Mr Swarbrick – I was surprised at the level of my fitness. I had expected to have lost a lot of it as I hadn't been in the water for many months. But it would seem my long, bracing walks along the promenade had done a lot for my cardiovascular system and leg muscles. I'm moving as well as I did a year ago. Better possibly, as I'm leaner from our rationed diet – there's a little less of me to pull through the water.

Today though my nerves were jangling a little ahead of the five miler from Preston to Lytham.

'It's busy,' I commented to Mr Swarbrick, and we looked at the crowd of onlookers gathered on the bank of the River Ribble, ready to cheer on myself and the other twenty or so swimmers who had agreed to swim down the river and out to sea a little way, before we finished our swim at Lytham.

'People want something to celebrate, you're bringing joy to these crowds, Lucy. Remember that.' Mr Swarbrick smiled at me and patted me on my shoulder.

'It's a long way,' I admitted, worried I hadn't done enough, though I'd trained every day since Mr Swarbrick suggested the competition. And I'd done it mainly in the sea – giving myself markers along the shore to swim to. I'd discovered I could swim four miles comfortably, the fifth had caused me issues – mainly due to cramping in my sides. But I was hopeful that seeing the end would spur me on to forget the final mile and just keep going.

'I'm sure your sheer bloody-mindedness will get you where you need to be.' Mr Swarbrick grinned again. 'Best of luck.'

Best of luck.

'Why must it always be luck? Best of expertise is more accurate,' I replied grimly. My teeth were beginning to chatter a little. I preferred to just get in the water and get on with the job in hand than stand around talking.

Fortunately the organisers agreed, and, not long after we'd all stepped into the water, the starter pistol fired and I plunged properly into the river, the water flowing over my shoulders as I pushed through. We began to find our rhythm and the group of us gradually made our way down the river.

There were mile checkpoints along the way which helped to gauge how we were doing, and, rather wonder-

fully, we seemed to have collected a procession of onlookers and well-wishers along the bank.

'Go on, ladies, keep going,' a young girl shouted. She
had to be around eleven or so and was sat astride a bike
that looked far too large for her, a big grin on her face and
her skirts tucked around her to give her the freedom to
pedal. I waved quickly before continuing with my me-
thodical strokes and she whooped at the recognition. 'I'm
a swimmer too,' I heard her yell. I wondered for a moment
whether this would be the day that made her decide to
become a competition swimmer. It was pleasing to hope
we may have inspired one or two young swimmers such as
ourselves.

When we reached the Bottom of Hutton, it was a
relatively small but patriotic crowd that greeted us from
the banks – all waving Union Flags and cheering and I
realised, a little belatedly, just how right Mr Swarbrick
was. I was selfish to think swimming was for me. This
competition, this performance, was for the spectators. It
gave something joyful for people to feel part of. Even if it
was just for one day. They all got to see something they
didn't usually and for a moment they didn't have to think
of their husbands, sons, lovers, brothers, off fighting with
no knowledge if they'd return.

The realisation spurred me on. I wanted to do well for
them. For the crowds. I pushed through the water, enjoying the pleasant sensation of very slightly being carried
down the river, and not having to fight my way against
waves or a tide, as I did when swimming in the sea. It was
calming and although there were cheers from the river-

bank as we went past clusters of people and houses, dotted along our route, they didn't distract us from the swim.

When we reached the three-mile mark, four swimmers stopped and pulled themselves out onto the bank. One looked like she was in a great deal of discomfort whilst the other two cheered on the rest of us and yelled to keep going. I didn't change my strokes, just kept pulling through, though there was a splash near me and I spotted an otter in its nest as I whizzed past. He eyed me keenly as though he was wondering why humans were trying to share his space. His fur was beautifully sleek and reminded me of the coats I'd seen some of the more well-to-do women wearing in the town. It looked better on him.

As we passed the official three-mile marker, I looked ahead to see the pack of swimmers had stretched out in front and behind me some way, dotted across the water like a string of pearls with me in the middle.

I was distracted from keeping the lead swimmers in my sights when nearby, another competitor called Mary, was, I noticed, struggling against the debris which lined the edges of the river.

'Are you all right, need a hand?' I asked between gasps of breath as I noticed she was lagging behind.

'No, some blasted reed or something, it's –' she broke off mid-sentence and I saw she was treading water. I looked behind me at Mary to see what was going on.

'Are you stuck?'

'I'm not sure – something's around my ankle,' she explained, whilst she bobbed in the water, 'but don't worry, you keep going. Don't lose your spot.'

I looked around. There was still over two miles to go, but the rest of the swimmers were beginning to get a little further from me.

'No, hang on.' I swam over to her, and as I neared the edge of the water I spotted the problem – there were long winding river weeds flowing with the water in the murky depths and Mary must have swum too close to the edge and become caught in one.

'Nowhere else I can go, is there?' she laughed, then spat out the water she'd gulped down at the same time.

'Just hold still, I'm sure I can get you out of there.' I took a deep breath and dove below the water, much to the interest of the crowd of onlookers who gathered nearest to us. The water was churned up with our movements and it was hard to see anything, causing me to grope around in the smudgy brown light, trying to work out where Mary was. Where her leg was. And where the reed was that was attached to it. Gradually the water cleared a little and I made out Mary's form treading water.

I felt down her leg, making her jump a little, then felt to her ankle. Sure enough there was a reed wrapped tightly around her calf. I gave it a yank with all my might, but it didn't yield. I tried again, this time with all the strength I could muster, conscious I needed to get to the surface soon for a breath, but in an instant she was freed.

As I pushed to the surface, breaking the tension of the water and gulping the air down, there was rapturous applause from the sides.

'Thank you, Lucy, you saved me,' she said with relief, swimming over to me. 'I can't thank you enough – come on, we must go, or else we'll be getting in hours after the others.'

Looking down the river I could just make out the forms of the rest of our group making their way around a bend, it was going to be a big ask to get back in the pack again.

'Come on, Lucy, if you follow me you can be in my wake. Hopefully you can regain some strength from being behind me for a while. We'll be back up there in no time,' Mary yelled, already making some distance with her strong strokes. With little to lose, I swam into her slipstream and powered as hard as I could through the river. It felt like I was in the final hundred metres of a competition, but I kept pushing, and so did Mary until eventually, after much effort on both our parts, we reached the back of the group, breathing hard. It wasn't until I gathered my breath I noticed something strange.

'Where's the rest of them?' I panted at Mary, who shook her head.

As I looked around I counted just three other swimmers, five including Mary and me. A much depleted group than the twelve that had started.

I resumed my strokes and powered through the river until I spotted the last mile sign. Relieved Mary's incident didn't become something worse, I vowed as I passed a windmill, its sails turning in the breeze, that I'd do a water life-saving course this year, so I could be better prepared in the future.

But as we made our way through the mouth of the river and into the Irish Sea, all thoughts were swept from my mind as the tide took us all by surprise and we battled to stay on course. The waves were choppy, white foam crashed over me, covered me entirely and I felt as though I was being raised through the water by Poseidon himself as I was thrust forward by the waves, trying to get to shore. I lost sight of the other swimmers and fought to stay on course.

We only needed to complete one thousand metres out at sea before turning into our final destination of Lytham, but they were the toughest I'd ever swum. I noticed the crew from one of the small fishing boats that were bobbing around us was pulling two of the competitors out of the water. Keeping my focus on the shore, I tried to ignore the chaos around me and coughed out the seawater which had caught me in the back of the throat.

Just as the thought had crossed my mind that I should just give up, I spotted Mr Swarbrick jumping up and down on the shore, his cane in the air as he hollered in my direction. 'Go on, Lucy, you can do it.' The sight of him gave me a much needed boost and I used him as a pinpoint. Something to aim for. I kept pumping my arms through the water and eventually, sweet, sweet heaven, I felt the bottom of the sea floor with my feet and swam, paddled, stumbled, and hauled my way out and onto the beach, my chest heaving. The crowd on the beach was jumping up and down, cheering, and I looked around, unsure of what was going on.

I couldn't see any other swimmers.

'Mr Swarbrick?' He had thrown a towel around my shoulders and was beaming. He rubbed my head as though it was a lucky charm.

'You did it, Lucy – you're the only one to complete the course,' he laughed hard, 'not just win it. It's only you here.' He laughed again as I looked around, taking in the scene properly.

'What? Why?'

Mr Swarbrick shook his head.

'Don't ask me. You were out there – all I know is, when you entered the sea there were five of you. When you got to the shore it was just you left. All the others have pulled out.'

'No.' I couldn't believe it. 'Are they all right?'

Nodding, Mr Swarbrick pumped the arm of an official who had come to make my win official.

'They'll be fine. They've just met their match, that's all.'

Chapter Thirty-Four

JULY 1916, BLACKPOOL

'It's happened, Lucy.' Alice came into our bedroom where I was darning one of my skirts. I really needed something a little longer, but I'd managed to let down the hem which would give me a little more use out of it. My sister slumped on the bed opposite me and sighed.

'What?'

'James. He's been drafted, he's going to the front.' Alice had barely got to the end of her sentence when she let out a wail. 'Oh Lucy, I can't bear it. I really can't.' I watched as she threw herself onto her bed, face down, the quilt muffling her words and tears. Standing up from my own bed and leaving my sewing on my nightstand, I sat beside her and lightly patted her head.

'You knew this time would come,' I reminded her soothingly, talking to the back of her head. 'Do you know where he'll be stationed?'

She turned over and I could see her puffy and tear-stained face, she'd clearly been crying more than the last few minutes I'd seen.

'He's going to France, he doesn't know where. I'm not sure he'd be allowed to tell me anyway.' Alice began another series of wails. 'I can't begin to think of life without him, Lucy,' she admitted, her hazel-flecked eyes boring deep into mine.

'Now, who's to say he won't make it? He's going to fight, but they will come back – we have to believe that,' I reasoned. 'We can't think every man and boy will die. It's just too ghastly to think like that.'

Alice sat up to look at me, biting her lip and looking for all the world ten years younger and as though I'd told her she couldn't have a toffee apple.

'You really think he'll come back?'

I paused before I answered, not because I didn't think he would but because I didn't want to give her false hope. There were already many casualties, and we'd seen for ourselves the many wounded men returning to Blackpool ready to be patched up and sent back.

I chose my words carefully.

'I really hope he will.'

She gave a whisper of a smile, and then looked at me with a determined expression on her face.

'I'm going to write him a hundred letters, so he can have something of me with him all the time.'

'That's the spirit, though a hundred might be a lot, even for you.' I hastened at her pained look. 'But do the very best you can, and maybe a photo of you too? I'm sure he'll like that.' She grinned, and with a sense of purpose, plucked out her notepaper from her side table, found a pen, and began to write the first missive to her love.

***

A few days later and it was Alice's turn to wave her love off, as so many had done before her. At Alice's request I accompanied them both to the station, but stood away so they could make their goodbyes in the relative privacy that a huge crowd of strangers gave.

Watching them tenderly saying farewell, I fought the lump in my throat at the thought of Alice watching her love leave her and clutched the piece of paper that I'd buried in the pocket of my thin coat. The envelope had arrived for me that morning as we were due to leave. I'd recognised the handwriting, of course, but I couldn't bear the idea of what I was going to read in its contents. Fortunately the morning had been busy and Alice had taken much of my time, so I'd allowed myself to make excuses for why I wasn't opening the envelope immediately. Instead, I'd shoved it hastily into my pocket, crumpling it up in the process.

As I saw Alice kiss James on the cheek for one last time, I rubbed my thumb and forefinger over the light envelope in my pocket and fancied I could hear the faintest rustle. For a moment I considered pulling it out and reading it there and then, but almost as though Alice had a sixth sense for my need to not see it, she arrived at my side and clutched me for support.

'Let's go, Lucy, I can't wave him away, it'll be too painful.' She wound her arm into mine and cast one longing look in the direction of the train, then, as though it physically hurt her, turned her head away and looked towards the exit. 'Come on, we should go.'

I nodded, I wasn't enjoying watching the hundreds of men being bid farewell at the station, watching the sobbing fiancées being walked away or worse, watching the mothers who kept a stoic expression whilst hugging their child, but who then dissolved into hot, wet tears as they left. It was all too much.

'Is there somewhere you'd like to go? We can go home, or...' I left the sentence, unsure of how Alice was coping. She gripped me ever so tightly around the arm, and I realised she was using me to hold herself up.

'Can we just walk?' she replied quietly, and I guided her out of the station, through the throngs of people flowing through to catch various trains away from Blackpool. As we moved away from the station the crowds began to thin out and I could feel Alice release her grip on me a little. We rounded the street corner and began to make our way down Talbot Road, which would eventually bring us out towards the beach and the pier.

'Do you want to go?' I looked in the direction of the pier but Alice shook her head. She remained quiet for the next half an hour as I took her on a meandering wander of back roads and side streets, in a bid to lose ourselves and our thoughts. Eventually we happened upon the cinema, something I realised held significance to James, as they'd met there, just as soon as I realised where we were.

I held Alice tightly.

'I'm so sorry, I didn't mean to take us here. I could have sworn we were a road up,' I gabbled, then looked at her. She was just staring up at the golden façade. 'Please, Alice, I am really sorry. It was an honest mistake.'

She looked at me and smiled sadly.

'I know it was, don't worry. I'd like to go in though.' She pulled on my arm and we wandered in. The interior was decorated with red velour across all the surfaces including the walls. There was an aged glamour to the venue, its hushed surroundings acting like a barrier to the world outside. Alice spoke to the woman at the box office.

'Anything on that isn't news?'

'Yep,' the woman replied, nodding, though unhelpful.

'And that would be?'

'*The Girl Who Loves a Soldier.*'

Both of us groaned on hearing the title.

'We don't need to watch it,' I suggested, aware it might be too much for an already fraught Alice. But she shook her head adamantly.

'Two please,' she ordered for us, but looked to me for the money. I searched in my handbag, but there was only enough for one ticket.

'I don't have it, sorry.' Alice looked despondent. 'Why don't you watch it and I'll wait out here, it's not a problem,' I suggested.

Alice looked unsure. 'I don't know, will you be alright?' she asked.

'Of course.'

'And you're sure you don't have any more money?'

'Not on me, I didn't think to pick up any. Bit of a busy morning, wasn't it?' I said as I made as much of a show out of it as possible. I pulled out the pockets of my jacket to prove I had no money. In so doing, the crumpled-up envelope fell to the floor. I gasped and went to grab it, but Alice was quicker. She snatched at it and inspected the looping cursive on the front.

'What's this then? Not money?' she said as she turned over the precious paper in her hand. I extended mine towards her.

'Not money, can I just have it back?' We stood locked in the usual sibling battle. We might have got on a lot of the time, but if there was something to get over the other, we'd still do it. We enjoyed exploiting secrets the most and wondered if there was leverage with which to use them. I could see Alice weighing up what was in the paper along with what she could get out of it.

I couldn't bear the waiting. But I couldn't look too keen.

'Please, Alice,' I asked, as gently as I could. She looked at the envelope.

'It's from the front.' A statement, not a question. I nodded.

'Who's sending you letters from the front?'

I snatched the envelope from her.

'I don't know. I haven't opened it yet.'

She looked at me, reading the truth in my face.

'It's from Harry isn't it?'

I shrugged.

'Like I said, I don't know. I've not opened it yet.' I blew out the breath I'd been holding for too long. 'But I think it might be from him. Yes.' I shook my head to try and rid myself of the thoughts I'd been having about Harry lately, the fears I'd been ignoring.

'Wow. It's been what, two years since you two last spoke?'

'At least.'

Alice looked puzzled.

'So why's he writing to you now? Have you been in touch with him?' I shook my head again.

'I don't know. I knew he'd be fighting somewhere – he signed up about three years ago, but I don't know where he is now. I'll know once I open it. But I don't know whether I want to know what he's going to tell me,' I admitted.

Alice shook her head, despite her being two years younger than me, it often felt as though she were the more sensible one.

'Let's sit here and take a look – it'll be easier if I'm with you, right?' I nodded and she smiled quickly in response. 'Good. Let's sit on one of those benches.' She pointed to a bench inside the theatre's foyer.

'But what about the film?' I tried.

'I need to take my mind off James and if I can help you, even better. And anyway, I've seen it already.' She steered me to the wooden bench and we sat down, shrugging off our coats and laying them next to ourselves.

I sat and stared at the envelope in my hands. It had worn edges, a collection of colourful stamps and water-marks and the address was lightly smudged. I rubbed my fingers over the stamps, imagining where Harry had been when he had put them on.

'Open it then,' Alice's impatience was brimming to the surface. 'Do it quickly and the worst will be over with.'

I closed my eyes for a moment, drawing on the calm I brought to myself when competing, then reopened them, ready to tackle whatever the contents were.

Chapter Thirty-Five

M y hands shook as I gave the letter to Alice. 'You do it.'

> *Dearest Lucy,*
> *I'm guessing this letter has come out of the blue for you, and, it is my hope you have indeed opened it, otherwise my attempts to secure paper and pen via a jolly unfavourable barter system in the trenches would have been futile.*
> *I'm in France. I suspect you'd guessed as much, though maybe it is too presumptuous to assume you've spent time thinking of me and if you have, where I may be.*

'Have you thought about him?' Alice stopped reading the letter out to me, after my failed attempts to look at the words, the handwriting. His handwriting. Blurring in front of my eyes.

I nodded gently. I wasn't prepared to admit I had thought only of him these past three years, and I'd become used to the light pain that came with thinking of him. I tried to put thoughts of him out of my mind as often as they came in. But with every intrusion I batted away, another three thoughts would take its place.

It had almost become a sick trick I played on myself. To test whether I still felt something for him – anything – I would tease myself with thoughts of him and me when we courted, as well as more up to date versions when I would play out other scenarios.

Then the war started. I knew he'd signed up a year before, of course he would be posted out to fight. I began to force myself to understand there may never be a chance to accidentally bump into him in a shop, or on the street ever again. That all opportunities of seeing him could well have gone. Completely. And if the thoughts before had hurt, those thoughts, the ones which whispered to me in the dark depths of night, they tore through my heart. The prospect of never seeing him again, even if was just amicable was too painful to consider.

And now this. This letter, postmarked three weeks ago, which claimed that – three weeks ago at least – he was alive. Alive and thinking of me.

'Shall I continue?' Alice was as gentle with me as she would be a new-born.

I nodded again. She looked at me, carefully judging whether I was of sound enough mind for her to continue.

Satisfied with whatever she saw, she nodded, almost imperceptibly.

'Right you are then.'

> *We made our way to France from Dover, near to where I'd been posted three months ago. Of course, at the time we were under the impression we go out for a few weeks, and we'd return fairly quickly. Most of the lads and I had been told the Germans were on the retreat, but it didn't feel like that when we arrived.*
>
> *I don't know what to say to you, Lucy. I'm sorry. That's one thing I'm keen to tell you. I want to tell you of everything I've seen, I need to share it with someone, but I don't know if the first communication with your...*

'It's a bit smudged, I can't read it.' Alice peered at the letter. 'It could be "grind" or "gerbil".'

I smiled a little, Harry's handwriting had always been poor. 'Let me see.' I looked at the word and my heart flip-flopped at what I'd read. '"Girl", Alice, he's referring to me as his girl.'

Alice looked again, first at the letter, then me.

'So he has.'

...but I don't know if the first communication with your girl should contain the reality of my day-to-day. Do you mind me calling you my girl? I still think of you as mine. I probably shouldn't. You've no doubt been swept off your feet by another man, someone who saw you for the person you are. Big-hearted, generous, and most importantly, not like other women. You saw me for who I was. I saw an age gap and it worried me. I know two years isn't a great deal now but it felt insurmountable to me when you were fifteen and I was seventeen, and wanting so very much more from you that it was right of me to expect.

If I'm to carry on writing to you, and I'm keeping everything crossed that you reply to me, Lucy, I will be honest. I signed up to keep myself from getting you into trouble, like so many of the girls round our way. I didn't think we would know our own hearts and minds as much as we did at those ages. But I look back now and realise we knew. I knew. I just wanted to keep you safe, I thought me signing up would do that. And after Mother died it seemed the most appropriate answer to living with Father and the children whilst I waited for you to get a little older.

I may have forgotten to tell that part to you.

. The waiting for you part. I've waited for over three years and never strayed. But now you're eighteen and I'm twenty, I think we can be trusted to know our minds. If nothing else because war doesn't give us much of a choice.

I wonder how you're taking this. I wonder if you're angry with me now. Angrier even than when I left. I wonder if you've asked Alice to read this as you can't trust yourself not to rip the paper up. I wonder if you're in your room, or raking your hands through your hair, or biting your lip with irritation. I wonder all these things and more, with every waking minute that passes without you in it.

Look, Lucky, I know I'm making some big assumptions. Presumptions. But if you can't make presumptions from the trenches, I don't know when you can. So if you can find it in your heart to forgive me, I would receive a letter from you with such joy it will be unmatched on the field. If you can't, I'll understand.

But I will always remain, forever yours.

Harry xx

'Well,' Alice whistled low through her teeth, 'that's some letter.' When I didn't reply, she folded it carefully and handed it back to me. 'You're going to want this, I think.' She pressed it into my hand, where it stayed.

'I think it's wonderful he got back in touch,' Alice continued. 'I hope half of what James sends me is as kind.'

I cleared my throat.

'It will be. I'm certain.' I took the letter and replaced it in my pocket, Alice watching my every move. 'Look at me hijacking your tearful farewell,' I apologised, 'you must think terribly of me. I promise you I wasn't planning to read it until I'd looked after you properly today.'

Alice batted me slightly.

'Oh, nonsense. I'm glad to have something to take my mind off James. Even if it is love declarations to my sister.'

'I think we should head home,' I suggested, realising I couldn't sit in the foyer of the theatre any more than Alice could sit in the darkened recess of the cinema auditorium. 'We need to be at home, and I need a tot of brandy,' I admitted. 'You could have a small one too – we've both had a tough day.' I stood up, trying to be the one in control. The older sister in charge of the younger one.

'Fine, but only if you promise you're going to write to him.' Alice remained seated.

'I...' I faltered, 'I haven't made a decision yet. He hurt me a lot when he went away, Alice, you know that,' I reminded her.

She nodded sagely, all shred of girl had disappeared, I realised. War had made her a woman.

'Yes. And now he's apologised. You have to forgive him. You have to write to him. Now isn't a time to overthink things.'

I looked at her, realising what she was saying.

'I have to take every opportunity?'

She nodded.

'You have to whenever it presents itself, otherwise it might be taken away from you.'

Chapter Thirty-Six

September 1916, Blackpool

I didn't write immediately. It wasn't that I didn't want to, it was that I didn't know what to say. Three years is a very long time to not speak to someone, and now, with a blank page in front of me, all at once I felt as though I had so much to tell him. And so little.

How could I possibly tell him the humdrum realities of my day, when he was living in pitiable conditions? He was fighting for King and country. I was doing my bit, of course I was, but I actually enjoyed my work as a sorter in the Post Office. It was humbling, knowing I was doing something to help the war effort and I had found I enjoyed the work. I suspected if I told him that life felt somewhat, ironically, freer for me than it had a couple of years ago, he wouldn't understand.

I sat at the desk I shared with my sister in our bedroom and looked out the window at the street below, hoping for some inspiration.

I could tell him about swimming. That was something I knew he'd be interested in. I didn't think I should share that I was still irritated the 1916 Olympic Games hadn't gone ahead, owing to the war, and that I was pinning my hopes on the games in 1920 before I got too old and unfit to compete.

> *Dear Harry,*
> *I must confess, I was shocked when I saw you had written to me. I suppose I thought I would never hear from you again, though writing those words down looks quite dramatic, it had been how I felt until Alice and I read your letter.*
> *I hope you don't mind. I had to have Alice help me, I wasn't certain I wouldn't rip it up, sight unseen, but she – forever in your corner – stopped all thoughts like that and urged me to listen to what you had to say.*
> *I have. And I've listened to her too. She had to bid farewell to her sweetheart not long ago – that's right, little Alice is in love, and she has urged me to accept your apology. I will. Though you must know to have been gone for so long without a word has hurt me deeply. I didn't mind you leaving, I knew you needed to help your family, but I had*

thought you knew I'd always be there for you – whether as a friend or anything else. It saddens me you left.
Still. Let's leave it there, shall we?
Would you like to know how I'm doing? I'm going to pretend you and I are strolling along the seafront as I write to you, so you will be asking a lot of questions, I hope. We're strolling arm in arm, and are near to the beach, the waves are crashing and you're considering whether to buy us an ice.
I have redoubled my efforts with my swimming. Last year I rather drifted. It felt silly to focus on something which wasn't related to the war, but I've found by keeping it going my head feels clearer. I enjoy the focus that comes with it too. Do you have anything like that?

I broke off and looked back at the window. Yesterday, I visited the strangest of tourist attractions which had been placed on the promenade. We have replica trenches on the seafront, mimicking the Loos trenches. They're to help train those who've signed up but also to raise money from visitors, with the entrance fees going to the convalescent hospital for wounded soldiers at Squires Gate. I didn't like the idea anyone was profiting from such a macabre tourist attraction, but when I realised the money was to help our boys recover, I went along with Greta and her little one,

Michael. Greta's husband has gone to war and although I'd had my misgivings we visited.

I'm not sure if it was the right thing for Greta, the reality was too grim. She could imagine how her husband was living and it devastated her, but for me it made me realise that with such an unpleasant daily life it was my duty to send Harry a letter with droplets of home sprinkled amongst it. Hopefully to give him some joy from what had to be a truly dreary existence. I took up my pen again.

> *I'm at a championship in a month where I'll be hoping to set a good time. Mr Swarbrick thinks I'm in the best shape I've ever been in – he's talking of world records, but I'm not sure. I did win the Northern Counties Amateur Swimming Association's championship, and was awarded the Breaststroke Championship 1916 First Prize War Time Medal. It's quite a hefty medal. Gold. I've added it to my collection – does that sound boastful? I hope not. I am proud of it though.*
> *Do you ever think on how we met? How funny to think eight years ago you were pulling me out of a pool as I was unable to stay afloat, and now I'm hoping to break world records. Seems a little ridiculous if you ask me. There's no Olympics, of course. Not that I could have competed anyway as I'm not practising the 'right' strokes for*

them, but it would have been something to see – I've competed against a few of the women who were expecting to take part. I know the lack of a sporting event pales into insignificance when we think of world events, but it would have been something. Wouldn't it?

Do you hear anything from your siblings? How are they?

I think our walk is coming to an end now, Harry. You've walked me home. We're in front of my door. You're suggesting you could pop in for a slice of Mother's cake and a pot of tea. I'd pretend to think about it, and then we both know I'd let you in.

I miss you deeply.

Yours,

Lucky

xxx

I had pondered how to end the letter, there was a lot I wanted to say. As I folded the note to place in its envelope, I lightly sprayed it with my perfume. I knew it was a touch trite, but hopefully if it remained by the time it made its way to him, he'd get a little memory of home. Before I sealed the envelope, a thought occurred to me, and I quickly scribbled a PS on the back of the page.

Satisfied, I sealed the envelope and carefully wrote the complicated foreign address he'd included in his letter.

France seemed a very long way away.

Chapter Thirty-Seven

SEPTEMBER 1916, BLACKPOOL

I don't know what I was expecting when I posted the letter. Actually, I do. I was expecting an instantaneous response. I expected the rules of time and distance to not apply, and I expected to receive a reply the following day. But nothing came. Of course it didn't. Then nothing came for a further two weeks.

I began to realise that what I had done was potentially reply to a man who'd died in the intervening weeks. How would I know? I wasn't his next of kin, so no one would need to inform me. Indeed, no one would know I would wish to be informed, as far as anyone was concerned there was no Harry and I. That thought weighed heavily. So I did what I always did when I needed clarity, or distance. Or quiet.

I swam.

Mr Swarbrick was pushing me to go faster. He counted the amount of strokes it took me to get to the end of each length of the pool, working out how many breaths I needed to take. He enjoyed it, the science behind me swimming, whereas I was pretty certain a good breakfast and a dose of hard work would do the job.

'You're so close, Lucy.' He crouched down beside the pool, the effort on his face plain to see. His injured left leg refusing to bend as much as the right one. He never would tell me what had happened, all that my father said was that Mr Swarbrick fought in the Boer War, and there was nothing else to say. I'd learnt not to press the matter. When I was eleven I was desperate to ask him about the limp, the constant twist of pain on his face as he moved, but I knew better than that now.

'Do you feel it, how close you are?' he was asking, a look of urgency in his eyes. I nodded. There was little else I could do, I was breathing hard after a particularly pelting two hundred metres of backstroke.

'You're this close, Lucy,' he held his thumb and fore-finger close together in front of me. 'This close,' he re-peated, shaking his hand at me a little in his excitement, 'to getting it. You just have to push.'

'I am pushing,' I replied, offended he didn't think I was trying.

Mr Swarbrick raised himself to standing.

'I know, but I think you can dig a little deeper. Think of all the long distances you've managed to do, this is a piece of cake. Two hundred metres? You could do this in your sleep – you just need to do it quickly.' He grinned, then his face turned serious. 'And whatever it is that's on your mind, let it go, we need focus.'

A lump formed in my throat and I tried to swallow it away. Was I that transparent? Rather than argue with him, I nodded.

'You have my word.'

Satisfied, Mr Swarbrick straightened up and smiled.

'Good. The competition is just three days away. I suggest you finish up here today, swim Thursday, then give yourself a day off. I'll meet you at the station Saturday morning to take you.'

I watched him walk away. His shiny black shoes and smart tweed suit at odds with the scruffiness of the poolside. The clop of his heels and the scratching of his walking cane lightly echoed against the walls as he made his way out. Deciding I'd done enough for the day, I pulled myself out on to the side and began to towel off a little.

As I made my way to the changing area, stopping off to shower in the freezing water and get rid of the briny water, my thoughts of Harry came to the surface again, despite my best efforts to ignore him – and them – for the last couple of hours in the pool. Though, I acknowledged, not as well as I'd have liked, given Mr Swarbrick's comment.

Drying off in the changing room, I pulled a dress on over my head and caught sight of myself in the small mirror affixed to the wall. Shaking my head at the forlorn face I could see, I spoke to my reflection.

'Enough. Get a grip, Lucy Morton.' I vowed I'd focus entirely on the competition on Saturday, and whatever happened during it, I'd have something to write to Harry about. But until then, I would put all thoughts of him out of my mind as they were not helpful.

***

Dearest Harry,

A wonderful thing has happened. Well, two actually. I WON! You are now receiving this letter from a WORLD RECORD HOLDER of not one, but TWO records!! That's right, I'm the official World Record Holder for the one hundred and fifty metre backstroke and the two hundred metre breaststroke. I'm thrilled!!! As you can probably tell.

I looked over the words, there were light smudges of ink which had dripped in my haste to get my thoughts down on paper but what of it? I was excited.

The competition was exhilarating. There were eight of us competing in both events – not all the same women, though a few competed in both like me. But I felt SO GOOD when I was in the water. Mr Swarbrick thinks it's because I had a good mind-set, I think it's because Mother managed to get hold of some sausages and bacon for a top breakfast before I went off. They're a rare treat nowadays, but they were welcome.

I wondered if that was too much of a reminder of home. Whether he was missing fry-ups.

I bet you'd appreciate an English breakfast – when you come home I promise to make you one.

When we arrived in the pool it was a little different to previous competitions. As the war is on there are, of course, far fewer men around, so it's mainly women competing and women cheering, but I rather enjoyed the camaraderie of it. The first competition was the two hundred metre breaststroke and I STORMED off, Harry, I pelted down the pool like I was being chased – which I suppose I was – and I went at such a lick. So I flew down, then did it another two times, before the final stretch and boy (!) did I push it. Agnes – the American, one of my main rivals at the moment whose record I was trying to take – was hot on my heels, but I dug deep and then I thought I'd won, but I didn't know if I'd managed it until the referee came over and told me I had the world record. I was elated, of course, but I had to remain composed as my next competition was just half an hour later.

I stopped to refill my pen, and looked at the cream diamond-shaped fabric badges sat propped up on my desk near to me. I'd be sewing those onto my suit soon. Both were embroidered with the NAFI red and blue logo, both saying *World Record*. One with two hundred metre breaststroke, and the other with one hundred and fifty metre backstroke sewn on the bottoms of each of them. I allowed a moment of pride to glow through me.

> *I hope you're enjoying the thrill of this as much as I did, Harry, it was stupendous. Though I must admit I was concerned for the backstroke. I'd put so much effort into the first competition I was rather convinced I had outdone myself. But, I'm pleased to say, I pushed as much as I could – I thought of you and what you were enduring and thought, come on, girl, yours is just a swimming race – so I went off again, as fast as you can imagine. And, well, the rest you can guess. I won, and I gained the world record. Mr Swarbrick is SO proud – as are Mother, Father and Alice, of course (she says hello by the way).*
>
> *We celebrated this evening with the most delicious stew. Mother has become accomplished in finding food. We grow a lot in our garden now, most of it is turned over to vegetables, I think Father likes that he's doing his bit. He's got green fingers so we're*

*spoilt by what he can grow – we share a lot
with neighbours, of course. I imagine you
don't see many fresh vegetables where you
are?*

*As I suspect this may cross over with any
reply to my first letter, I've asked around
for ideas of what to send you to keep your
spirits up. I hope I've guessed correctly –
though do tell me if there's anything else I
can get hold of for you.*

*I must go to bed now. I think today's ex-
citement is rather beginning to take its toll.
I think I will sleep for many hours. I hope
wherever you are that you can sleep too.*

Thinking of you always,

Lucky

xxx

Chapter Thirty-Eight

OCTOBER 1916, BLACKPOOL

O ur home was filled with waiting. Alice was waiting for news of James, I was waiting to hear from Harry, and Mother and Father were waiting to hear whether they were going to have two wrecks of daughters.

'Ethel was in the grocers, her boy is on his way home – shot,' Mother told us both bluntly as we ate our breakfast in the kitchen, the warmth of the range taking the chill from my bones. October had settled like a damp blanket for the past few days and I'd felt it in my body for the first time. I wasn't even nineteen and I was beginning to act like my mother. Mr Swarbrick was sure it was to do with the volume of swimming I'd done these past years, but to me it felt like my body was rejecting the grey around it.

'Mother, you can't come out with something like that.' Alice was looking up from her bowl of porridge I'd only seen her stir. She barely ate anything these days and was beginning to look as bony as the sparrows we'd rescue from the grips of the neighbours' cat.

'No, it's a good thing. He's been shot, enough to take him off active duty and away from the front, not so badly he's going to be in a wheelchair all his life,' Mother mollified. Though to me being shot, whether in a good or bad way, didn't seem all that appealing and I said as much. But Mother shook her head from her position at the fire, as she threw on more wood.

'No, dear, this is a good thing. It means Ethel will have her son at home, she doesn't have to worry about him at least.' She looked at our Father who was reading his paper. 'She has her husband fighting too, it's been a very difficult time for her.' We nodded in understanding.

There was a noise at the front door which caused Alice and I to both look up. Mother shook her head.

'I'll go.' We watched her walk out of the kitchen, and I heard her footsteps in their slippers along the staircase to the porch, then her return, padding back through to the warmth of the kitchen. She had a small handful of post which she leafed through as quickly as possible, settling on a grubby cream envelope. My heart instantly leapt, it looked very similar to the one Harry had sent me. But at the same time I realised it could be any missive from the Army. They probably had a standard paper and envelope.

'For you.'

Mother held it out to me and my heart thumped. I turned the envelope over and there, in his scrawl, was our address in Harry's hand. I couldn't help it, an enormous smile spread over my face and the tight grip on my heart that I'd carried this past six weeks loosened. Only to glance up at Alice and face her look of sadness that yet again, there was nothing for her.

I reached for her hand and gave it a squeeze.

'You'll see, you'll get a letter soon. I'm sure of it.' She looked away and I withdrew my hand. I was desperate to rip open the letter straight away, but didn't want its contents to be seen or read by my family, not until I'd digested them. Instead, I wolfed down my porridge as quickly as possible, under the ever watchful eye of Mother. She nodded, understanding, when I pushed back my chair, the scrape of the feet against the cold flagstone floor, and ran out of the room. I didn't stop running. I ran up the two flights of stairs to get to our room, then flopped onto my bed still clutching the letter in my hands.

I studied his handwriting, the three colourful stamps, the watermarks embossed across the paper. I took in the smudges of mud, flecked here and there, and then I allowed myself to carefully slit open the envelope and pull out the sheets of paper held within.

> *Darling Lucky,*
> *First off, I am utterly thrilled you decided to reply. I cannot thank you enough. To read the words you'd penned, your thoughts, and our 'conversation' brought such joy to me, you cannot know. Today, whilst I write, it is three weeks since the date on your letter, so I believe you must be competing in your world record competi-*

tion roughly now.

I am keeping everything crossed – so are the other lads, I've told them all about my golden girl. I hope you don't mind that description, but I think it fitting for you. I've told them of your achievements, and that you're due to compete. One of the privates here, Sam, says he can hold his breath underwater for a minute. I told him that was nothing – you could do two! I hope to hear you've become a world record holder, so I can boast to the boys, I don't doubt your ability for one minute.

I don't doubt you, Lucy. I'm so sorry I didn't give you the chance to make a decision about our future, instead choosing what I thought was best. I did think I was doing the right thing. Evidently I wasn't. If only... well... if onlys are no good are they right now? If onlys won't give me time with you instead of time spent here, in the mud. It's so   here, Lucy.

The words were smudged and I tried to work out what he'd written. Hard? Dark? I wasn't sure.

I can't tell you where we're going today, it'll get censored, but I don't think our lot will improve when we get there. Many a good man I've known has gone there and not returned. I'm sorry to say this to you. I truly am. I just want you to know the reality of what we're facing. It's not easy here. No one said it would be. But every day is a battle and that's before you begin to fight. Please know I will do all that I can to come home. I want to come back. I want to come to you and hold you and know you. You are what I think of when everything around has gone to hell. When I close my eyes for a moment of sleep, it is your face I see and it warms me.

Forgive me, Lucy. I begin my note so full of joy at your endeavours, and then see where it leads. My pity. Ignore me. Ignore a rambling old man (I am older than you, so I can say that!). Ignore all my ills. I want to know all the good in the world. I want to know about you. Is Alice well? Your parents? Are they well? Tell me, has your father begun in the Home Guard? I know of many others who have – a jolly good job they do too. Tell him that from me. Embrace your mother for me. She was always so very, very kind to me.

You asked if I'd like anything. I'm not sure YOU can fit in an envelope but other than that, tobacco is good. So is chocolate. Anything that can bring a smile would be ap-

preciated.
I don't want to end this letter, but they're
telling us we have to ready ourselves to
march. Onwards, Lucy. Keep Lucky.
Harry xxx

I held the paper tightly to my chest and could feel my eyes brimming with tears. It had to have been a fortnight at least since he'd posted me his letter, looking at the date. Last night we had been listening to the wireless as the newsreader spoke in a sobering voice of the battle continuing in the Somme. Thousands of British men were dying.

I couldn't bear the idea that mine could be one of them.

Just then, Alice burst into the bedroom.

'They're bombing the channel.'

Chapter Thirty-Nine

NOVEMBER 1916, BLACKPOOL

T he battle in the Dover strait though hundreds of miles from Blackpool, brought the war to our doorstep.

Whilst the fighting was awful and so many people knew of someone who had died in the war and although we'd seen the soldiers around the town and heard of those returning to the hospitals around us, the fact was – we'd not seen the war. It wasn't that we didn't believe it, it was just that our war wasn't looking the same as the millions of men who were fighting theirs.

Our war meant working in jobs which men had vacated, being sensible with food and practical with our clothes, but there was a sliver of freedom I was experiencing that I knew I wouldn't have done if the war hadn't taken place. I'd have been close to married by now at least. But instead, I got to work and swim. The only fly in the ointment, and it was a big one, was knowing that Harry was fighting and I couldn't help him.

We'd been aware of zeppelin raids. Of course we had and we lamented the losses. But they became a way of life and it was as though we'd grown somewhat complacent over the past few months. There'd been some bombing in the south east from early on in the war, but it hadn't felt as planned. Or as timed as the attack from the Germans on boats just a little away from our shores.

The day the bombing took place in the Dover Strait with German torpedo boats attacking, was a sobering one and the following month was much harder. By mid-November the papers reported that the Battle of the Somme had concluded, though it seemed unclear whether we'd won it or not. What was clear was how many of our boys had died. Then, near the end of the month, a biplane dropped six bombs near a train station in London and that cemented it, our lives would never be the same again.

I took to writing to Harry every few days. They became more like diary entries than letters, but I thought if he received them – I had to believe he would – that he'd enjoy them as a snapshot of our lives. I tried to keep things light, amusing titbits I'd collected, bits of gossip I'd overheard, music Alice and I had heard on the wireless, that sort of thing. I didn't share my fears for him, or for us, much as I wanted to.

> *Dearest Harry,*
> *I've had a go at knitting. I know what*
> *you're going to say and I absolutely agree*

– I'm not a knitter. But, Mother has given me some jolly good lessons and, you'll be thrilled to know, you're the first lucky recipient of my creations. You should find enclosed a pair of gloves and a scarf. I'm sorry about the colours, it was all I could get hold of, but hopefully muddy green and yellow will work in your favour as a form of camouflage? Anyway, my greatest hope when I made these was that they may help to keep you warm over the winter, I can't think there's much warmth for you over there.

As you can see from the date, I'm writing this at the end of November, and I'm very hopeful that means this will arrive ahead of Christmas – the Post Office have told us all to get items out to you, they're encouraging us to send nice things, so hopefully that means the deliveries will be quick. I've also found you a box of chocolates – which you're very lucky I've not pilfered any from – and some baccy and tea. I've added some fun things too, I hope you'll enjoy them with the other men with you.

I'm sorry you won't be home for Christmas, but I'm keeping everything crossed you will be home soon.

It's quiet around the town now. Many of the soldiers have gone, and of course, there

253

d of course, there are very few tourists. I'm looking from my window where I can just about make out a few comings and goings in the dark, but it's quiet out on the street. I walked along the seafront earlier and looked at the amusements. It reminded me of our first kiss – I hope you remember it – we were on The Flying Machine. When you kissed me I thought my heart would explode. I felt so lucky that you'd chosen me. I still do. I know our relationship, as such, is merely letters right now, but I'll wait for you. I've been waiting for years.

Gosh, I sound like an old lady, don't I? Well, I don't intend for it. But I don't intend to be alone when I grow old either, so hurry up and get back from the blasted war.

I miss you, Harry Heaton, with all my heart.

Lucky

xxx

As I wrote the address on the front of the parcel and looked forward to posting it the following day, I caught Alice's eye. She'd written to James. He'd started writing back, though his responses were more erratic than Harry's and she was going through the ringer with the ups and downs of having a sweetheart in the forces.

'Are you sending anything to James? I'm doing mine before my shift, you can give it to me?' I suggested carefully, aware she was very delicate just now. Ready to shout at us at a moment's notice.

'Yes, please. I've written to him and have a few things to send on – nothing as horrible as those mittens you're forcing on Harry though.' She laughed.

'It's good to see you laughing, it's been a while, little sis.'

She smiled again.

'James has told me to enjoy living and enjoy life. I think he means apart from him – you know, completely – but whilst I don't agree with that sentiment, yet, I do think he's right. I need to stop moping, and yes I know you've been saying the same,' she added before I said anything, though my mouth was open to speak. 'I've decided to go to the pictures this weekend, if you'd like to join me? And then I should like to see if I can secure a bottle of scent for Mother for Christmas – hopefully if we start early we have a better chance of finding her perfume and other gifts.'

'I think that's a jolly good idea.'

Alice raised her cup of cocoa in my direction.

'To hope, and rubbish knitting.'

I laughed and raised my cup in her direction.

'To hope, and rubbish knitting.'

Chapter Forty

May 1917, Blackpool

When war was declared in 1914, we all supposed it would be over within a few months.

Instead, I'd celebrated another birthday, my nineteenth, in the shadow of it, three years later with the introduction of bread rationing.

'How am I to eat enough to get energy to swim?' I complained to Mother who merely nodded at the sink, where she was washing up and I was drying.

'I know, love, but we've plenty of other food – your father has turned the whole of the garden over to vegetables, which will keep us going. And Ethel has said we can swap some of our potatoes for some of her eggs. Don't forget there's a war on.'

I rolled my eyes. How could I not forget?

'I know. I'm well aware, thank you,' I replied curtly, replacing a plate in the cupboard, 'and I know my hunger pales into whatever the boys are putting up with but I feel like all my opportunities are being taken away.'

Mother looked at me.

'And what sort of opportunities do you mean? You have a roof over your head, a job – a good job I might add that you'd never have had if men were around – you have a loving sweetheart who continues to write to you from the front. You are growing up with more than I did at your age, despite a war. I should think you would be grateful.' She thrust a cup on the drying rack with such force I thought it would shatter.

There was a silence between us as I dried and she continued to wash up.

'I was so excited when I won the world records,' I began, tentatively.

'We all were. We're really proud of you,' Mother said quickly.

'But I want more. Agnes is still competing in the States. She writes to me to tell me how she's progressing – but she's so young, Mother, and I'm worried that that's it, I've missed my chance at anything more than what I've achieved. Eventually, when this war ends, I'll be too old to take part in anything else, or win any records because other, younger women, will be outperforming me. It's not fair.'

Mother turned so I could see her. I was two inches taller than her which continued to surprise me. This woman I'd looked up to all my life was now short enough for me to be able to see the numerous grey hairs flecking her once dark-brown hair. She pulled me in for an embrace, her wet hands dripping lightly down my back.

'Maybe this is it. Maybe you have achieved everything you could. Who knows? You were introduced to swimming to stop you from failing everything at school and look how far you've taken it. You're a world record holder – whether or not someone else takes it from you,' she hurried her words as she could tell I was going to say something. 'You should hold yourself up straight and proud and know what you've done is incredible. If you get a chance to do anything else, great, you can do that. But if, instead, you begin to give yourself more time on other outlets, such as settling down with Harry when he comes home, then that's fine too. There is more to life than just swimming, Lucy, even if you can't see it.'

I leant in and allowed the embrace. I didn't agree that if I didn't swim my only other option was to get married, but I did realise I needed to consider that at nineteen I had to think of other things to do, aside from swimming. I decided against telling Mother I was still holding onto the hope the 1920 Olympics would go ahead, and I would be able to compete in them. I didn't want her quashing my hopes for that competition. Instead, I'd focus on life.

Which was all well and good, until a couple of months or so later, when Mr Swarbrick announced I'd been invited to a competition at Lambeth Baths in London. I'd be competing against chosen swimmers from across the country.

'London?' I'd repeated, dazed at the idea of going to practically the other end of the country, 'but won't that take a long time?'

'Not just that, but is it wise?' my father asked over the pot of tea we'd set out for my coach. 'I've been hearing and reading about a lot of the raids taking place over the south-east, that's where the Germans are focusing their attacks.'

Mr Swarbrick wiped his moustache with his handkerchief.

'I know. I've read of them too. We all have, but the British have fought off the zeppelin attacks, the Germans know we can shoot them out of the sky. Millions of people are still living in London, Alfred. We're only going to be there one night, and we'll travel back once she's competed.'

When my father didn't say anything, Mr Swarbrick changed tack. Leaning a little closer to him, and loosening his tie a touch – even the cool of the kitchen couldn't diffuse the warmth from outside today – he smiled. 'Arthur, Lucy has been invited to this competition and I will personally make sure she is safe. At nineteen I believe it would be detrimental to her swimming career if she said no to this, I think she should be taking all of these opportunities – we don't know how many more will be left for her,' he added, looking not unkindly in my direction.

Father looked at me, assessing what he was being told and nodded, almost imperceptibly.

'As you wish.'

259

With a whoop of glee, I ran up the two flights of stairs to my room and grabbed some paper.

> *Darling Harry,*
> *Well, you would never guess what. I'm going to LONDON. I know! I'm so excited. I've been invited to a swimming competition there at Lambeth Baths. I will be joining the best in the country!*
> *We go in June. Father is understandably concerned owing to the capital being a target, but I can't wait to see the city. I wonder whether there'll be a chance for a tiny bit of sightseeing or if it'll be all swimming and no looking?*
> *I'll have to find out how long it'll take us to get there – a while I should guess. Still, it'll be an adventure. I will, of course, send you a letter with how I get on. I'm hoping to win, of course.*
> *How are you my darling? I'm so very sorry to hear you'd lost Sam, he sounded like a wonderful man. I'm keeping my fingers crossed you'll come safely home soon.*
> *Lucky xxx*

Chapter Forty-One

JUNE 1917, BLACKPOOL

T he next few weeks flew by, though not without event. A group of American soldiers arrived in Blackpool and caused quite a stir with their tightly carved jawbones, exotic accents and ability to look as though they'd just walked off a film set.

Alice and James's relationship had fizzled out over the last few months. She'd put it down to the irregularity of his letters, but privately I was of the opinion it was because the romance of having someone away had become rather tiresome for my sister. She never was the patient sort, and I think she fell out of love with love. At least the long-distance variety. Her letters had been far less frequent, until eventually I was just posting mine.

'Lorna, tell Lucy she should come with me to the dance this evening,' said Alice, cajoling my friend who had stopped by to drop off a few magazines. We had been standing in our hallway discussing the fashions on the front of one of them when Alice had popped her head around the door-frame from the kitchen.

Lorna shook her head.

'If I know Lucy, and I'm pretty sure I do, if she's said no, she means it – she can be a bit of a stick-in-the-mud,' she laughed as I scowled at the description.

'Oh yes, and I suppose you think its fine to go to dances with American soldiers? We know what they're after.' I crossed my arms.

Lorna stuck her tongue out.

'Only some of them – and anyway, we can't all be as lucky as you. With such a devoted sweetheart,' she raised an eyebrow at me. 'It's alright for some.'

I blushed a little.

'It's not just that. I'm competing in two days' time, I can't have a late night.'

Furrowing her brow, Lorna looked confused.

'I don't know of any competitions – where are you doing it?'

'Lambeth? I had an invitation,' I admitted, a little embarrassed. Lorna was still competing, and doing well, but I didn't know why she'd not been invited to the same competition as me.

Lorna's face cleared. Oh, yes, I think Phyllis mentioned something – wrong competition for me. Crawl only.' She pointed at herself and I nodded with understanding.

'Ah, of course.'

'Still,' Lorna looked concerned, 'Lambeth. Is that wise?'

'Shush, we're not meant to question it.' Alice had squeezed into the hallway with us and was flicking through one of the magazines. 'Father isn't happy, but Mr Swarbrick thinks it'll be all right.'

'Shoo, go and make yourself pretty for the Yanks,' I told Alice, irritated at her presence. Lorna made a face.

'I know that look. But Lorn, what else can I do? I may not have many more chances to compete, you know that.'

She nodded.

'I know. But I can be worried for you,' she watched as Alice made her way up the stairs. 'I know you're worried about her. How about I go to the dance tonight and keep an eye on her, and those soldiers.' She raised an eyebrow suggestively, causing me to smile.

'Thanks that would be great.'

She leant in and embraced me and I squeezed her back.

'Just look after yourself.'

'Always.'

I didn't want to admit I was worried too. I had a sneaking suspicion I was allowing pride to get in the way of making a sensible decision, but it was too late now. I couldn't back out of it. Plus, I reasoned, after Alice and Lorna had made their evening's plans and I'd waved my best friend off, I deserved to compete. I owed it to myself to keep pushing what I could do.

Even when the world was closing in and I was beginning to question whether I should be doing it anymore.

A few days later and I'd wonder at the lightness with which I'd taken my decision.

Dear Harry,

*You ask me how I'm doing, when in the
next sentence you speak of such misery and
loss that I wonder what you must think of
me concerning myself with such luxuries as
swimming competitions. My hope is that
my letters give you an element of joy and
that maybe you ask me about my efforts as
a distraction from your own.*

*With that in mind, I shall honour the
question and tell you how Lambeth was.*

I paused to look away from the paper for a moment. Remembering what London had been like when we had arrived after a day of travelling from Blackpool. I was intrigued by the change of scenery as we'd approached the city. Whilst Blackpool was bustling, and Liverpool had always struck me as a busy town, I hadn't prepared myself for the enormity of the capital city.

Or the destruction.

*Where there had been zeppelin attacks
previously there were rows where houses
used to stand that are utterly destroyed.
Just rubble. I hadn't realised it would be
like that. I'd read the papers and spoken
with Father about the attacks, but seeing
a grainy image in a paper and seeing the
reality are two different things. I suppose*

you'd know that.

I realise just how protected we've been so far. I had no real idea of what you and the other men were going through.

Whilst we had been travelling towards London, news had reached us that there had been a Gotha attack on the city. We had many hours to go, but we'd also been travelling for quite some time and Mr Swarbrick felt we should carry on regardless. I admit I was nervous about it and slept fitfully on the train that night. Mr Swarbrick and I arrived at 6am just as the all clear had been given after the first daytime air raid over London.

We discovered later that day that over one hundred bombs had been dropped, killing almost two hundred people including some children who were at school.

I looked up again from my letter, tears in my eyes.

They were AT SCHOOL, Harry. Such young, innocent lives, lost just like that. And there I was in London, to swim. And for what? To show I could. Mr Swarbrick seemed shaken too, he was quiet for most of the day.

I did wonder if he was concerned for the

danger we were voluntarily putting our-selves in, but when I asked him he shook his head and told me to rest.

The next day, after another bad night's sleep, we went to Lambeth Baths – it's quite an imposing building, Harry, very grand. It's no Blackpool Tower, but then, what is? It had a really high, ever so decorated ceil-ing in the pool area and the noise from the crowd felt like it was coming from all directions.

When I was ready and poolside, eyeing up the competitors, I noticed for the first time that I was substantially older than many of them. I'm convinced there was a smatter-ing of girls who'd not even seen their thir-teenth birthdays yet.

I also couldn't help shake the feeling how futile this all was, in the wake of the bomb-ing. Mr Swarbrick had, I believe, guessed I'd feel this way so he came over to me for a pep talk. He pulled me in close and I realised I was now taller than him too, then he'd whispered, 'Don't let all our ef-forts go to waste, Lucy. It won't have been worth anything, all the hours trav-elling, the worry of your parents, if you throw it away today. Do you hear?' I'd nodded, aware he was saying something that seemed profound although I struggled to get my thoughts in place. Nothing felt right.

But as soon as I hit the water all thoughts of my age, the war and the bombs, all left me in the cool, calm. I won't beat around the bush any longer, I won. I beat the girl into second place by just a few seconds and I was thrilled to win, and relieved, but I didn't feel the same glee I had felt when I'd won the others. It was a relief mainly, that it was over with and I petitioned Swarbrick to get us back to Blackpool as soon as possible.

As we travelled back we were both quiet. Mr Swarbrick read his paper, read his book, completed his crossword. But very little was said. I asked him when I'd next be competing and all he could say was he hadn't heard of any other competitions taking place this year. I think, though he hasn't said it, it might have been my final competition for a while.

That thought leaves me a little lost to be honest, what do I do if I'm not competing? If I had something to aim for, some competition to train for, I would know what to do. But at the moment there's nothing. Maybe that's it? Maybe I need to think of something else to keep myself busy. Have you any suggestions?

I'm sorry to not send you a more uplifting letter, but you may as well know how things are going for me right now.
Yours, as always,
Lucky
xxx

Chapter Forty-Two

AUGUST 1918, BLACKPOOL

'But which one?' I held up two dresses. Neither of which I liked that much. The first was navy blue with white spots. I disliked it because the collar was slightly frayed and I thought it made me look like I was twelve.

Alice frowned at me.

'I like the yellow one. It's a bit more...'she wafted her hand around to imply something which I didn't understand.

'What?'

'Friendly,' she finished airily, 'makes you seem more welcoming.'

I folded my arms and stared at her. 'I am welcoming. I'm very welcoming.'

Trying to not giggle, Alice nodded slowly. 'Definitely the yellow.'

I harrumphed and pulled the yellow one over my head. It was looser fitting than the blue and the colour of buttercups. It was a pretty dress.

'But I've worn it so many times,' I pleaded, before slumping on the floor. Alice joined me, her shoulder pressed against mine. The scent of her lilac soap was so familiar. She took her hand in mine and pressed it gently.

'He doesn't know that though, for him it's the first time. It's the first everything – it's the first time you've seen each other in what, five years? You've kept up an impressive pen friendship but now you get to be with each other. It'll be the first time he sees you as a woman, and you'll see him as a man.' Alice swooned as though she was a hammy film actress and I tapped her playfully.

'Stop it. But yes, I get it. First everything. No pressure,' I sighed and smoothed my dress with my hands, a little nervously. 'Of course, he may not like this Lucy,' I pointed at myself. 'It's been a long time since we saw each other last. I've got older. More opinionated.'

'More annoying,' agreed Alice and I tapped her again. 'More beautiful, more successful, more you. I think he'll be thrilled. It's you who should be worrying.' She raised her eyebrows at me.

'Me, why?'

Alice cocked her head on one side and assessed me, trying to decide whether she should be honest or not.

'What?'

'Look, we know he's injured and he's at King's. So it's a good sign because we know it's not a serious injury, otherwise he'd have gone elsewhere. But he might be, I don't know, missing a limb,' she suggested and I shook my head.

'Doesn't matter to me if he's missing all his limbs. I love him, Alice.'

She nodded.

'He could be blind. Or deaf.'

'Good, it means I can wear this dress a thousand times over, and he doesn't need to listen to me whinging about it,' I replied defiantly.

'Or,' she paused for theatrics, 'he could be missing... his... appendage. Oof,' she groaned as I hit her squarely with my pillow.

'Enough of that.' I giggled, then hit her again as she cried with laughter. 'No discussion of anyone's "appendages". All right?' Alice stood up, rearranged her hair and pulled me to standing in front of our mirror. She began to brush my hair.

'Fine, agreed. But I wanted to prepare you, he might not be the boy you remember or the man you've fallen in love with. There may be events which have affected him.' She looked knowingly at my reflected self and I nodded in understanding. Men were returning regularly from the frontline now who had a far-off look in their eyes. You would make conversations with people who you grew up with or who you'd known from the neighbourhood and they'd be easily startled by a noise in the street, or not be able to hold conversations. Then others who came back in wheelchairs, or with just one arm.

She fussed with my hair.

271

'I don't think I can do much more than this,' Alice apologised as she gave my hair a final brush through, and tried to flick it under so that the length was in line with my jaw. Finding a clip of hers which had a dainty turquoise blue flower on it, she pushed it in just above my right ear and looked at the finished product.

'Beautiful,' she said, just as Mother came into the room. She looked at me and smiled broadly.

'Well, Alice has worked wonders.' She laughed at my scowl.

'It's only a little make-up,' Alice explained but smiled. 'I had a good base to work on.' She squeezed me and said to Mother, 'I'm sure you have a blue handbag to match the clip, don't you? We can't do much about the shoes, but she looks smart enough. A handbag would finish off the outfit,' she decided and I nodded, finding it easier to go along with the preening than to not.

Mother looked thoughtful.

'Yes, I think I do – it's been such a long time since I've had dressed up properly, I've forgotten half of what I used to wear.' She looked sad for a moment. 'I'm glad that you get the chance today though, Lucy.' She took another lasting look at me, then disappeared down the flight of stairs to her bedroom. Moments later we heard her feet on the wooden floorboards as she made her way back to our room at the top of the house.

'Found it,' she puffed a little, 'I'm getting too old to keep going up and down this many stairs. By the time I've come up to tell you it's lunch and gone back down again,

I'm exhausted.' She shook her head. 'Old age. Don't let it happen to you,' she advised and we both nodded.

'Noted, Mother. So, lunch is it? Best pop down then. Lucy's meeting Harry at three o'clock, she'll need to leave by two o'clock to make sure she's on time,' Alice advised Mother who nodded.

'Of course, and I've put together a few bits for Harry. You know, just a cake, some sandwiches.' She smiled. 'I managed to get enough together from rations. I hope he enjoys them – he'll need building up.'

I felt a lump in my throat.

'Thank you, Mother. He'll be really pleased.'

'Hang on.' Alice was standing, hands on hips. 'Does that mean we don't get any of it? Is it your boiled fruit cake? That's my favourite.'

Mother smiled. 'Don't worry, I've managed to make the ingredients go some way. We have two small loaves, they'll need to be thin slices, but we'll all get some.'

Alice looked relieved.

'Phew, goodo.' She made her way out and headed off down the stairs. I made to do the same but Mother stopped me.

'Lucy,' she began, then just embraced me and I held her too. 'It's been a long war for all of us – we don't know when it'll end. Just be there for him, as I know you will. And tell him we're here too – I know his family life is, or was, unsettled, tell him he can always rely on us.' She spoke into my hair, the words lightly muffled, as I burrowed my face into her shoulder.

I held her and we stood there in the doorway of my childhood bedroom, the dust motes catching the light, throwing sparkles across the floor where my blue dress lay discarded.

'Thank you, Mother.'

Arriving at King's Lancashire Military Convalescent Hospital, I stilled my nerves with a huge, deep breath. It was the sort of breath which could take me from one side of the pool to the middle, but today it got me no further than two short steps and yet it still did nothing to calm my rapid heartbeat.

I didn't know why I was so nervous. Harry had invited me to King's, I'd been sending him letters for two years – and him me. And we knew each other. I didn't need to be nervous. But I was. A lot.

'Miss?' There was a guard on the door, someone installed to stop nosy passers-by dropping in, and stop the soldiers leaving, I supposed.

'Sorry, I'm Miss Morton,' I replied, as I hastily flattened my hair with the palm of my hand.

'Yep, you're on the list – visiting Harry Heaton?' the guard double-checked and I nodded, his name throwing my stomach into such disarray I feared I may lose my lunch.

'Lovely, if you just follow Nurse Malone, she'll take you to his ward. He's in Room G.' The guard nodded to a pleasant-looking nurse in a starched white uniform with a dark-blue cardigan slung over her shoulders.

'Of course, follow me,' the nurse replied and took off at speed. I tried to keep up, aware of my heels click-clacking across the floor of the corridor. We went past room after room of patients. All men. All in various states of injury and dishevelment.

The nurse stopped to talk to me. 'Just be aware that some are a bit chatty. Ignore them if they say anything coarse. A few years on the front line will do that to you,' she advised. 'Just try not to provoke anything,' she added and I swallowed. I wasn't sure what I'd be provoking but I hoped I looked demure enough and unlikely enough to encourage unwanted attention – which is what I assumed she was alluding to.

'Right, this way, here we go,' she said. 'Through here.' She nodded at the door which had a small square window with black gridded lines etched on it. 'I'm sure he's awake, he was half an hour ago.' She smiled at me and walked away.

I watched my hand reach the door-handle and I willed myself to open it. But I was frozen.

Instead, it opened from the inside and I was met with a tall, bare-chested man wearing light blue-and-white-striped pyjama bottoms, his arm in a sling, in apparent mid-sentence to someone else in the room, '... think there's someone...'

We stopped and looked at each other. Me, still going to open the handle. Him, with his hand on the door to keep it open. Both staring at each other in disbelief.

It was him.

His face broke into a huge smile.

'It's you.'

Chapter Forty-Three

SEPTEMBER 1918, BLACKPOOL

We spent weeks in our own bubble.

It didn't matter that I had to work at the Post Office during the day, Harry used that time to rest and recuperate. The hospital said he may never regain a fully functioning left hand, after a bomb blew up near to where he'd been sleeping and shrapnel embedded itself in his lower arm, rendering most of his muscle function useless.

Fortunately for him he'd been protected from the blast by his location in the trench. Many others who he counted as friends and brothers hadn't been as lucky and lost their lives that day. The doctors said with regular exercise there was a chance he could retrain his hand to remember how to work, but they couldn't guarantee and, because it wasn't life-threatening he was not the top of their priority list. Understandably.

Whenever I visited the hospital I had seen many men in much greater need than Harry. Men with bandages wound around their heads, or both legs covered with a blanket to prevent people staring. Harry's injury was slowly improving.

Whenever I visited the hospital I brought as many biscuits and cakes as Mother, Alice and I could make with our meagre rations, along with anything else we could barter for. Lorna, who was working in the Land Army, was able to get hold of more eggs than our own share and even a little butter every now and then, so we swapped things with her. I'd even found sugar through one of the girls at work, though she told me it was better I didn't know how she was getting it. I swapped the sugar in exchange for Alice's dressmaking skills, so everyone was happy.

All so we could ensure the lads were well-nourished. It all started when I returned home from one visit, and told Mother how thin they all looked. Never one for allowing people to go without, she saw it as her duty to feed them. Despite me telling her they were pretty well fed at the hospital, it was just months of fighting that had taken its toll, she wouldn't hear of it. So that's why I turned up daily with tasty treats, and that's why I knew so many of the men.

None as well as Harry though. His face would light up when I came into the room and he'd stop whatever he was doing, whether it was a conversation, a card game or writing in his journal – something he did regularly – to walk over to me where he'd kiss me firmly on the lips. It always made me smile, that kiss. I think that's why he

277

did it. Yes, there was a little ownership in front of the other guys, but more than that it felt like it was his way of anchoring himself here. Away from battle. He was here, with me, he was kissing me. I was real. I was solid. All this was real, and the war was far, far, away.

Our days followed a similar pattern, with every visit from me meaning a walk outside for him. We would walk around the grounds of the hospital, but not on very wet days. Those days, when it was throwing it down, they were the worst ones for Harry. He wouldn't say why. Only that he'd spent days soaked through in France. His eyes said more, but I didn't press him. Those days we sat in the window and looked at the weather whilst we held hands.

On the other days though, the sunny and the dry ones, we'd walk. We'd talk. We'd catch up on the past few years. We'd laugh.

'Am I keeping you from swimming?' he asked abruptly one day as we were sat on a bench in the grounds, sipping on cups of tea a nurse had provided for us, and I took a moment to reply.

'There's no swimming to keep me from,' I eventually admitted, to which he turned and looked at me, his face giving me the look that I could never hide from.

'Of course there's swimming – Lucky, you're always swimming. You're a swimmer, what's going on?'

I paused, unsure how to explain.

'Last time, in London – I think I wrote to you about it, there was a bomb. Children died. When I came home, I just didn't see the point of it anymore.'

Harry shook his head, his disbelief obvious.

'But what does that mean? You can't have quit swimming? I'm sure you've mentioned it in letters – it's been, what, nearly two years since that bomb.' He paused and looked at me. 'I remember every letter you sent. They're what stopped me from getting completely lost in the war. I felt as though I was with you when you wrote. I was so proud of all your achievements, even though there's a war on, there you were, pushing forward. Making strides. Don't tell me you've given up.'

I looked across the grounds. The wind was getting up a little, blowing the leaves on the trees and hastening autumn along. It would be October soon and more wet days would be on the horizon. I hoped Harry wouldn't have to go back to France. He needed to be here.

'Lucy?'

I turned to face Harry and held his good hand.

'They shut the baths when I came home and they've only opened erratically. Since there have been very few competitions this past eighteen months or so it hasn't been a priority for me to seek out those which run. I love swimming.' I spoke quickly to try and intercept any of his questions. 'But swimming isn't the most important thing right now. Living is,' I reminded him and he shook his head.

'But your living includes swimming. You're telling me you've not swum for a year and a half?' he asked, incredulous.

I shook my head gently.

'No. When the baths have been open I've been down. When they're closed I've swum in the sea – I've enjoyed the freedom of just swimming as far as I like, and I've done a couple of life-saving courses so my swimming is useful.' I paused again. 'The Olympics in 1916 didn't happen and it's not looking likely that the 1920 ones will either, so, what's the point? I've taken it as far as I can. Now I need to do what everyone is always suggesting I do. Move on, grow up, marry, have children. That's if this blasted war ever ends. I'm not bringing a child into this world for them to know this...' I realised I was beginning to sob and tried to stop myself with quick, short breaths.

Harry leaned over and put his arm around my shoulders.

'Lucy. My darling, darling Lucy. All this time you've been holding all this back from me. Why didn't you tell me what was going on? Your letters were always so fun and enthusiastic.' He squeezed me lightly. 'Though now I come to think of it, I didn't think about the lack of swimming news. I was taken by everything else you were telling me. Your job, your family. The town.' He shook his head sadly. 'I wanted to believe what you told me, and you told me what you wanted me to believe.'

I nodded, what else was there to say?

'I'm here now, let's not pretend anymore, all right? You can always tell me anything,' he tipped my face and kissed me lightly on the lips. 'Whatever your hopes, your fears, your worries. I want them all. I want to be there for you like you've been there for me these past couple of years. Your letters kept me going in the darkest of days.'

I smiled and kissed him back.

'And yours mine, I always imagined us walking along the promenade arm in arm, dressed in our Sunday best, telling each other everything,' I admitted.

'Well, how about we do that this Sunday?' Harry asked quietly, a light grin playing on his lips.

'You're not allowed out unless you're discharged though,' I replied, hope soaring that he'd be all mine, then extinguishing as I realised if that was the case he was another step closer to returning to the frontline.

He nodded.

'They're letting me out for good behaviour, Luce, though they're encouraging me to continue my stay with them in the hostel wing, so they can keep an eye on how I heal. It does mean though, that I'm allowed to leave whenever I want – we could even take ourselves out for a day trip somewhere. 'I returned his smile. Whatever happened in the future, I wanted this to be the moment I remembered. This happiness and light and hope.

He kissed me, gently.

'My Lucky.'

Chapter Forty-Four

NOVEMBER 1918, BLACKPOOL

I t came, like so many things in this war, as a shock. On the eleventh month, on the eleventh day at the eleventh hour, the announcement came that the war was over.

'Harry,' I dashed into his hostel room, elation written on my face, 'it's over.' He was already in my arms and kissing me with such joy, I couldn't hold back my tears.

'Everyone's going to the town hall, Father says there's going to be a party there,' I told him speedily. My father had recently been made Mayoral Attendant and had moved from his groomsman job. His work kept him at the town hall for many hours of the day, but he enjoyed it so much that whenever he returned to Brighton Cottage it was always with a slight jaunt in his walk and a grin on his face.

I kissed Harry deeply on his mouth, wondering when the novelty would wear off.

'You know what this means, don't you?' He nodded, kissing me with enthusiasm.

'They're not sending you back.' I held him tightly and tried to actually believe what I'd heard. Could it be true? Was it over?

Harry brushed my cheekbone lightly with his thumb, calloused from the days he spent whittling wooden sculptures to pass the time and I enjoyed the feel of it on my skin.

'It's true. It's over, Lucky.'

Our moment was interrupted by an enormous roar from the corridor and when we stuck our heads out to see what was going on, it felt as though the entire hostel was emptying out in one long line of the walking wounded. Soldiers on other's shoulders jostled, cheered, shouted and drank. The relief of the terror that had hung over us was so palpable it was hard not to get swept up in it all.

'Come on, Harry, party's this way.' One of the lads, Jimmy, threw his arm around Harry's neck and pulled him into the fray. He was still holding my hand and I was pulled into the group too. It felt as though I was in the middle of a current, being pulled out to sea.

As we made our way down from King's towards the centre of town, our group swelled to include other people who streamed out of hotels, homes and cafés. Already, ribbons and bunting were being thrown out of windows and strung up in the streets. People were jumping and cheering with joy and when we reached the town hall I gasped at the sight.

'It's like all of Blackpool's here.'

Harry grinned at me and kissed me again. We watched as flags were hoisted above the municipal buildings in Talbot Square and the prickling of tears started to itch my eyes at the sight. I wiped them with the back of my hand, when Harry nudged me.

'Your father's up there. Look, Lucy.' He pointed towards the town hall and I broke out into a huge bubble of laughter, because there was Father stood next to the Mayor at the front entrance looking as pleased as punch. There were a few other officials standing around the front too, but then it was like someone had told the whole town that an announcement was due because within a few moments the whole of Talbot Square was rammed with people, all filled with hope and expectation.

The Mayor held his hands out to hush the excitable crowd and a silence fell. We were ready to hear what he had to say. We wanted the reassurance.

'It is my great honour to tell you that the armistice was signed at five o'clock this morning and today, at eleven o'clock, fighting ceased.' He broke off as the crowd roared. Wave after wave of cheers swept over us and Harry held me tightly. I held on too, concerned I'd be swept away from him.

'Silence please,' the Mayor said and gradually the noise around me abated, albeit interspersed with pops of mini cheers from people and yells of 'Hooray'.

'At noon I shall be attending a special thanksgiving service at St John's Parish Church, and I ask that you all accompany me. It's an opportunity for us to give thanks for all the men and boys who gave their lives for peace.' He paused. 'All shops should close at one o'clock today, so that we may mark this historic occasion.'

'Hip-hip,' one of the soldiers near to me yelled, and the whole crowd, it seemed, replied, 'Hooray.' Two more cheers, each bigger and louder and rawer than the previous one, rolled across the crowd. As I looked around I saw women in tears and couldn't help but allow mine to drop freely.

'Chin up, Lucky, it's all going to be better now.' Harry squeezed my hand as we walked, with the rest of the crowd, towards the church.

I looked up at the buildings as we walked by, the whole town fluttering with flags, streamers and pennants – it was truly wondrous to see and the sight of our Union Flag standing proud on the pole near to the church gave me pause. There was something so grounding, so patriotic, so wonderful about our flag it made me proud to live on our small island.

It was clear, as we made our way into the churchyard there wouldn't be room for everyone looking to give thanks inside the church, and instead we joined the hundreds standing outside it. At some point all the children in the town seemed to have acquired their own mini Union Flags and were waving them frantically, with such vigour that I was sure someone would receive one in their eye.

An old man, with ingrained lines around his eyes and medals on his jacket, pressed a patriotic favour into my hand and smiled. 'We won, young lady, may God bless us all.' He spoke gruffly and continued handing out the rosettes in red, white and blue. I pinned mine onto the collar of my coat, aware of Harry's arm around my shoulders.

'When we were fighting, I kept two things with me at all times,' he muttered under his breath to me, so that I, and I alone, would be privy to his thoughts. I held my breath, aware he rarely spoke of his days in battle, and let him continue.

'I had a photograph of you, Lucy, that I'd cut out of a newspaper years before, when you'd won a prize, and I had this.' He held out a crumpled postcard, which he unfolded carefully. It was a landscape of the South Shore, which had been coloured in, complete with promenade and rides. When he turned it over, all that was written on it were the words '*I'm sorry,*' and a large H, scrawled in a similar hand to his, though more childishly.

'I did try to send it. I promise I did. But I couldn't bear to think of the hurt I caused you, so eventually I stopped trying. Then when we were in France, I realised I may never get to say those words to you. Or any for that matter. I couldn't face going into battle knowing I'd hurt the one person I truly loved. I hope you can forgive me.' He looked hard into my eyes.

I held his hand, which was clutching the worn-out postcard.

'Harry, I forgave you years ago. We've all been through so much, I wouldn't wish to hold onto any bad feelings. I'm just relieved you managed to write to me, and that's what brought us back together.'

A wave of excitement began to ripple through the crowd and as we looked up we noticed the Mayor on the steps of the church.

'I know we're all so very relieved to have the end of the war,' he began and as a large cheer threatened to wash out the rest of his speech, he raised his hands for quiet, 'so I ask you to come to the town hall at three o'clock this afternoon for music in the square. We shall have bands and songs and merriment.' He smiled widely and everyone cheered again.

The next couple of hours passed by quickly. Harry and the rest of the soldiers returned to their hospital to collect beer and cigarettes, I dashed home to put on my most patriotic blue and white dress over which I slung my raincoat and found a red scarf to fling around my shoulders. Alice was there too and we kept bumping into one another as we looked for dresses, shoes, coats and whatnot, giggling at the excitement.

'Lucy, don't tell Mother but I've already had a glass of sherry,' she hiccupped as she was doing the straps on her shoes. 'I hope I'll be able to get a dance with Arthur. Remember that soldier I told you about? The one who always waits for me when I deliver cakes and biscuits?'

'Just be good, not too much sherry and don't let him persuade you to go off somewhere, just the two of you,' I advised, though at the same time thinking how she was seventeen and could do whatever she liked. The war was over. We needed to celebrate.

'I'll be good if you are.' Alice raised her eyebrows and we both laughed. We walked together towards Talbot Square and I looked for Harry near the statue we said we'd use as a landmark. It was heaving already but as we got closer I spotted him, and many of the other soldiers, standing around the statue, laughing and drinking beer.

'There he is.' Alice disappeared from my side and quickly reappeared in front of Arthur who took one look at her and swept her into a deep kiss, to much applause and whoops from the men standing nearby.

I found Harry, and he passed me a beer.

'I'm not sure,' I stuttered. I didn't drink much, apart from an occasional sherry.

'Just take a swig, it'll get you into the party spirit – I won't tell anyone,' he smiled warmly and I realised he'd already had at least a couple of beers. I took a deep gulp of the warm, brown ale and spluttered at the taste.

'Oh, that's awful,' I winced as he laughed heartily, 'no more.' I held my hand up and he laughed again.

People were closing in on all sides, thousands were filling the square and, from our vantage point on the statue, we could see them streaming down Clifton Street and Talbot Road from the old bank to the walls of the town hall. And everyone had the same idea – to cheer and let loose the smothered feeling of nearly four-and-a-half years' war. How they cheered. In one vast volume, the cheers roared and crashed.

The bands from Harry's hospital played and we danced and danced. I felt as though I'd never been happier, or freer, than I felt just then.

It was only when the national anthem played, and we all stood there, sombrely thinking of those who wouldn't be coming home, only then when I heard those words and thought of how important representing your country was, only then did I think, once more, about swimming. About hearing this anthem, stood on a podium. Being the best of British. The surge of pride I'd felt earlier on seeing the Union Flag resurfaced, quashed under the last couple of years of restraint. Restrictions. Rations. A time when dreams and hopes no longer counted because you needed to just keep on going, because so many other people were dying so you could keep living. A time when thoughts of a future seemed reckless, futile even, given how little hope there was for a decent one. And yet.

'And yet, here we are.'

'What's that?' Harry had turned from the chaotic dancing of so many soldiers and people in the crowd, as the sound of bagpipes played from the steps of the town hall.

'I said, to the future,' I replied, hastily.

Harry raised his beer.

'To the future,' he paused and looked at me, 'and to hope.'

Chapter Forty-Five

AUGUST 1920, BLACKPOOL

A s I walked out of the town hall, I marvelled once
again at the turn our lives had taken since the end
of the war almost two years ago.

Father's role had been added to, and now, as Mayoral
Attendant and Town Hall Keeper, we had moved out
of Brighton Cottage, my home for the last twenty years
or so, to the town hall itself where we had been given
accommodation on site. We had a suite of rooms that were
beautifully furnished and it felt as though we lived in one
of the smart hotels that had popped up on the seafront.

Mother was very happy telling people she lived at the
town hall, and it had given me an opportunity to be in
the middle of the town, with as much independence a
twenty-two-year-old could ask for. I could walk to my
recently promoted job at the Post Office and generally
enjoy the liberty of a war-free Britain.

Everything was perfect. Sort of.

What mattered was that I was swimming again. A lot. The pool reopened in May 1919 and I hadn't looked back. Competitions were back up and running and I'd managed to place first in two breaststroke events, which had fired up my enthusiasm once more. I'd come second in the Kew to Putney five-miler so it felt like my body was allowing me to work properly, to behave how I wanted it to.

'Lucy,' Harry was a little breathless when he caught up with me, 'didn't you see me, or hear me? I was calling for you.' He fell in step with me, though I didn't make any effort to slow my pace.

'Oh, sorry. Hi, Harry, off to work?' I carried on walking quickly along the pavement and across the cobbled street. He kept up, though there was a slight sheen to his face due to the exertion and eventually I relented and slowed a little so he didn't have to work quite so hard.

'Of course,' he looked baffled. 'Why are you rushing to work?'

'I'm trying to see if it helps my lung expansion. Mr Swarbrick has read that walking briskly does wonders for one's lung capacity. He thinks if I walk quickly I should see an improvement in my time.'

Harry raised his eyebrow, as I knew he would.

'Fine.'

'What? What does that mean?' I asked, intentionally speeding my walk up again. He fell into step with me once more, swinging his arms as though marching in the Army again.

Harry looked at me as though he was going to say something, then bit his tongue. I wanted him to say it, willed him. But he wouldn't. And I knew he wouldn't. And because he wouldn't, I wouldn't. Which meant we danced around each other, and our issues, neither of us willing to say what needed to be said.

'Well, if he thinks it'll help. Remind me what you're training for now? I thought you'd just had those competitions,' he asked, and it irritated me. Irritated because he knew. But he wouldn't say. And he wouldn't agree or disagree with my decision. So he made me repeat my plans. My choice. I sped up a little more, and even though I began to feel breathless it felt good. I could feel the blood pumping in my veins, throbbing into my heart and awakening my brain.

'I'm going for the world records again – in breaststroke and backstroke. The competition is in two months' time and I need to shave eight seconds off my time to be in with a chance of knocking Agnes off her perch,' I replied as I stopped sharply at the front of the Post Office and checked my reflection in the window. I rearranged my hat a little, pulled my jacket straighter and, satisfied with my appearance, pushed the door open to begin my shift.

'I thought we'd agreed you weren't going to do that.' Harry caught my elbow to stop me from walking through the door and we stood there, half in and out of the door-frame. I, in the Post Office, Harry in the street.

'I don't think we agreed anything of the sort, Harry,' I replied, my anger rising. 'I think you said you'd had enough of sharing me with swimming, and I said you needed to get used to it.' I paraphrased the argument we'd had over the weekend. The last in a long line of arguments we'd had the past six months or so pretty much in direct correlation to how much I trained. The more I went swimming, the higher the level of arguments. Harry shook his head sadly.

'Lucky,' he began.

'Stop calling me that. I'm not a child anymore, Harry. I'm twenty-two. I'm a woman and I'm called Lucy,' I replied, stepping back onto the street to be with him, mainly to get away from the audience we'd attracted in the Post Office.

I immediately regretted saying it at the look of hurt on his face. I didn't mind his moniker for me usually, but today it felt grating.

He sighed, exasperatedly, and ran his hands through his hair. As I had done in the past. In the year following the end of the war, when the world felt upside down. Where I found I had to make way for the man whose job I'd kept open at the Post Office, like many of my female friends. I was one of the lucky ones though, through some kind of fluke I'd been moved into a different section. Allowed to remain as I was, unmarried and childless. It wasn't the happy year we'd hoped for after the war. Certainly not for the men who'd returned, weary and who needed something to distract themselves from the horrors they'd seen. A year which saw rationing continue because there were so many lives lost affecting farming and shipping.

The same year which laid out to me that it didn't matter how far us women had gone these past few years, we were about to watch it all get wound back as the men in charge feared we were getting too used to the freedom that came with their jobs. To trousers. The glory of wearing trousers, and yet now we were being called to dress 'properly' again, with articles in the *Daily Mail* and *The Express*, explaining how we needed to make an effort for 'our boys'.

'Lucy. You know I've supported your...' Harry struggled to find the right word. 'Hobby, but I think you need to start thinking about your future – our future.' He held my left hand and rubbed my naked ring finger. 'There's a time for distractions and there's a time for – us,' he explained.

I stared at him. At the face I loved and loathed. At the person who above all other people should understand that swimming wasn't a hobby, it was a passion and something I wanted to see through as far as I could take it.

'I've been asked to take part in Olympic trials,' I replied flatly. 'The games are in Antwerp in August and a team is being put together. There's talk of breaststroke being included, so I'm being invited to test out for it.'

Harry lowered his head sadly.

'So you're choosing swimming?' he replied quietly.

'It's not a case of choosing. It's a drive in me, in here,' I pointed to my heart. 'I have to see what I can do – whether I can be the best. I have to know, Harry, surely you must understand that?'

He shook his head.

'I think you'll never be happy. Even when you're the best in the world, you'll still want more,' he replied, 'and I just want you, so that means one of us is going to have to be unhappy, and I don't want it to be you.' Harry let go of my hand and I let it drop to my side.

'No, Harry, I will be happy – I am happy,' I replied, though I realised I didn't know if I wanted to fight for us. 'I just want to see how good I can be, surely you want that for me?'

He stepped past me and placed his hand on the door-handle.

'I wish you all the luck in the world and that you find what you're looking for. And maybe, once you've found it or won it, maybe I'll still be waiting for you and I'll be happy too. Or maybe I'll have found happiness else-where.' He shook his head and went inside.

Left on the pavement I tried to reconcile his words with his actions. I wanted to be sad. I was remorseful – I loved Harry but if he wouldn't accept me for who I was, truly, and what I wanted to achieve, maybe he wasn't the person I wanted by my side.

'You're on your own, Lucy Morton,' I told myself. Taking a deep breath I pushed the door after him to con-tinue with my day job.

Chapter Forty-Six

BLACKPOOL TIMES

*W*ORLD RECORD BROUGHT BACK TO
BLACKPOOL

*THE town is rejoicing today as lady swimmer Miss
Lucy Morton has triumphed once again in gaining a
world record.*

*Miss Morton, who takes her competitions very se-
riously, competed at the weekend at the Cocker Baths
against many other ladies who are the best in their
areas. However, our Miss Morton, who strode out in
her usual haughty manner, her head held high, stood
elegantly by the side of the bath taking no heed of the
competitors around her.*

*As soon as the official for the competition had shouted
loudly to 'go', Miss Morton dived into the pool, barely
breaking the surface as she disappeared in the water,
arising a few metres later and beginning her breaststroke competition.*

Three other ladies were neck and neck with Miss Morton for the first fifty yards, however, it soon became apparent that Miss Morton was not to be outdone. With determination in her eyes and a steely manner, she ploughed her way through the water as though she was born to it, quickly pulling away from her competitors who could only look on as she disappeared into the distance.

The final fifty yards were a 'how to' in winning a world record, for Miss Morton carved her way through the water, looking serene and controlled throughout and when she slammed her hands on the side and was told she had achieved the world record, she merely smiled and looked satisfied with herself, allowing the home crowd to do the cheering.

Upon exiting the baths and taking her world record badge and medal from the Mayor, Miss Morton looked weary and a little tearful, as ladies are wont to do upon achieving such greatness.

She posed, albeit a touch unwillingly, for photographs for The Blackpool Times, holding her pennant up for all to see as she shivered a little.

Unassuming and of pleasant personality, when asked how she felt about regaining the World Record she was short, yet sweet with her honest answer, 'Relieved to have beaten the American.'

Next for Miss Morton is an Olympic-sized opportunity, where she will be competing for a place on the ladies team going to Antwerp this year.

Chapter Forty-Seven

OCTOBER 1920, BLACKPOOL

'I've had an idea.' Alice came into my room at the town hall where I was lying on my bed, staring at the ceiling. She was dressed top-to-toe in dark purple, her low-slung sweater hiding her bump, which was also concealed under her long pleated skirt. She had finished off her outfit with a pair of black shoes, a black handbag and a beautiful clip adorned with feathers, affixed onto her recently bobbed blonde hair.

'Oh yes?' I replied.

'We're going out today. It's a Saturday, we're both off. You're not swimming – I think we should go out like we used to,' Alice urged and I grimaced. She caught my look. 'You know we haven't gone out nearly as much as we used to,' she paused. 'It'll be good to go out and do something – for both of us. Goodness knows I won't be doing much in a couple of months.' She beamed, rubbing her belly fondly. I noticed her wedding ring catching the light.

'How's Arthur?'

'He's wonderful, Lucy, and looking forward to meeting this little one. He's building a cot today and I told him I was going to take you out for the day, to cheer you up.'

I stared back at the ceiling.

'I don't need cheering up. I'm fine.' Alice sat, a little heavily, on the end of my bed. She looked tired and drawn and I wondered how much of a toll the pregnancy was taking. I hadn't seen much of her over the last few months, since she married and moved in with Arthur. But now, upon seeing her for the first time properly in a long while, I noticed the pale complexion, the sweat patches under her arms, her laboured breathing as she sat, watching me.

'Everything all right?' she asked as I looked at her.

'You look ill.'

She rooted in her handbag for a compact and eyed herself in the mirror.

'Yes, well, that's what happens when the blasted morning sickness actually hits all times of the day – and doesn't want to stop,' she added, powdering her face and applying a little colour to her already lipsticked and lightly chapped lips. Satisfied with her appearance, she returned to looking at me.

'So, are you coming out with me or not?'

'Where?'

Alice huffed.

'It's a surprise, that's where. Something to take your mind off the Olympics.'

I scowled.

'I don't need my mind taking off anything. I'm fine.' Alice shook her head and got to her feet slowly, before pulling me up on mine.

'Sure, I'm absolutely certain this... cloud...' she wafted her hands around my face, 'which you're walking under is nothing to do with the fact you've not been accepted on to the team. But humour me and come out. You'll like it, I promise.'

I realised I would never win against a pregnant, insistent Alice, and nodded. She let out a little squeal of joy and began to throw clothes at me from my wardrobe.

'There, that'll do. Pop that on and do something with your face. I'm going to have a cup of tea with Mother, then we're off. It'll only be for a few hours, so you can come back and be despondent in a bit.' She walked off before I could show my irritation and I did as I was told.

When I entered the living room a little while later, my mother and sister were leaning in closely to each other, smiling and laughing over their tea and I felt a pang of envy. I'd never found my relationship with Mother to be as easy as Alice found it. Maybe it was something to do with being the eldest and the burden of being the first. Or maybe it was just because I'd taken a different route to hers in this world, whereas Alice's was closer to what Mother saw as normal.

'Here she is,' Mother smiled and I responded with my own, then reached for the teapot but Alice stopped me.

'No time, come on, we need to go,' she kissed Mother on her cheek. 'I'll see you soon – it's your turn to come to ours for lunch next.' She smiled and shooed me out of the room and into the public space of the town hall.

We walked down the corridors, our heels clipping on the shiny floors and as we rounded into the entrance hall, Alice waved at Bill who looked after the Mayor's car. 'We're ready for it now,' she said grandly and he nodded.

'The car?' I asked, surprised. We were very rarely allowed to use the car – it was a privilege and only to be used when Father was carrying out a mayoral duty.

'You didn't think I'd be walking like this, did you?' Alice admonished and exaggerated her duck-like waddle I hadn't wanted to comment on.

'Well...'

We walked out onto the steps and down to the car where Bill was holding the door open for us. 'Thanks, Bill,' Alice said kindly to him and stepped in. I nodded thanks as well and sat alongside her.

'Where are we going?' I asked, growing tired of the surprise.☐

Alice clasped her hands together, a gleam in her eyes.

'What do you most like to do?' she began, then hastily added, 'Aside from swimming – I'm not getting into any bath for the next few months, goodness knows what lurks in those waters. But aside from swimming, what do you most like to do?'

I frowned.

'Erm...'

'Eat?' prompted Alice, tickling a small smile out of me.

'I suppose.'

'You more than suppose – you're always going on about how hungry you are, and I happen to know what you love eating more than anything else in the world.'

I smiled. She was winning me over.

'Chocolate cake?'

Alice nodded. 'Chocolate cake. We're going to a hotel with a restaurant which, I'm told on very good authority, serves the best chocolate cake. We are going to sit at a smart table, with a starched tablecloth and silverware, and we're going to order chocolate cake and champagne. Then we're going to eat it until we're sick, wash down the bubbles and have the best time. With no discussion of swimming at all.' She sat back, pleased with herself.

'That's pretty good – how have you swung that?'

Alice looked mortified.

'How dare you suggest that I've swung anything?'

'Arthur helped, didn't he? Is it the hotel where Arthur works as a chef usually?' Alice tried not to smile but she never was good at hiding her feelings.

'Maybe.'

I laughed and sat back, relieved it wasn't anything too over the top. I was concerned for Alice's condition, and I wanted to be able to get her home as quickly as possible, but Arthur's hotel was lovely and we could easily while away a few hours there. Which was definitely a good thing. I needed a chance to get my thoughts in order.

There was a moment of quiet between us and I realised I needed her to know something.

'It wasn't that I wasn't accepted onto the team.' I looked out of the car as we pulled away. 'It was that the

Olympics committee decided not to run either of the strokes and distances I compete in,' I said, correcting her earlier comment. 'So unless I somehow manage to persuade them I can be on the freestyle team, despite never swimming it, my involvement is just not a factor. It's not a no, it's a "not applicable",' I explained. I wanted her to understand that I was good enough for the team – still was – but circumstances beyond my control were preventing me from reaching my dream.

She reached over and took my hand in hers.

'You're allowed to be mad, just don't be sad. And don't take it out on Mother,' she advised.

'Since when did you become all wise and knowing,' I huffed, ignoring her gaze and continuing to stare out the window. 'You're the younger sister, I'm meant to advise you on life matters. Not the other way around. It's not the way things are done.'

Alice smiled thoughtfully.

'I don't think anything you do is particularly "the way things are done". Look at you, one year back into swimming properly and you've got world records, a chance for the Olympics and you seem to be adding long-distance open-water swimmer to your list of achievements.'

Just as I turned to look at her, her face impassioned with the speech, it was her turn to look away, out the window.

'It's not easy being the other sister, you know? The one who never does as well. My medals are outnumbered four to one,' she reminded me and I opened my mouth to reply, but she shushed me. 'It's not easy,' she repeated, 'but I am exceptionally proud of you, in everything you do.'

She turned to look at me. Her gaze intense. 'I'm your biggest fan and will tell everyone about my big sister. The one who gets on and achieves things she sets her mind to. The sister who has chosen the other path, the awkward, sometimes trickier one. But she triumphs. Even in her darkest times – I tell people – even then, just you watch her.'

She looked at me, eyes glistening. 'You watch, because even then she shines.'

Chapter Forty-Eight

July 1922, St Annes

'You did it, Lucy.'

I crossed the line and tried to focus my breathing for a moment, trying desperately hard to ignore the people talking to me, whilst looking for the other competitors and spitting out some of the seawater which filled my mouth and nose.

'First lady to cross the line, again,' said Greta with a grin, now an official at the long-distance races I'd shown a knack for.

'You don't look tired,' Greta shook her head, 'you've swum ten miles and you look like you could do it again.' She laughed, then looked at Mr Swarbrick. 'I think she needs a towel,' she reminded him and he pulled himself from the conversation he'd been having with a reporter from *The Blackpool Gazette & Herald*.

'Apologies.' He wiped a handkerchief over his forehead, the August sunshine not suiting his constantly worn attire of a three-piece tweed suit. 'Lucy, they'd like a chat with you when you're ready.' He handed me a towel and I dried off on the beach, trying not to spray Greta in the process.

'I could swim further,' I admitted, 'though truth be told one can get a little bored just constantly swimming. It's nice to have a finish line.' I smiled at her. 'But it's good to be first, again.'

Greta embraced me.

'You're smashing. I hope you know that. Truly smashing. I know you were annoyed not to win against Connie in the Kew to Putney.'

'Again,' I added, to remind her I'd finished second to Connie Jeans in the same competition in two years, though it was hard to be irritated with her – she was a superb swimmer – I had expected a first and was starting to wonder if my age was catching up with me. My twenty-four years was certainly beginning to look elderly compared to the fourteen, fifteen and sixteen-year-olds I was up against in competitions. They weren't even novices, they'd been swimming for years and they had more in them than I had.

'Even still,' Greta continued, handing me a robe to put on. Despite the August warmth I was beginning to shiver a little. 'I think you're truly making a name for yourself in this area. No one else can come close to you at these distances. You'll be looking to cross the Channel next.'

I laughed as I squeezed out water from my hair.

'Oh no, it's fine – I'll leave that to Mercedes. It's twice what I've swum. Too long, even for me – don't get me wrong, I've thought about it, but I don't think I fancy my chances. What if I got lost?' I added, making Greta laugh.

'A good point, let's stick with these distances. Oh, I have to keep an eye on the other ladies, they're all beginning to get in now. Well done again.' She dashed off to maintain her role which she enjoyed so much and Mr Swarbrick came over to me.

'Are you ready for that chat? The chap wants to know if you plan on doing it again,' his voice was muffled as he dabbed sweat away from his top lip with a handkerchief.

'Today?'

Mr Swarbrick's laugh took us both by surprise.

'No, I don't think he means today – probably next year.' He patted his forehead with his handkerchief and I nodded.

'Of course. What else am I going to do with my time?'

Because the fact was, as much as I enjoyed the long-distance swims and was good at them, there was only a handful of competitions a year I was eligible to compete in – many of them were men only – so I didn't have many opportunities.

'Miss Morton, if I may?' The cub reporter, who had to be no more than sixteen, was holding his notepad and pen, staring keenly at me. 'May I ask a couple of questions?'

I nodded. There was a shout from the crowd who had been watching as a gull stole someone's chips, followed by a ricochet of laughter.

'Of course.'

'Excellent,' he consulted his notes, 'well done on the win by the way.' He spoke a little self-consciously and I smiled in a bid to make him feel less nervous.

'Thank you.'

'Do you find it easy to swim those distances?' I shook my head slowly readying an answer.

'I wouldn't say easy, but I train a lot and that makes it easier when I get to the competitions. But no, not easy. Nothing like this is, we just make it look that way.'

He grinned whilst making notes.

'Would you say you prefer these competitions because you have a better chance of winning them?' the cub reporter asked bluntly, and before I could answer he blundered on. 'Because it's been noticed that you've not been on your best form for a while, placing third or not at all in the last few two hundred yards competitions you've taken part in.'

I looked at him again. He had acne. His wispy blond hair kept trying to get in his eyes. Rosy-cheeked and eager for the quote, I fought to maintain the serene replies Mother told me sounded best in the interviews.

'Erm, I wouldn't say I do these to ensure I win,' I answered trying to appear measured.

'All right, so you choose to compete in all of them for a better chance of winning?' he pressed. 'Because for the last three you've placed bronze or,' he made a show of checking his notes for the answer which we both knew. 'Or not at all. Fourth, fifth and so on.' His young, expectant face looked at me for the quote.

'I swim. I don't need to give the reasons why I choose competitions.' I tried to reply calmly. 'I don't mind if I lose to good competitors either. It's what makes the sport interesting.'

Before he could say anything else, I turned and walked away, keeping the tears down – they wouldn't have fixed anything.

I'd noticed that my times were slipping. Whilst the girls around me were getting quicker, I didn't need a hatchet reporter telling me. I didn't need Mr Swarbrick's overly enthusiastic smiles, or Greta's platitudes. I needed more wins to stay relevant, to ensure ASA thought of me when the Olympics came round in a couple of years.

Although I had won today's event, it was clear I was no longer the golden girl.

Chapter Forty-Nine

MAY 1923, BLACKPOOL

'What do you think, Hannah?' I gave a twirl for my niece's approval, and she clapped her hands together emphatically.

'Auntie Looosey is bootiful,' she told me, solemn-faced, in a way only a three-year-old can, which I took to mean she agreed with my choice.

'Thank you, though I think I need a necklace maybe?' I held up a string of pearls and she blew her tongue out at me. 'Fine, no to these. How about this one?' I held up the peridot-decorated silver locket Harry had bought me during our time together and Hannah's eyes lit up.

'Mine,' she demanded, holding out a chubby hand to take my necklace, which I quickly scooped out of her way.

'No, Hannah, mine,' I told her, and did it up. Just then, Alice came in. Six months' pregnant with her second, she was finding this pregnancy harder than the first one and the strain showed on her face. She slumped on the chair by my dressing table with a sigh and smiled a little sadly.

'I miss dressing up. I miss dances.' She pouted at the mirror, fiddling with her hair around her ears in the hope it would stay put. It wouldn't. It never did. I stood over her and took my hairbrush, lightly brushing her hair so it would stay still, slid a Kirby grip in for extra hold then sprayed a little hairspray to keep it in place.

'There, neat as a pin,' I said, looking at her in the mirror, then leaning down to give her a peck on the cheek. 'Beautiful Alice.'

'Not so beautiful Alice,' she huffed. 'More like bloated Alice. I swear I'm having a litter this time.' She sighed again and I lightly squeezed her shoulders, rubbing her neck a bit to soothe her. I looked over at Hannah, playing peacefully on the floor in a patch of sunlight by the window. She had some of my old beaded necklaces and was grouping them in colour. The reds and yellows shone with the daylight, delighting her, whilst the blues and greens sparkled gently, like water, as she rolled them around happily.

'You're a wonderful mother, Alice. If the next one is half as fantastic as Hannah is, you'll have done a pretty decent job,' I supplicated, hoping she'd agree. We'd spent a large portion of this second pregnancy discussing whether she should have stuck with the one child. She wasn't sure, whereas I was of the opinion if you're given the blessing twice over, you should accept it.

She looked at me and I knew the matter was closed, for now.

311

'What time is the dance?'

I checked the slim gold watch Father had given me for my twenty-first birthday. '7.30pm.'

'And is everyone going?'

I nodded.

'Yes, everyone. It's a Post Office party, all the girls will be there – in fact, I'll need to make a move soon,' I realised, but Alice shook her head.

'Not the girls, is everyone going?' She emphasised the word 'everyone' and I knew what she was trying to imply.

'Yes, Harry will be going too. He works for the Post Office, it's nothing to do with me whether he goes or not,' I explained reasonably, but Alice wasn't convinced.

'Uh-huh.'

I looked at her.

'And what's that supposed to mean?'

Alice pretended to think.

'Remind me, does Harry have a fiancé?'

'No.'

'A wife? A girlfriend?'

'No, and no. Which you know.' I shook my head in despair.

Alice smiled.

'And you've been single since you split up which means...' She left the suggestion in the air and I decided to ignore it.

'Which means nothing. We're on our own. We've been broken up for longer than we were ever together. We've moved on, you should too, Alice. You should just concentrate on your own family.'

Alice looked hurt.

'You are my family,' she reminded me. I pulled her to sit next to me on my single bed. I still found it odd that I was the one left living with Mother and Father and Alice had moved on and led her own independent life. I felt like I'd missed my window

'Of course I'm your family, but you need to recognise when to leave things alone. Concentrate on lovely Hannah and wonderful Arthur,' I advised. 'You're a lucky woman, Alice, you've got all of it. Enjoy it.' I squeezed her hands gently and she looked at me silently.

She remained quiet as I fastened the straps on my tan shoes and stood up, ready for her approval.

'Beautiful. Just missing something.' She looked around the room and then, spotting my lipstick on the dressing table gave it to me.

I slicked it on, gave myself a once-over look in the mirror then grabbed my handbag.

'Bye, Hannah, be good for your mother and I'll see you both soon.' I blew a kiss at the two of them, then headed out into the night air to catch a bus to the party, but as I left the town hall, I almost walked straight into three of the girls from the office. All telephonists too, we spent most days sat in a room together and could easily slip into conversation without much as a hello.

'Look who it is,' they whistled, 'ready for the party?'

'Yes – you all look amazing.' I replied joyfully. We all fell into step and walked as a four along the pavement, chatting about hairstyles and the latest moving picture, big-busted Betty leading the way, twirling her handbag around and talking ten to the dozen.

Yvonne leaned in. 'I swear, it's been like this all the way. I've decided to just nod,' she admitted and I snorted a bit.

'There was me thinking I'd need to get a word in.'

Yvonne shook her head. 'No worries there, they can carry on a conversation with a wall. Come on, let's go.' It had only taken ten minutes or so and we'd arrived at the tower ballroom where the dance was being held. I had a flashback to the dance I went to with Alice during the war, a night of laughter, where we ignored the atrocities and tried to focus on happiness. But tonight there was nothing to worry about, nothing to ignore, just fun.

Grasping Yvonne's hand, I walked into the ballroom, gratefully accepting a glass of champagne from a passing waiter for myself and for her.

'Don't mind if I do,' she laughed and took a sip. Her midnight-blue dress fell to her knees where the tassels danced with every movement. Her length of midnight-blue beads hung low too, the whole effect was mesmerising when accompanied by her blonde bob and bright-red lipstick. It wasn't long before she was waving apologies at me and heading off to dance with one of the clerks from the sorting office.

I didn't mind too much, I stood there and took in gaiety, listening to the Robertson Trio playing a swing number.

'No woman should be left watching the dancing,' said Jack, one of the older clerks, who stood next to me. 'Would you mind?' he asked, extending a hand, and I smiled, not ungratefully – it was, after all, much nicer to be part of things than not. It turned out, what Jack lacked in style he made up for in exuberance when it came to dancing and soon I was being swung around the dance floor with gay abandon.

'I think I'll need to catch my breath.' He puffed a little as the number came to an end and I shook my head.

'Not fair, you'll leave me out here on my own.'

'Oh no, old girl, I'm sure there'll be suitors ready to take my place.' He looked over my shoulder. 'In fact, here's one now.'

I knew, of course, who it would be behind me. I'd known from the moment we'd walked into the dance hall where he was. I'd seen him looking resplendent in his sharply tailored suit and crisp white shirt, talking to Betty. He had looked so at ease with himself, so confident, it was hard not to be drawn to him but for the fact we'd gone our separate ways so very long ago. We locked eyes, as we had done so many times over the past eighteen months or so. Though this time neither of us looked away.

But still I waited for him to tap me on the shoulder. My stomach lifting so much with possibility and butterflies I stood stock-still. I could barely breathe I was so taut with the knowledge it was him.

He tapped me on the shoulder and I turned slowly around, my face flushed and my hair out of its style from the exuberance on the dancefloor. I wondered, briefly, whether any lipstick was still on my mouth, having noted earlier how much had transferred to my champagne glass. He, of course, looked handsome. His fine features, dark eyes and dark, heavily slicked hair giving him an air of a silent film actor.

'I believe this is my chance to cut in,' Harry said to Jack, who just nodded and walked away. I merely gazed up at him, taking in the faintest hint of grey at his temple, which hadn't been there before, the tiny lines around his eyes marking the time since I'd last been this close to him.

I breathed in his scent, a familiar mixture of hair balm, starch and the Acqua di Parma cologne I gifted him at Christmas two years before.

'You're wearing the necklace.' He touched the beads that rested heavily against my clavicle with such tenderness I shivered.

'Are you cold?'

'No.' I shook my head but couldn't find the words. What words do you use to the man you walked away from? How do you say you were wrong? That you missed him every day of every month? Or that you made the wrong decision? That no amount of hobbies or pastimes could make up for the time you'd lost with him? That even though he had apologised you'd been too foolish, too selfish, too proud, to make up.

How do you tell him you still love him? That you need him and hope he needs you too. That you hope he hasn't found someone who fits into his body like yours does.

Instead, I just stared at him, into his beautiful dark-brown eyes that showed the concern I'd seen when I'd almost drowned all those years ago. The eyes I fell in love with at twelve.

I couldn't breathe. My throat was tightening with sadness at what I'd chosen to throw away and for once, I didn't know what to do.

'Hey Lucky.' He leant in and wiped the tear which had fallen on my cheek. 'Want to dance?'

He kissed my face where the tear had been just moments before and I beamed at him.

'More than anything.'

Chapter Fifty

APRIL 1924, BLACKPOOL

'We think you should give it a try.'

'But I've just turned twenty-six. They'll all be younger than me.'

Mr Swarbrick nodded.

'That's as maybe, but this is the Olympics, Lucy. You've done enough with your swimming that the Amateur Swimming Association have asked you to take part in a trial.'

'In which stroke?' I was still put out that the 1920 event hadn't included my strokes, keeping me out of the competition when I'd still had an outside chance of winning. Now I was a good eight years older than most of the competitors – Agnes, the American, was nineteen, she'd been breaking and setting records for years and was at the top of her game. She would be the person to beat, I was sure of it.

If I took part.

'Breaststroke, two hundred metres.' Swarbrick smiled. 'A good one for you, and it's a marginally shorter distance as we've been measuring in yards. But let's see, shall we? The trials are a month before the Olympics. You'll need to give up open swimming for now and concentrate again on bath swimming.'

I nodded. 'I could make a fool of myself, of course.'

Mr Swarbrick nodded back.

'Of course, but you've not managed to so far. I have faith in you.'

'When is it?'

Mr Swarbrick patted me on the shoulder. 'Four months from now – at the open-air baths, here. Home ground, you'll smash it.' His excitement was infectious but I had other priorities. Turning to the other man in my life, I looked at him with hope beginning to brim.

'What do you think, Harry?'

'I think I can't wait to see my girlfriend on the podium at the Olympics,' he said smiling, and swept me up in his arms. 'Then when you get back, I'll get to see you at the altar.' He raised his eyebrows at me. 'Deal?'

I nodded. 'Deal.' Then I turned to Mr Swarbrick.

'I'm in.'

'There was never a question in my mind, but you'll need to get your time up. They're all quick.' Mr Swarbrick's words weren't helpful.

'Really? And there was I thinking the Olympics was a walk in the park.'

'Should be for a world record holder – know any of those?' Mr Swarbrick replied, turning on his heels before making his way out of the door. Before he closed it, he turned round, a determined expression on his face.

'Four months, Lucy.'

'I know,' I replied.

Blackpool Council – via Father – discovered I'd been invited to compete and although, it being February, it was out of season and the Cocker Street Baths where I'd usually train were closed until Easter, Mr Swarbrick was given permission to open them for me.

In that way, between training before and after work, pushing myself harder and harder under the watchful gaze of Mr Swarbrick, demolishing the nourishing meals made by my mother, and the support when I was so tired I could barely stand from Harry, the four months disappeared quickly.

***

All too soon it was Friday 13 June and I was in the changing rooms, preparing to take part in the trials. If I got through, the Olympics was only a month from now.

'Good to see you, Lucy.' Verrall, a diver who I'd seen at various swimming and diving competitions over the years, had stopped to towel off her hair. 'There's a big crowd out there, you know.'

'How did you do?' I was always in awe of the divers who threw themselves off boards ten metres high. I still found it odd measuring everything in metres too - yards and feet made much more sense. But that was the way the Olympics was measured, so I was forcing myself to get used to it.

Verrall grinned.

'I got through. I'll be representing the ten metre platform event – Paris, here I come,' she said, then gripped me with both arms. 'You've got to get through, Lucy, the rest of them are all so young. I'm the oldest diver I'm sure of it. We twenty-somethings need to stick together – we'll never get the chance to compete again, let's face it.'

The butterflies in my stomach threw in a couple more tumbles than I needed which just added to the pressure.

'Thanks, V, I'll remember that,' I grimaced.

'You'll be great, Luce, I know you will.' With that she left to change into her clothes, with the assurance she'd cheer me on.

I wasn't surprised, most of Blackpool had turned out for the final trials. These were the final selections of the swimmers, divers and polo players to represent Great Britain. It was a Friday night in midsummer. The air was warm, the sea was sparkling and the crowd were enjoying the entertainment.

'Swimmers,' a woman with a clipboard barked as she came into the changing room. 'Time.' I walked out dutifully with the other women who were either competing against me to get a place in what I privately called 'my competition', or were looking to place in one of the other races.

There were three heats to decide on the Great Britain swimming team with just eight of us to be picked. We'd also have to compete in heats at the Olympics to progress to the final.

If I got there.

Looking at the other competitors I rolled my shoulders back and stretched out my arms. I worked some feeling into my hands and rolled my neck a little to ease the tension which had crept into the right side. I hadn't slept well the night before, I just kept imagining what would happen the following day.

The majority of the other swimmers were, as I'd feared, much younger than me. It hadn't been so apparent in open swimming, they'd regularly been a similar age, or male, but here, looking down the line, my twenty-six years looked positively fossilised compared to the four-teen-year-olds. There were quite a few roughly seventeen, eighteen, but, I was definitely the oldest.

'Good luck, Lucy.' The yell from the crowd broke into my thoughts and I turned around to see who it was. When I spotted the girls from the Post Office, I grinned and stuck a thumb up. They all cheered, along with a crowd near them and I spotted Harry and Alice, with Mother and Father and Mr Swarbrick all waving excitedly.

'Right then,' I said quietly, psyching myself up. 'You're the outside chance, but you're the local girl. You've got nothing to lose, and a lot to gain.' I knew I'd put the hours in. I knew I could do this in a good time. But could I do it in a better time than the rest of them? I needed to place in the top three to get through to the Olympics.

'Ladies, it's time,' the announcer's voice crackled through the megaphone and the crowd began to cheer. I was reminded of the opening of the baths just a year ago, when I'd given an exhibition of my 'motionless swimming', a form of artistic swimming. Then though it had felt celebratory due to the novel nature of the baths, now there was a change in the air. Anticipation from the crowd.

A shiver went up my spine. The place hummed with electricity – everyone was excited. Not necessarily for me, I was perfectly aware but they were all excited for the sport. I inhaled the scent of the pool, enjoying the late-evening warmth on my skin.

Then I focused on the water in front of me.

I realised the width of the baths was longer than most of the pools I was used to swimming in and the length was the biggest I'd seen in all the competitions. It was awe-inspiring standing at one end of the baths, with the other end almost out of sight.

One dive, two lengths.

I was ready.

Chapter Fifty-One

H arry had wrapped his arms around me, despite me soaking him through, 'Lucy, you've done it – I'm so proud of you.' He was punching the air with joy as I caught my breath.

'Where did I place?'

'Second. It was phenomenal, you did such a good swim.' His eyes sparkled with the reflections of the water. 'Your mother and father and Alice are jumping around somewhere over there.' He pointed to a very jubilant part of the crowd. 'They're all very excited for you, Lucy.'

I looked down at the ground, watching the droplets of water fall from me.

'Damn.'

'It's good, Lucy, it's good enough, don't worry – enjoy it,' Harry soothed gently, but I shook his hand off my arm.

'It's not first, though, is it? I'm going to need to go even quicker to beat anyone at the Olympics.' I smarted, irritated that I hadn't won though not, if I was honest with myself, surprised. Harry looked at me a little strangely.

'You need to remember this and feel proud. We have no idea how far you'll go in Paris, but enjoy this moment, Lucy,' he urged, 'you won't have another Olympics.'

I nodded. He was right, of course. At the same time Mr Swarbrick arrived with my dressing robe.

'It's been confirmed, Lucy, you're in,' he handed me my robe. 'You're going to Paris.' He shook his head a little and spoke fondly. 'I'm so proud of you. Everything you've achieved – it's been no mean feat to get here, I know it hasn't. But I have such belief in you.'

It could have been the cheering, the exhaustion from the race, Harry's joy, Swarbrick's pride or a mix of everything but I did, at that point finally feel proud of what I'd achieved. And nervous of what was ahead.

'There's so much to arrange. I've got to be over there in three weeks to compete in four. I need to organise travel, accommodation, a chaperone...' I tailed off. 'And I need to train. How will I get it all done?'

Harry smiled. 'When has she ever done all this by herself, Mr Swarbrick?' My coach shook his head and looked fondly in my direction.

'I don't know, Harry. I think Lucy's under the mistaken belief that we would leave her to her own devices on the run-up to the Olympics. Never going to happen. Someone's going to have to take the place on the trains I've booked, and stay in the hotel that's been arranged for you.' He laughed as I cottoned on.

'You've already booked it? That was...'

'Positive thinking,' Mr Swarbrick finished. 'And yes, I've sorted out your travel. ASA have said you're rooming with some of the other swimmers in Paris and they'll get that bit done for you, as well as a chaperone. Cocker Street remains open to you whenever you want it, and that, as they say, is that.' He clapped his hands together with glee.

Disbelief flooded me.

'You were never in doubt?'

'Never.'

The next three weeks passed by in a flash. There was coverage in *The Times* about me. Mother added all the clippings alongside the collection she'd already built up over the years in a scrapbook. She spent a lot of the time sourcing all the items I would need for my time in Paris.

Every day when I returned home, exhausted from a training schedule that was still sandwiching eight hours of Post Office work in the middle, she'd have something or other she'd picked up that she was adding to my trunk. We'd be expected to attend a variety of dinners and attend formal occasions, and Mother bought me silk stockings, new dresses and matching accessories so I wouldn't feel out of place.

'I know you're not too bothered about how you put together an outfit, but you'll be in Paris and, quite frankly, darling, those women really know how to dress,' she explained as she hung another new outfit on the front of my wardrobe to allow the creases to drop a little. This dress was an emerald green and it made me smile to know Mother was enjoying her contribution to my trip to Paris as much as possible.

I moved from where I'd been standing in the doorway and crossed over in three quick strides to embrace her gently. She squeezed me back and I inhaled her scent, a mixture of Yardley's Lavender and Nivea face cream. I promised myself when I got a little time off in Paris I'd find a shop and choose her a perfume. She'd adore having her own Parisian scent. Just the thought of the surprise made me smile.

'What?' Mother had spotted it.

'Nothing, it's just good to be so well looked after,' I noted, holding her a little tighter.

'Well, it'll be your turn to look after someone when you get home I should think,' she replied, and I frowned.

'Of whom?'

Mother drew me over to my bed and sat me down.

'Lucy, you and I know that if Paris hadn't been on the menu these last few months that you and Harry would have married and settled down. He's already asked your father for your hand. We've all allowed you to postpone that next point in your life whilst you,' she searched for the right words, 'take advantage of this final opportunity.'

'I see.'

'Lucy, you love Harry, don't you?'

'Yes, of course, what sort of question is that?' I replied, hurt at the suggestion I didn't.

'Then sooner or later you're going to need to make it more permanent. Goodness knows your father and I could do with the space.' She smiled softly. 'Alice is settled and happy with her children. It would be good if we could see you both happy.'

I forced myself not to roll my eyes.

327

'I am happy. I do plan to marry Harry. I know I've had some sort of reprieve these last few months...'

Mother was aghast.

'I wouldn't suggest it was a reprieve darling that makes it sound like some sort of prison or death sentence.' She shook her head. 'And we'll be having none of that nonsense.'

I thought then of the suffragettes. Of everything I'd seen over the last few years. Of my role shifting again in society. Yet here we were, still assuming I was better off in wedlock, rather than out of it.

'Mother, right now, all I'm thinking about is Paris. Harry knows that, he understands. He and I are happy and when I return, whatever happens, I'll marry him.'

My mother, a woman from a different generation, smiled at that.

'Good girl. Just as long as we're clear on all that.' As she got up from her position on the bed, another thought appeared to cross her mind. 'And no funny business in Paris. There'll be a lot of male athletes there who might try and take advantage of you,' she began and I raised my hand to cut her off.

'I just want to swim.'

Chapter Fifty-Two

JULY 1924,
BLACKPOOL-PARIS

T he day came when I needed to make the journey
from Blackpool to Paris. It was going to take
three days to travel to Paris and Father had said he'd
accompany me the short distance to Preston. After
that, I was to be met by some of the other swimmers
and our chaperone, and from there we'd travel the
length of the country to Dover in the south, then on
a ferry to Calais, France. Then it was a few more train
journeys and we'd eventually arrive in Paris.

Mr Swarbrick was at Blackpool train station to wave
me off, along with Harry, of course, and a few other
well-wishers. The women from the Post Office had come,
Greta and her three children were there too, Alice with
Arthur and the children, and of course, Mother, hanky
in hand, a mixture of sobbing, waving and laughing. The

photographer from *The Blackpool Gazette* had me stand by the train, holding my luggage, then waving.

'Are you excited about the Olympics, Miss Morton?' the enthusiastic reporter asked, his notepad and pen attached to him, it seemed.

'Of course.'

'Do you think you'll get gold?'

'Every athlete likes to think they'll win, I'm no different.'

'Your main rival is Agnes Geraghty from America. Do you think you'll be able to beat her?'

'I wouldn't be boarding this train if I didn't,' I replied curtly. It wasn't that I didn't appreciate the interest, but I didn't like the fuss and I was keen to get going.

'That's enough now, she needs to go.' Mr Swarbrick had appeared at my side, gently moving the press out of the way. 'I'm sure you'll have plenty to write about soon.' He turned me away so only I could hear what he said.

'You're doing something we've dreamed about for years, Lucy. *Years.* If you can remember back to those first few months when I began teaching you, I was always hoped but never in a million years did I think this is where our journey would get us.' He kissed me gently on the cheek. 'You're already a winner as far as I'm concerned. Now all you need to do is show the rest of the world.' I nodded, a lump in my throat. Mr Swarbrick had been more than a coach, he'd been a constant, reassuring presence for the past fourteen years. I wanted to do him proud.

'My turn.' Harry had been patiently waiting just a couple of yards from me, allowing everyone else their time. I walked over and embraced him.

'I'm going to miss you, Harry Heaton.' I leant against his chest and enjoyed the familiar solidity.

'I'll miss you too, Lucky,' he said quietly, 'but you can write to me – and you'll be home in a matter of weeks. Then we can begin our life together.' He slipped something into my hand. 'It's no gold medal, but I think you'll be happy.' Without looking at it, I knew what it was.

'Of course we will.' I squeezed the ring in my palm and kissed him gently on the lips. 'We're good at letters, I'll make sure to send you some.'

He grinned and brushed his hand through his hair, mussing it a little, then leant in and kissed me gently.

'All right, enough of that. You're not wed yet.' Father had appeared at my side. 'I'm going to have to take her from you, Harry.' Turning to me he spoke, 'We need to go, we can't have you missing any connections.'

I nodded, squeezed Harry's hand one more time and then broke free, following my father onto the train, into the carriage and found my seat by the window where I looked out at my friends and family gathered on the platform.

'Bye,' I yelled, waving eagerly as they waved back.

'Good luck!' Alice bellowed loud enough to hear through the window, and I laughed, sticking my thumbs up at her. The motion of the train began our journey and Father settled next to me, beaming.

We both enjoyed a cup of tea from the trolley and I could tell Father was trying to work himself up to say something. He kept clearing his throat and fiddling with his tie.

'What is it?' He was beginning to make me feel nervous.

'I don't think I ever thought it. You, going to see the world, pet,' he replied, a little sadly.

'It's hardly the world, Father, it's only Paris,' I reminded him, smiling and fiddling with the engagement ring on my finger.

He smiled back.

'Ah, but that's further than your mother or I have ever gone. It's a very exciting adventure for you. I suppose I'm just disappointed that we can't all be there with you,' he admitted, finishing the dregs of his tea.

'I know, and I'll miss having you there. You've – all of you – always been there for me, I couldn't have asked for a better group of supporters. You, Mother, Alice, Harry, Mr Swarbrick, I'm going to Paris because of all of you. I'm doing it for you.'

Father slowly put his teacup down into the saucer and looked at me with an urgency in his eyes I hadn't seen before.

'No, do it for you, pet. Don't swim for us. Swim for you. You're worth it. You deserve to give yourself the best chance possible. Just go for it. No looking back or hesitations?'

I nodded.

'Whatever happens, we're really proud of you, lass. And we're going to keep telling you that.' He looked out of the window to save my embarrassment. 'Oh, look, we're here.' We'd arrived in Preston and Father jumped up to gather my bags.

'Come on, we need to get you to the group.' He strode away from the train in search of my chaperone, me walking in a slight daze behind him. Suddenly the enormity of it all became real and I needed a moment alone to gather myself.

We walked over to the group of women who were clearly divided into the shorter, lighter ones that were in the diving team and the taller, broader-shouldered ones who were on the swimming team, like me. Gripping my shoulder Father said, 'your mother wanted you to have this, by the way, and don't forget to write.'

I looked down at a small parcel and was surprised at the lump that formed in my throat, I was going so far away from home.

'Of course.'

Father spoke with my chaperone, a fierce woman called Joan, who looked like she could lift two sacks of coal without breaking a sweat, then returned to me. 'Right, I'm off, love. My train leaves before yours. Good luck, Lucy.' He kissed me on the cheek, then walked away, his familiar gait disappearing into the distance.

'Hi, I'm Gladys.' A Lancashire accent came from the left of me and I looked to find its source. A willowy brunette, roughly around twenty years of age, had her hand extended to me.

'Lucy,' I replied.

'Hiya, how are you? Are you excited? I am so excited, and terrified. But mainly excited,' she babbled nervously and I smiled back, aware I would be sharing cabins and rooms with a lot of these women over the next few weeks.

'I'm not nervous yet. But I am looking forward to getting there,' I admitted. 'We've got a bit of a journey before. I hope you've brought some books.'

'Oh yes, my ma packed so many I can barely pick up my trunk – thankfully Joan can help with that.' She indicated the chaperone who was standing watch over the chattering group of women, and I laughed.

'Yes, I think she'll help with any heavy lifting.'

'It's a pity though,' Gladys admitted.

'Pity?' I asked.

'Well, with her around I definitely won't get the chance to meet any nice men, will I?' She pouted a little and I stifled a giggle.

'We're not going there for that – we're going for medals, aren't we?' I reminded the younger woman. 'I for one am not going to concentrate on anything else apart from that.'

'Ooh, I can see you're going to be my main competition.' Gladys gently nudged me in the ribs. 'I like it.'

'Ladies, we need to get the train now. We have to make several connections to London before we can get to Dover. Come along, these,' Joan snapped her fingers at two porters hovering by the cases, 'will bring your luggage. Follow me.' She walked off at such a brisk pace, even my long legs had a challenge keeping up. I could only imagine how the shorter girls were coping.

'I want you partnered up. Choose a girl and sit with her. She'll be your buddy for the journey. You must all keep an eye on each other's belongings and each other wherever you are. I can't watch all ten of you at once,' Joan's voice rose above the bustling crowd on the station's platform. She reminded me of Mrs Phillips, my old headmistress who introduced me to swimming. 'Do remember you are all grown-ups, you are all respectable ladies. Please act like them.'

I heard a stifled snort from Gladys.

This was going to be interesting.

Chapter Fifty-Three

JULY 1924, PARIS

Quickly I realised that my world had been very small up until that point. I'd often thought how quaint people were visiting Blackpool for their holidays, how the country folk must find our town too busy and bustling. I would think of them with a little pity.

I remembered this on our journey to Paris as we stepped off the train in Dover and made the short walk to the port, where our ship was docked. There was so much busyness going on, it made my neck swivel like an owl in a bid to take it in. From the billowing steam from half a dozen ferries, the chaos of the passengers alighting from trains, the cranes heaving vast cargo, the hammering from nearby, the stench of horses and the yellow-tinted water of the port itself. The whole feeling was one of intense confusion.

'Don't lose me.' Gladys looped her arm through mine and I was thankful for the reassuring presence next to me.

'I have no plans to, this is—' I broke off as a loud horn reverberated around the docks, 'exceptional.'

We followed Joan and the other women up the plank and into the belly of our ship. It would take just a few hours to reach Calais, and although I wasn't relishing the idea of the journey, I favoured it over staying any longer at the dock.

The saloon we were shown to was small, but comfortable for what we needed. Gladys and I shared with Phyllis – a swimmer I'd competed against in the past and who I'd struck up a friendship once again, this time over cards on one of our many train journeys. The last swimmer to complete our foursome was Irene, who kept to herself. The others and I already had a bond from our travelling, so sitting and chatting in the saloon was a gift for us. Whilst the three of us took tea together and enjoyed each other's company and arrived in Calais as firm friends, Irene continued to keep her distance.

'Golly, is this what dry land feels like?' Phyllis giggled as she tried to walk from the gangway to the pavement where we'd cross to the train station a few yards away. She wobbled as though she'd enjoyed too much champagne.

'Gladys fell over, so you're doing a whole lot better than she did,' I shouted in her direction from where I'd made my way to the end of the gangway.

Irene shook her head as she hung onto the railing to get to firm ground.

'That's not helpful, Lucy – I'm guessing you pirouetted down here?'

'Ignore her.' Gladys hugged me. 'We're jealous, really.' Irene aside it felt good to be part of such a fun group, I'd already grown very fond of them.

'Come on, ladies, keep up.' Joan began her now familiar march at a fast pace and all of us, now aware of the speed, walked quickly to keep up, but Gladys, not watching where she was going, bumped into a chic-looking woman who began speaking in harried French, whilst pointing angrily to her small fluffy white dog.

'Ah,' Gladys began, 'pardon, Madame.' This led to another outburst from the dog owner, and I grabbed my friend by the arm.

'Nous somme désolé.' I spoke carefully the French I could remember. 'Mademoiselle,' I finished, then led Gladys away. 'I think she was upset you called her Mrs.'

Gladys shook her head.

'I think I'd forgotten everyone would speak differently to us. Home feels quite far away, doesn't it?' she finished quietly and I nodded. It was alienating as I looked around. All the signs were of course in French, most of which made very little sense. I had a French phrasebook, but although I'd read it on our journey over, I couldn't recognise the words I'd learned on any of the signs or posters that welcomed us into the train station. The station announcer's voice was male and crackly, and he spoke too quickly. I could only make out a word or two, neither of which were useful as we rushed to catch up with Joan and the other girls.

'We need to keep up with them, the last thing we want to do is get left here.' I chivvied Gladys and we picked up the pace. When we arrived at the train, panting with exertion, the other girls had already boarded and our faces were shining with sweat.

'You'll need to get in the pool soon,' Joan pointed out, 'you don't seem that fit to me. We were only walking.' She spoke with her nose in the air as though she was sniffing something unpleasant.

I caught Gladys's eye and we both stifled giggles.

All the girls had the same level of excitement and our chatter filled the carriage, despite Joan's regular shushes. We looked out the windows and took in the tiny country stations where the ticket offices were trimmed with delightful window boxes filled with brightly coloured flowers. Our squeals of delight sent the two non-swimmer travellers out the carriage when the food trolley arrived.

It was breakfast time and we fell upon the delicious pastries that had been given to us, held in small white serviettes, accompanied by steaming mugs of thickly scented hot chocolate.

The trolley lady kept making an odd gesture at us when she gave us our pastries and chocolate. She kept making a fist, turning it over and gesticulating with it up and down into the left fist.

Phyllis raised her eyebrow comically.

'What is she saying?' she asked Joan who was fussing with the right amount of francs and centimes from the kitty she used for all our food and drink.

'It looks like she's being very vulgar,' Gladys suggested. Joan looked up and took in the gesture, then gave a rare smile.

'She's saying to dip your pastry into the hot chocolate, it's the French way apparently.' Our chaperone returned to counting out the change as we all looked at each other to decide whether to dip or not. I shrugged my shoulders and did as I was told. When I bit into the flaky, buttery pastry it had taken on a hint of the hot chocolate and reminded me a little of the texture of porridge. It was heaven.

Seeing I hadn't choked with disgust, the rest of the girls fell on theirs, doing the same.

'So delicious,' Gladys said with a full mouth, much to Joan's obvious distaste. 'What are these called again?' she asked the trolley lady who was grinning widely. 'Erm, le nom?' she asked hesitantly, pointing at the pastry.

'S'appelle une croissant,' the lady replied. 'Et chocolat chaud,' she finished, pointing at the hot chocolate.

'A croissant. Amazing,' Gladys replied. 'I could eat these every day, and *chocolat chaud* sounds much more interesting that hot chocolate,' she commented. 'I could definitely live like this.'

'Your waistline couldn't, Gladys,' Phyllis said. 'You're all right now as you'll be burning it off in the pool but I can't think these are good for you when you're no longer swimming,' she finished, and Gladys poked her tongue out.

'For your information, I'm fairly certain I'll be coming back to the Olympics in four years. I've got plenty of time left to eat these.' She underlined her point by pushing the rest of her croissant deeply into her mouth and reaching for the rest of Phyllis's.

I enjoyed my pastry, but vowed not to eat many. I knew I was lucky to be at this Olympics, there was no way I'd be competing in four years. The likelihood was I'd get slower whilst the girls around me would get faster. I wasn't retiring from the sport like that and I wasn't ruining this one chance by overindulging. I'd hold off until the competition was over.

'Ladies, we're here.'

Joan didn't need to announce our arrival into Paris. The Gare du Nord did that for her. A silence fell over all of us as we viewed the monolithic structure of the station, nothing that we'd seen so far had compared to its size and beauty. The roof was patterned with ornate metal girders, cast about as though knitted in an intricate design. As we walked from the platform to the concourse we took in the size of it all.

'Can you believe we're here?' Gladys whispered to me, and I squeezed her hand in reply. There were no words.

'Ladies, keep up – we shall be taking three taxis from here to the hotel, I will tell the drivers where we need to go and I'll pay when we get there. Just hang on,' Joan barked. 'The driving here is nothing like you've experienced, just find something in the taxi to hold tight,' she advised.

Gladys laughed with Phyllis.

'Lucy, you can be in a taxi with those three,' she nodded at them. 'You four in there,' she pointed at the taxi behind the one we were getting into. 'You lot, with me,' she told the remaining girls. We all did as we were told and the taxis exited the station in a synchronised move.

'Look at those women, they all look fabulous,' Gladys groaned. 'I'll never look like that – look at that waist,' she simpered.

'She probably doesn't eat croissants for a start – and they're not all fabulous,' I argued, looking for someone on the street to support my argument. I was distracted from people-watching when Phyllis shrieked, causing the driver to touch the brakes briefly, and us to lurch forwards.

'What is it?'

'Look.' She pointed behind us at a billboard.

'Wha—?' Gladys broke off as she saw what Phyllis had seen. 'Whoa.'

Turning my head this way and that, I couldn't quite see what they could from my middle seat.

'What is it? Everything all right?'

'More than all right. Look.' She pointed in the direction to the left of my shoulder. I looked and then saw what she had.

A group of men, with naked chests, all raising one arm in a way which could be waving or saluting, with the French flag in the background, and the simple words, *Jeux OIympiques* written at the bottom in capitals. It was enormous. It was grand. I felt light-headed seeing it.

'Monsieur – c'est—' Gladys broke off from trying to communicate to the driver. 'What's *us* in French? I want to say we're taking part to him.' I shook my head.

'Sorry, my French doesn't get further than asking for wine. Plus, I don't think we can explain it's us – it's a poster of men, we don't exactly look like them, do we?'

Gladys frowned. 'That's nothing to apologise for. We've gone past now anyway, it's not worth me saying anything.'

'We know though,' I nudged her, 'exciting isn't it?'

'Very exciting. Look.' Irene pointed at the Eiffel Tower. The Blackpool Tower was said to be based on this design, but I was shocked at its grandeur. The driver, who forced the taxi into a lane of traffic, slammed his hands on the horn and yelled a rapid fire of French assault at another driver, who retaliated and I swung forward in the cab as he punched the brakes. Fortunately Irene shot her hand out and caught me across the stomach to hold me in place.

'That was close.'

Shocked at the outburst, the four of us remained quiet as we watched the sights of Paris flash past, until we began to slow as we drove down the Place du Palais-Royal, and our taxi stopped outside of the Grand Hôtel du Louvre. The name was emblazoned on the front in large, lit-up letters.

'We're staying here?' Phyllis gasped, awestruck.

I was in shock too. 'The whole British team is. Most of the other athletes are in the Olympic village near to the stadium, but we are...' I looked up at the arches that fronted the pinky cream bricks, a stone which seemed to be used everywhere across the city, 'here.'

'It really is quite remarkable,' Gladys agreed, as we were beckoned out of the taxi by our now, much calmer driver. 'I wonder what the rooms are like?' she asked as we craned our necks to take in the enormity of the hotel. From what I could see from the pavement there were at least three floors with many windows spread across the building, each, it seemed, flanked by its own balcony.

'Better than the Olympic village,' Irene said quietly. 'I hear there's just lots of wooden huts there, sounds a bit miserable to me.'

'Ladies, come along.' Joan's voice cut through our conversation and we joined the other girls in front of the hotel, as a bellboy arrived to take our bags. We followed her into the hotel, which contained enormous palm-fronded plants, placed equidistantly to the desk, where Joan announced 'The Great British swimming team are here,' to all that would listen.

'Do you think she could draw any more attention?' Phyllis said nervously clutching her handbag in front of her. 'We may as well have entered with a marching band and fireworks.'

'I wonder if we're here, rather than the Olympic village because not all the teams are fielding female athletes. Maybe they're looking after us all because of that,' I suggested, having considered it a while.

'Maybe – I wonder when we'll meet the rest of the team. It's a week until the opening ceremony, I would have thought we'd see them before then,' Irene said as we watched Joan at the desk. The long journey was catching up with me and I craved a soft bed and a chance to sleep.

Eventually, after the commotion had settled down, Joan had located keys for all of us and we were shown to our floor – two of which had been taken over by the Great Britain team in their entirety. I was sharing with Gladys.

'Right, make yourselves comfortable – this will be home for the next few weeks. Feel free to unpack and get yourselves settled. I'll come back for you in two hours and we can all go out and look around together. Do not leave by yourselves, you understand?'

We nodded dutifully.

She really did remind me of my headmistress.

Chapter Fifty-Four

July 1924, Paris

O ut of more than three thousand athletes that took part in the Paris Olympics, one hundred and thirty-five of us were women. We were somewhat of an oddity and an attraction, with our presence tolerated by some and humoured by others.

When we walked around the hotel, Joan told us we had to have at least one other person with us to ensure our safety. Eating in the dining room could, we discovered, be a bit of an ordeal owing to the design of the room. We were all meant to share one long table. However, it often meant some of the girls got separated and they'd have to sit with male competitors, who would make lewd and suggestive comments about why we were there. So the British swimming ladies team tried to all go together, at the same time. That way we could find spaces in the restaurant that didn't include mixing with the men.

A lot of the female competitors from the British team were taking part in swimming events, and, by and large, they were a good bunch. Though it was the Americans who were the ones to beat. The way they took to the pool, even the way they walked into the Piscine des Tourelles when we trained, gave them a winning air.

There were issues when we made our way from the changing rooms to the pool, along a cool, concrete corridor, when we would cross over with the male competitors in the tunnel. Sometimes there would be a level of, what Joan termed 'jostling' or what we referred to as 'keep your hands to yourself'. Our presence in our silk swimsuits appeared to cause the men to lose their heads. It was as though they hadn't seen a woman's legs before, so had to touch us to make sure we were real.

'Must we?' I implored, as Joan held up one of the enormous towelling robes she carried at all times when we were poolside to immediately cover us, to protect our dignity. 'I'm so hot, I can't put it on – not yet.' I put my hand up to stop her and just held the robe. I was still getting my breath back from my last practice length.

'Do you wish for your privacy to be interfered with?' She put the emphasis on the final words, and I rolled my eyes.

'No, of course not. But like it or not, to swim fast we have to wear as little as possible so we don't drag through the water, and these are the suits we're wearing. I don't have a care that when I get out my legs can be seen – nothing else can be. I've these knickers on underneath too, as have all the girls and no one can see these.' I glanced down at my breasts, causing Joan to colour and look irritated.

'Well, if you're content to give everything away, that's your choice, but as your chaperone it is my duty to protect you all from wandering eyes and wandering hands, so you will wear the robe or you will not compete,' she replied crossly, folding her arms over her chest.

'Fine. But I need a towel or something, I can't wear this as soon as I get out, I'll overheat. At least find us some lighter robes, like the Americans have,' I pleaded. 'Come on, Joan, it's thirty-two degrees. Even though the water's cold, as soon as we get out the heat hits you and it's boiling. We can't wear these – they're like winter coats.' I smiled, hoping she'd understand, whilst wrenching the swimming cap off my head and giving my hair a good muss.

She took a moment to consider the options. 'Very well, I'll look at what else we can provide – but for now, you have to wear this.'

Satisfied I'd been listened to, I walked over to one of the benches to sit next to Gladys, still holding my robe. The pool was open-air and the shape of it acted like a basin, with the heat reflecting around it.

'She's good.' Gladys pointed at an American, Gertrude, who was hacking down the swimming lanes, marked out by cork floats – a novelty as we'd never had segregated lanes in any competition before – and she was going at a cracking speed.

'Hope she's not participating in my event,' I whispered.

'No, she's in the freestyle and the relay,' she whispered back in admiration. 'She's good though, isn't she?'

It was so impressive seeing these women in the pool at the top of their game. And I was one of them. I had to pinch myself to remind me this was definitely real. All of it.

'Good, isn't she?' Phyllis stood over us, dripping. 'Just done my fastest time, hope I can manage that in the heats.' She breathed heavily and drank swiftly from one of the glasses on the table. Phyllis was competing in the one hundred metre backstroke. I'd have liked to have given that one a go, too, but I tried to remain satisfied that what I'd be doing was enough.

'She's coming,' Gladys whispered as Irene walked by, not looking in our direction. Irene, it had turned out, was my main rival for the breaststroke as the current world record holder and despite my best intentions, we hadn't really seen eye to eye.

All the women were leaving the pool so the men could begin their practice session.

'Gosh it's hot,' Phyllis fanned herself. 'I almost feel like just walking about in my swimming costume.' Gladys and I laughed at the possibility, though I felt the same.

'Can you imagine? If the men are struggling with our costumes in the pool, how they would cope if we were to just saunter round the hotel dressed like this?' I shook my head at the thought.

'That'll be the day.' Phyllis grinned. 'But I could cope with it right now.'

'Ready for the opening ceremony tomorrow?' Gladys asked me whilst eyeing one of the male swimmers taking to the pool, an American called Johnny. He dived in so elegantly all of us watched with admiration, as he began to rocket through the water, making no bones over the fifty-metre lengths.

'Ready as I'll ever be,' I replied honestly. 'I'm nervous though. You?'

'Same.' Gladys said.

'Same.' Phyllis spoke over Gladys. 'Well, that makes three of us then.'

'Time to leave, ladies.' Joan had arrived with four of the swim team in tow. 'We need you back to the hotel, an early dinner. Big day tomorrow,' she announced, though I was pretty certain none of us needed reminding of what we were to do.

The next morning came and Gladys's nerves had turned from gentle jitters to full-blown shudders of anxiety. She watched me as I dressed in our uniform of a white dress, with pleated skirt, a navy Great Britain blazer with our flag, which felt a little on the large size, a blue and white diagonally striped tie around the collar of the dress and a straw boater decorated with a navy ribbon and flag. Our hats were slightly rounder than those of the men, but apart from that – and the dress of course – we were in very similar attire. As I buckled my pristine white shoes, I noted Gladys hadn't moved.

'Come on, Joan will be on at us if we're not ready,' I prompted, already beginning to perspire under the weight of the blazer's material and needing to leave the warm room so I could wait in the lobby area where there was a cool breeze.

'I don't feel so good, my stomach is churning something terrible,' Gladys moaned and I shook my head.

'No, you're not getting out of this – we've all got to be there, it could be a once-in-a-lifetime opportunity,' I reminded her. 'There's no guarantee you'll be back in four years. And anyway, I for one will definitely not be, so I'd like to experience everything I can.' I spoke primly, irritated by Gladys's nonchalance.

'You're right. Sorry, Lucy, I'm just feeling ever so queasy at the idea of walking out into the stadium – in front of such a big crowd,' she admitted.

'And the press,' I reminded her. There had been talk that there were a thousand members of the world's press at the games.

'Stop it,' she replied, pulling her white dress over her head.

'Sorry – if it helps, I don't think anyone is too bothered by us female competitors, so they won't be looking anyway. We'll just turn up, walk around the stadium, pose for any photos if anyone actually asks, then return to the hotel. We can have a nice glass of lemonade when we get back, and maybe they'll let us have a sandwich,' I said, a touch wistfully, as I hadn't enjoyed the food the hotel had provided us.

'Lucy, you're terrible – you're not giving the food a chance,' Gladys began and I held up my hand.

'No, give me meat and two veg any day – none of this over the top frippery, too much cream, and too much butter. I can feel it swimming in my arteries long after I've finished.' I watched as she pulled on her white stockings as slowly as I'd ever seen someone move, especially a competitive racer. 'But I tell you what. I'll give another plate a go, if you hurry up and plaster a smile on for the ceremony,' I bargained.

She looked at me then jumped over the gap between us and gave me a hug.

'Oh, Miss Morton, you do strike a hard bargain, but all right.'

I laughed and went to the mirror to apply a small amount of lipstick.

'I was worried you might be a bit austere as a roommate,' Gladys began, 'you know, being a bit older than us.' She stumbled over her words a little as I looked at her from the mirror. 'And you can be a bit short and offhand at times, but I think it's just who you are. You want to swim, you want to be the best and I really respect that. But, Miss Morton,' she said in a mock French accent, 'I'm thrilled you're my roommate, I couldn't have asked for a kinder, more encouraging friend. You'd make a great teacher, you know, after all this.' She waved her hand around.

'Now there's a thought. Come on, let's get this over with.'

If we'd thought the pool had been imposing, we had not prepared ourselves for the Olympic stadium. We arrived, as we arrived at anything in Paris, in a taxi complete with a furious Frenchman driving at speed. We had grown used to this and were having a spirited discussion as to who we thought would win the men's swimming, but fell quiet when we saw an enormous arena veer into view as we reached the outskirts of Paris in Colombes. The stadium grew out of the suburb, eclipsing much of the other architecture in the vicinity, throwing its shadow wherever we looked.

'Wow,' Phyllis managed, as I just looked on.

Many of the British athletes had already arrived when we reached the holding room, deep in the belly of the arena, and we joined them with Joan following close at hand. Our small group of four enlarged to include the rest of the female British athletes, all twenty-eight of us, but we were swamped when the men joined us, swelling our ranks to some two hundred and seventy competitors, preparing to walk into the tunnel and out into the arena.

'Ladies, at the front please,' a marshal addressed us in a thick French accent and we made our way through the group to find our places. My stomach had started to flip. We were going to lead the team out and somehow I'd found myself in the second row. None of us had realised and we all kept looking at each other in disbelief. I had to shrug my shoulders in apology to Gladys when I realised there'd be no hiding.

'The flag bearer 'ere.' The marshal pointed at a spot a few paces in front of the woman stood before me. I watched as a polo player, with the same name as my sister's husband, Arthur, walked proudly to the very front, holding our flag. The reality, the enormity of where I was, suddenly hit me square in the chest and took my breath away.

If only that ten-year-old dunce could have known where she'd end up when she began learning to swim all those years ago. I could hear the shouts and applause from an enormous crowd accompanied by wild claps and cheers which echoed around the stadium, and I felt the emotion in me rise up. Me, a girl from Blackpool, here in Paris, about to represent her country.

My throat was aching from holding back the tears that were threatening to come from the emotion, the realisation, of where we were. But I wasn't about to be seen by the press crying, I wanted to be seen – if seen at all – as proud, which I most certainly was.

'Lucy,' Gladys looked at me, her eyes watering, 'thank you. I can't believe I didn't...' Her words tailed off as I nodded. I reached a hand to hers and grabbed it, she squeezed it back and we both smiled tightly at each other, dispelling some of the heightened emotion I was experiencing.

All of a sudden, the marshal gave Arthur a sign, and he began moving forward and we followed as one. We walked slowly, but in formation and as soon as we stood at the mouth of the stadium our national anthem began, the familiar drumroll sounding comforting and patriotic at once. An announcement told the crowd it was Grande Bretagne and as we walked out, the wall of sound that hit us was something I hadn't expected. Roars of cheers. Enormous applause. People shouting and screaming and a few of our own flags flown within the crowd. The French flags outnumbered them, of course, but to see that people had made the journey to support us, the emotion of it all finally got to me.

As we stood in the middle of the arena awaiting other countries to enter, we all proudly looked forward. I glanced to the left to spot a press photographer who was capturing the event for the press and wondered briefly whether my family and friends would see it in the papers at home. The thought made me smile.

I hoped Father would see it in *The Telegraph* over breakfast, he'd be thrilled.

Chapter Fifty-Five

JULY 1924, PARIS

I t was eleven days later that I got the chance to take part in the semi-final for my own event. In that time I had been at the practice pool every day with the ladies and the majority of us had grown close. Even across the different countries we were chums. It felt good to have a group of women who were not only interested in the same thing I was, but as competitive, as excited as I was, to be part of this worldwide event.

On the day, though, I felt sick with nerves. I'd tried to eat the breakfast laid on by the hotel, but I was finding most of the food too rich. However, I settled on a plate of kippers and eggs, rounded off with a glass of orange juice, and it just about stayed down as we rode in the taxi to the Piscine des Tourelles.

'Are they all coming to watch?' Gladys asked excitedly when we glimpsed through the taxi windows and saw hundreds of people flowing towards the pool, dressed in their Sunday best. There was still another hour before we were due to compete, but there was, we saw as we drove to the back of the stadium, a lot of people queueing to enter the viewing gallery.

'Looks like it,' replied Phyllis, who was accompanying us for moral support as her heats were taking place at the weekend. 'You've got to put on a good show today, girls,' she said seriously. 'The Americans are favourites to clean up – we need to upset things.'

I was aware we were slowing to a stop and trying to ignore the butterflies in my stomach. 'I'll remember to quote that back to you when it's your turn.' I stepped out of the taxi and Gladys followed and as we began to walk towards the changing rooms at the swimming pool, she touched my hand gently.

'I just wanted to say thank you – I'm glad I get to do this with someone else.' The younger gripped my hand in hers.

'Likewise. It's a relief to share it all.'

When we reached the changing rooms, we spotted Irene, who smiled broadly.

'Why's she so happy?' I spoke quietly to Gladys.

'She's the world record holder, she's favourite to win her heat – and I think the final.' Gladys muttered tightly. 'I think she's trying to put us off.'

'Right you are,' I replied absent-mindedly as I looked at her. I wasn't going to be frightened off by some childish changing-room chatter.

There were three semi-finals to take place that day in my discipline. Fifteen swimmers from eight countries would compete in groups of five. The top two would qualify for the final, and the best third place would get added to the mix. I had to get one of those places.

'The first semi-final is due to take place in ten minutes. Can you all make your way poolside please, so we can have you outside, ready to compete,' a smartly dressed official said, having knocked on the door, and was talking to us with his eyes closed – lest he saw something.

Draping the towelling robe with an embroidered Union flag over my head and allowing it to drop to my shoulders, covering my body, I saw many others doing the same with their own countries' uniforms.

As I walked out to the poolside, something we had done almost every day since we'd arrived in Paris, I was surprised at the level of support we received, with many of the thousands of spectators standing and blowing whistles. It wasn't as overt as I'd seen when the men had competed two days previously, but it felt good that our competition was recognised.

I took a seat on the bench, along with the other competitors who were in my heat, mouthing 'Good luck' to Gladys as she went and sat on her own bench with her competitors.

'Hey.' Eleanor, from the USA, sat next to me and grinned. She was fresh-faced and full of life. 'Excited to get in the pool?'

'Yes – though I sort of want to get it all over with, and experience it forever at the same time,' I replied honestly. 'Is that weird?'

'Nope, I agree.' She turned to see the woman next to her. 'Bonjour.' I did the same and waved down the line at the French entrant, Alice.

'Bonjour,' she replied, then continued to look straight ahead, clearly not wanting to make any conversation in the time running up to the competition. I preferred my Alice in Blackpool.

'Suit yourself,' Eleanor replied, turning back to me. We watched as the first five women walked to the edge of the pool. 'Go on, Agnes,' Eleanor hollered and I cringed a little, so crass.

'Good luck, Irene,' I called, as politely as I could but she was staring towards the end of the pool and chose to ignore me.

There was a silence across the crowd, but as soon as the starter pistol fired and all five women dove in, the cheering started. It was fantastic to watch, the rhythm of all five was almost hypnotic as they rose out of the water as one. It was clear there were three fighting for the top spot as they raced down the final fifty metres. Marie from the Netherlands was a few strokes ahead of Agnes, who in turn was marginally ahead of Irene.

'Go on, girl,' I heard Eleanor yell beside me, and I couldn't help it, I leapt to my feet – I wanted a Brit to win, even if I didn't much care for them.

'Go on, Irene, you can do it.'

In a flurry of foamy white water, Marie came in first, with Agnes a stroke or two later and Irene just after. I sat down, surprised. I'd assumed Irene would be through, though I knew even world record holders had off days.

'Look.'

Eleanor had grabbed my arm in the excitement and pointed to the officials. They were conferring over something, with some head-shaking, then the announcement came, Marie had been disqualified.

'They're saying she didn't touch one of the walls with both hands.' Eleanor leant in. 'Immediate disqualification.' She broke off to cheer as Agnes was put into first, and with a time of 3.27, setting the Olympic record. Irene went into second place. So they were through.

'Ladies.' The official from the changing room was to the right of us. 'It's time.'

I breathed out slowly. Leaving my robe on the bench, I heard a yell from Gladys who stuck her thumbs up at me and I nodded, though couldn't say anything. I needed to be at the top of my game for this. Focused. Agnes's time was the one to beat.

As we walked to the pool, I could feel the familiar rough stone which paved the area up to the water. The officials ticked each of our names off and I stood in my position in front of my lane. I looked at the length of the pool, the sun glinting off the water which I knew from experience would be cold – despite the heat of the day – and pulled my hat over my hair. A few men in the crowd yelled obscenities about our breasts but I blotted it all out.

No pressure, Lucy, but if you don't get through, that's your Olympic hopes dashed. I could hear Alice's voice in my head and I shook it, ignoring her. She wouldn't say that. She'd say she was proud of me, but that she knew I'd do well.

'Positions please,' another official said loudly from his end of the pool.

I crouched into my diving position, listened for the gun, then dove in and swam with no thought to what was going on around me. The water was as cold as I'd expected, but I'd trained in this pool over the last few weeks so I was used to it.

I focused on breathing and moving, and when I got to the wall, made sure I got both hands on before turning and battling down the next fifty metres. I returned on the third fifty metres, gulping large amounts of air but feeling good. I could sense there was someone behind me, but I tried not to let it distract me. Once, when pulling out of the water, I brushed against the corks that segregated our lanes, but I ignored the distraction and continued to focus on getting to the end.

It felt like no time at all when I reached the wall, confident I'd done enough to be in first place.

'Yes, Lucy,' I could hear Gladys hooting and hollering. Looking around, I spotted Laure from Luxembourg putting her thumbs up as we both got a look at the board.

'Yes,' I heard myself yell as I saw the time I did it in, 3.29. Less than two seconds behind Agnes's record time.

I'd made it to the final. As I walked off from the pool to dry off, Gladys's group were called to compete.

'Good luck, Gladys, let's make it three Brits in the final?' I shouted excitedly. I walked over to the rest of the swim team and became lost in a sea of embraces from the cheerful girls yelling out their congratulations.

'Ladies and gentlemen, time for the third and final heat of the women's two hundred metres breaststroke,' we heard announced over the speaker, and I stood, keeping an eye on the pool and keeping everything crossed for Gladys.

As soon as they heard the pistol, the women disappeared into the water, and the girls and I yelled and screamed for Gladys to win. I knew she wouldn't be able to hear us, I hadn't heard anything in the water and they'd told me they were doing the same for me. But it felt good to support her. I wanted her in the final.

'Go on, Gladys,' I yelled as we watched her coming down the final length. She was making great time and leaving the rest of them in her wake.

'She'll be competition for you, Lucy,' said one of the girls cheering.

'I like a bit of competition,' I said back at the same time as the whistle blew to say there was a winner, and we all whooped when they raised Gladys's hand.

'Wahoo,' Phyllis yelled and the rest of us joined in, cheering and jumping around as we waited for her to come over to our group.

'I did it.' She walked over just minutes later, still panting, and still dripping.

'Yes you did.' I ran to my friend and hugged her. 'You did so well, we're in the final. The final of the Olympics, Gladys.' I laughed with joy.

'So that's, me, Irene and you competing,' she replied, shaking her head. 'I can't believe we've all had so much luck.'

'Not luck, grit,' I replied, my teeth firmly set. 'We've worked for this.'

'Ladies, time to get to the changing room.' Joan had arrived in the midst of the excitement and you wouldn't have known anything out of the ordinary had happened. She behaved as though it was just another training day.

'We all won, Joan,' Gladys beamed.

'I know, and now we need to get you changed,' Joan replied curtly.

'Can we at least, I don't know, go for a meal or something to celebrate?' I asked sweetly.

Joan looked as though she was considering the request.

'You can't have a late night. You have training tomorrow and the final on Friday. How about you get changed and we head back to the hotel and we have a special meal there, with a little champagne to toast your success?'

When we didn't leap around at the suggestion, Joan softened a little.

'On Friday once the final has taken place we can go out and see the sights, and have a wonderful meal but I have to keep you focused until then. I'd have thought you'd all be excited about the champagne.' She raised a rare smile in our direction.

'Good, go and get yourselves changed.' We did as we were told, traipsing down to the cool of the changing rooms.

I left the swimming pool with Gladys a little later on having changed.

'Looks like Agnes is our main rival,' Gladys said between gulps of cola from a bottle, glancing over at me as I rubbed my temple. 'Got another headache?' She frowned in concern.

'A little, it must be the heat,' I conceded. 'I don't get them at home. But you were saying about Agnes?'

'I think she's our main issue, I get the impression Irene isn't quite on her game at the moment, and to be honest, everyone else's times lagged behind ours.' We stepped into the heat of the late-afternoon sunshine and both squinted at Joan who was flagging taxis down.

'Blast, I've forgotten my sunglasses,' I realised, scrabbling in my leather holdall, through the damp clothes and towel, in an attempt to find them. 'I'll need to go back and get them, the sun is worsening my head.'

Gladys looked over her bottle at me. 'Want me to come with you?' She looked tired and I shook my head.

'No, you go back, there's still a few girls who haven't left yet. I'll go back with them and see you in the hotel in a little while.' I waved at Joan and pantomimed sunglasses. She nodded and beckoned Gladys to the taxi.

I dashed back into the cool interior of the tunnel which led towards the changing rooms and made my way back to the room I'd been getting dressed.

'Lucy, great swim today.' Ellen, one of our much younger competitors, said as she tied her long blonde hair into a bun. 'Much better than my shambles.'

'Ellen, you're fifteen. Fine, you didn't advance today, but you're sure to be back in the '28 games, I'm sure you'll do well then.' I hugged her, thinking how young she was to be here. 'Oh, there they are.' I spotted my sunglasses underneath the bench and retrieved them quickly.

'We should get a move on, you know what moody Joan's like if we're late.' Iris, one of our freestyle competitors, had returned from the toilet and was packing up her bag. 'Come on, Ellen, and Florence, come on, what are you doing?' She turned to me, 'Honestly, I feel like their mother, I'm always telling them to get a move on.' She looked at them indulgently. 'But I love them both dearly.'

'Joan said she'd hold a taxi for us, as we're the last ones to go,' I said loudly enough chivvy the girls along and they laughed.

'Told off by both of them, we better get a move on.' Florence grabbed her bag, and the four of us returned down the tunnel, reaching the sunlight. Prepared, I popped my glasses on and felt almost instant relaxation as my eyes stopped squinting in the bright light. Joan was nowhere to be seen, but there was a taxi waiting.

As the most senior member of the group, I spoke to the driver.

'L'hôtel du Louvre? Oui?' I asked, hoping he'd understand my awful French accent. He nodded, removed the cigarette dangling from his lips and replied.

'Bien sur, vous etes chaperon – la grande dame – m'a dit de vous attendres quatre. Elle a dit qu'ell vous reverrait a l'hotel.'

I processed his words to try and understand what he'd said. He'd mentioned 'chaperone', and something about four of us going back to the hotel. I nodded, and thought it best to repeat the name of where we needed to go, to be sure.

'L'hôtel du Louvre? Oui?'

He nodded and indicated we should get in, which the four of us did, in high spirits.

'Are you excited about the final?' Florence asked as the taxi swung out into the main road. We'd all grown so used to the way the drivers tore around Paris, we barely thought about finding something to hold on to whilst we chatted.

'I am, I can't wait. Agnes is strong competition – aside from our girls, of course – and I want to know how I compare,' I replied, smiling, and shifting my position a little as the handle of the taxi door kept catching me on my hip.

Iris turned from her side of the taxi to look at me.

'It was wonderful watching you, I've heard a lot about the fantastic Lucy Morton. What with your world record holding and ridiculously long swims, it's a pleasure to be on the same team as you.' She reached out her hand and squeezed mine. The taxi shifted around a corner, scattering two pedestrians from the road.

'That's such a kind thing to say,' I blushed. 'Thank you. It's an honour to be on this team.'

Ellen was sat in front of me, leaning on the window, looking out into the street.

'I know I'm not progressing in this Olympics but I've had such a ball on this team just being here. What a place.' She grinned as we passed the Eiffel Tower, gleaming proudly in the July sunshine, flanked by tourists.

'It definitely beats school,' Florence said, a mischievous glint in her eye, causing us all to laugh.

'Merde.'

The curse came from our driver.

Another vehicle came in from the right.
My door bulged inwards as I was thrown sideways.
Then. Nothing.

Chapter Fifty-Six

July 1924, Paris

'She wakes.' Gladys was stood over me, watching me closely as I tried to open my eyes properly, and work out how it was that I was in bed.

'Eugh,' I attempted, but Gladys put her finger up to her mouth to quieten me. 'No speaking. Let me get you some water, you must be parched.' She held a glass of water up to my mouth in one hand, and pulled my head gently off the pillow with her other, so that I could swallow. The pain in my mouth was excruciating, even sipping the water hurt, but I knew I had to drink, my throat was so dry it grated when I swallowed.

When she'd decided I was finished, Gladys rested my head back on the pillow, then gently found another so as to prop me up a little. She helped me sit up, wincing every time she looked at me.

'What is it?'

I croaked, aware of a thumping ache in my right side.

She shook her head, not meeting my eye.

'What?' Fear gripped me. 'Have I lost a limb?' I instinctively stretched my toes, noting there was feeling in both legs, and clenched my fists, aware I could move both arms too. I felt sore. I ached all over but I had two working legs and arms, which was good. But still Gladys was looking oddly at me.

'Listen, Lucy. You were in a car accident just a few doors down from the hotel – another taxi drove into the side of yours,' she explained. 'Somehow you and the girls managed to get out of the wreckage and walk to the hotel. Someone heard a shout for help, and the next thing we knew we found all four of you passed out on the floor.'

I nodded, dimly aware of the memory, but it was fuzzy.

'A doctor come, and he gave you and Florence sleeping draughts as you got the worst of it. Lucy, I'm sorry, but you've lost a few teeth.' She looked at me, concerned. 'They've cleaned you up, but they were knocked out.'

I reached my hand to my cheek and felt the swollen lump on the side of my face.

'That's why it hurts, but what about swimming?' I croaked, 'I've come all this way. Am I out of the competition?'

Gladys looked at me for the longest time.

'You were in a lot of pain and you needed the sleeping draught. But the thing is, it knocked you out for longer than we thought it would.' She paused. 'It's Friday morning, Lucy, the competition is this afternoon.'

I shook my head in disbelief.

'I slept through a day? Why didn't anyone wake me?' I was beginning to feel angry. Why did anyone else think they could have a say over my competition I'd fought so hard to be in?

'We couldn't wake you, Lucy, be reasonable. It was strong medicine to make you sleep. You couldn't wake until the effects wore off.'

'Can I compete?'

Gladys shook her head and I began to cry. Light, soft, fat tears falling onto the primrose-yellow eiderdown and she rushed to sit next to me.

'No, you've misunderstood me. I was shaking my head at your determination. You're unstoppable, Lucy Morton. You can compete if you feel well enough. But you've likely got at least one cracked rib, and of course,' she looked at me. 'Your face. It'll hurt when you dive in.'

'I don't need reminding,' I growled, 'I just need to get up, and I need to get in the pool for a practice swim. What time is it?'

Gladys smiled.

'It's nine o'clock. I've brought you up some breakfast. You need to eat this first before you're going anywhere – we can't have you fainting if you don't eat enough, can we? We'll leave for training together.' She walked over to a tray she'd placed on a small table nearby, and brought it to me.

I gave in.

'Good. I want to win this, Lucy, but I don't want you making it easy for me, got it?' She grinned, and I smiled broadly back, forgetting the pain in my mouth which quickly took hold.

'Shush, Lucy, no need to talk. Eat your porridge, I should think you're peckish. And here.' She poured out a cup of tea from the teapot on the tray, adding a little milk. 'Drink this, you must be ever so thirsty.'

I did as I was told. She was right, I was starving, and quickly polished off the food, thankful Gladys had chosen porridge. My mouth hurt a lot. The tea went down quickly too. Whilst I inhaled my breakfast, Gladys returned with Joan in tow.

'Nice to see you awake,' our chaperone said gruffly. 'Had us all worried there for a moment.' She came over and cupped my face in her hand lightly to look at my mouth, causing me to wince. 'All right, you haven't got a fever, but you are going to be in pain the next few days. The doctor left me with some aspirin, which I suggest you take.'

I shook my head firmly.

'I won't take anything until after I've competed.' My voice sounded clearer now I'd had something to drink. 'I want to feel everything.'

'As you wish.' Joan replaced the pills in one of the cavernous pockets of her dress. 'We leave in half an hour.' She looked sad. 'I'm sorry, Lucy, I should have been there.'

Gladys came over to my bed.

'Come on, time to get up. I think you need to have a look in the mirror,' she added and I inclined my head in answer. I needed to know what I was dealing with. She helped me out of bed but I felt so wobbly when I stood up it caught me off guard and I grabbed Gladys for support.

'It's fine, I've got you. Slowly, here we go.' She guided me gently to the bathroom and switched on the electric light overhead. Usually so ornate and beautifully gilded, the fixtures glinted garishly in the light and I winced at its brightness. Then we stood in front of the mirror and I looked at what Gladys had wanted me to see.

'It's not too—' I started, studying my face and finding just a few navy-coloured bruises along my jaw and grazing across my cheek, but I stopped talking soon after my mouth opened. I had holes where my top two front teeth, and three of the teeth below had been. Dark, cavernous, bloody holes and bashed-up gums too.

'Sore?' Gladys looked concerned and I nodded. 'That's no surprise. Look, Lucy,' she spun me around to make me face her, 'I know it's not perfect, but you have to compete. It might be your only chance. Ignore the pain for now – you only have to hold it together for twelve more hours. After that you can give in to it all.'

I stared at the mirror, trying to smile and recoiling at the sight before eventually closing my mouth and remembering why I was here.

'No one needs me for my looks. Five more teeth won't make me go any quicker.' I swallowed painfully and looked away from the mirror to talk to Gladys. 'Whatever happens, I'm going to need to visit a dentist when I return home, before any kind of photos.'

Gladys grinned.

'That's the Lucy I know.'

Chapter Fifty-Seven

FRIDAY 28 JULY 1924, PARIS

'That was awful.' I hit the water around me in frustration, causing waves to wash over the side and catch Joan's ankles.

'Excuse me,' she looked at me sternly. 'That is no way to behave.'

I sighed deeply, the pain in my ribs catching as I exhaled.

'Sorry, Joan, but this is not how I expected the day's training ahead of an Olympic swim to play out.' I sunk below the water, pushing my head under until the whole world was diffused by the aqua light that surrounded me. Moving my hand in front of my face, I took a moment to consider what the rest of the day could look like. I could bash my hands in frustration, I could shout, I could stomp around the swimming pool telling everyone how unfair it all was.

Instead, I heard Mr Swarbrick's voice in my head. Every time I'd felt as though I couldn't continue in a long-distance race, or each second place that hurt more than third did. Every time, he'd tell me to look up, look around me and see all that I'd achieved so far. Take it in, breathe out the anger, and then use it to swim faster.

Pushing off from the bottom of the pool I burst out of the water, to see Joan's face change to relief.

'I thought you'd sunk. I was going to ask one of the girls to jump in and save you.' She shrugged a little desolately. 'I can't swim.'

'No, but I can,' I replied, pulling myself onto the side of the pool and standing tall. My whole body disagreed with me, but I dove back in.

That morning I swam the two hundred metres three more times, and each time I was slower than my qualifying time. Slower even than the women who'd finished well after me and not made the final. But I was in the final, and slow or not, I was going to give it what I could.

'You. Lunch.'

Gladys had been watching my training for the last half an hour. 'No more or you'll be exhausted – I want some competition,' she added, sensing I would continue until I dropped. 'You need to eat, Lucy. They've set up some food for us down there,' she indicated the tunnel. 'Near to the changing rooms. All the other girls are there. We need to eat, then it'll be all the pomp and whatnot, and then we get to race. Agreed?'

I shrugged non-committedly.

'Good,' Gladys replied, satisfied. 'Changing room, shower, dry off,' she said to me as we walked through the tunnel. 'Did you hear about Irene?'

'No, I've been asleep for a day.' I tried to grin but my face was too painful. 'What about her?'

Hooking her arm through mine, Gladys leant in.

'Word is that she's got tonsillitis, has been feeling dreadful the last couple of days.' She looked at me. 'Not as bad as you maybe, but pretty bad. She's not even sure she'll be able to compete.'

'But she holds the world record, she has to compete,' I replied. 'Surely she can give it a go?'

Gladys shrugged.

'She may do, but think about it, even if she does swim she won't be at her best. Agnes is doing well, but then it's you and I – I think we could do well, you know? Even if the Americans have swept the board this week.'

I shook my head. 'I think you'll do well. I'll be pleased if I complete it.'

Now it was Gladys's turn to shake her head. 'That doesn't sound like the Lucy I've come to know. All I'm saying is, you're not the only one feeling under the weather. It might make the race a little more even, that's all.' We stopped by the changing rooms. 'Ah, here we are. You get changed and I'll see you down the hall, just there, for food.' She pointed at a room a short distance away and I left to change, wondering whether Irene's illness would help me at all.

The next few hours passed quickly. All the women ate lunch together, a platter of what we'd come to recognise as abundantly French food – slices of their national loaf, a long thin baton with a thick crust. The baguettes could be found at every breakfast and lunch we'd had since getting to the city but today they were proving difficult to chew, owing to the loss of my teeth. The bread was accompanied by an unctuous, smelly cheese called Brie which I heartily disliked. I coped more with their *jambon*, thick slices of ham reminiscent of my mother's cooking, which I paired with bright, sweet cherry tomatoes. We were offered glasses of very dry white wine, but I couldn't face anything. I was already trying to avoid aspirin to manage my pain, I didn't want alcohol in my system too.

All too soon we were walked out of the tunnel, in our individual country's attire. The sun glaring down on us as we entered the Piscine des Tourelles to a surprisingly full crowd. It may not have been the full eight thousand people the pool stands could hold, but I guessed we would be watched by at least two thirds. True, they were there for the men's race, which was after ours, but it was good to know we'd compete in front of a crowd.

Absent-mindedly I stroked the Great Britain flag on my competition costume and a thrill of nerves and excitement shot through me. I, Miss Lucy Morton, was here, at the Olympics. Gladys squeezed my hand and I returned it, then we both withdrew – aware we were, for the next few minutes – in competition with each other. We'd be there for each other whatever happened, but for now, it was every girl for herself.

We were positioned on the side of the pool in order of our qualification times, putting me into the second lane flanked by Agnes on my right and Gladys on my left. Irene was to the left of Gladys and she stuck her thumbs up at me. I returned the gesture, then pulled my hat on and looked ahead.

The corks that separated our lanes bobbed peacefully in the water and I focused on the distance in front of me in a bid to ignore my pulsating mouth and the low ache in the right of my ribcage. Looking to my right briefly I noticed how steely-eyed Agnes was. She wanted this.

'Well, so do I,' I said out loud, readying myself for the challenge ahead.

'Ladies.' An official stood poolside. He checked something with the three male judges sat in their stand alongside the pool to keep watch for any infractions. More umpires and officials were stood at either end to ensure we stuck to the rules.

For the first time in our competition I realised we had members of the press here. We hadn't seen any cameras since the opening ceremony – apart from the formal team pictures our coach had us pose for. These press were taking notes, or wielding their cameras, ready to get a shot.

'Ready.'

The crowd began cheering, the noise was the loudest I'd heard since my Olympic trials back in Blackpool.

'Set.'

I arched my back in preparation to dive and winced in pain.

The pistol went and I instinctively dived in, just as I had hundreds and hundreds of times before. The water was cold but familiar.

My whole body wanted to fight me. It didn't want to push through the water, it felt like I was swimming through cement and my limbs had forgotten how to work. Trying and failing to find my rhythm, I misjudged my breathing and took in a mouthful of pool water which caused me to choke. Water streamed out of my nose and mouth and I watched as Agnes began to pull away from me.

Just swim.

The phrase reverberated as I continued in the water and breathed through the pain, the way I had every time I'd gone into the sea or the pool. This time, I felt like I relived every moment I'd ever been in the water. From the first time I went into the pool and almost drowned before Harry saved me, to my first competition, battling down the lanes, unsure why I was doing it but knowing I was enjoying it. To more competitions. Distances in sea, through rivers, up and down pools across the north. Every time I'd been in the water was leading to this very moment.

I kept pushing. End of first length. Both hands on the wall. Turn. Swim. Agnes's lead was stretching out in front of me. I could see her, but she had her momentum and I was struggling. Second length completed, hands on the wall, turn, swim.

That time, Agnes's kick put her further ahead and I watched as she began to pull further away.

It's no one's race but yours, Lucy. Mr Swarbrick's voice came into my head. I was not in this to lose against Agnes. I was in it to win for me. The strength of belief coursed through me, I began to ignore the pains and the cement water and instead made peace with the pool. I would do the best for me.

I kicked hard. The third length disappeared and I was on the fourth and final fifty metres in the two hundred metre race. Reaching into myself for something else I kicked again and I felt it this time, I could do this. Agnes had slowed, not a lot but just enough for me to be in hot pursuit of her, and gold. I pushed with everything I had left, I powered down the water.

This is for Mother. This is for Father. This is for Alice. This is for Harry. This is for Mr Swarbrick. This is for Joan who can't swim. This is for all the little girls who watched me in the heats in Blackpool, cheering me on. This is for me age ten. This is for me age sixteen. This is for me age nineteen.

This is for me now.

I threw my hands down on the side and looked up. I couldn't see anything.

'Who's won?' I shouted at the umpire nearest. 'Who's won?' I turned to Irene who'd only just come in and couldn't help me, she just shook her head.

Suddenly it felt like the whole bath was teeming with British swimmers trying to pull me out of the water – the whole team was there, all the girls, and they were leaping in the water causing it to froth and swirl as though it was as excited as us.

'You've won,' they cried, as my arms were pulled almost out of my sockets as the women still on dry land dragged me out onto the side, and then upwards so they could embrace me and shake me and generally turn me inside out with their joy.

'Have I? Are you sure?' I couldn't believe it. Wouldn't. Not until I'd seen the result for myself. Agnes, too, was out on the poolside with a look of disbelief and celebration.

'Look,' Gladys was next to me, breathing deeply, trying to catch her own breath. 'Look.'

On the board, my time 3.33, Agnes, 3.34 and Gladys in bronze position in 3.35.

'Oh my, oh my,' I hugged Gladys close. 'You did it too, there's two of us on the podium – we've broken America's monopoly.' I laughed joyously and Gladys joined in.

'Lucy.' Even Irene had come and hugged me, as had numerous other teammates. We were all jumping for joy and celebrating but something seemed to be wrong.

'Why haven't they hoisted the flag yet?' Phyllis asked an umpire nearest to us who had been watching our jubilation. He shrugged and continued talking to the man next to him.

I stopped jumping, concerned.

'What's going on? I have won – haven't I?' All the girls were stood around me as we tried to make out what had happened.

'You definitely won, Luce, I saw you – you were there first.' Phyllis stood by, her arms crossed in front of her chest. 'They can't say it was Agnes. It was you, then her, then Gladys, I saw it,' she stated firmly.

'Me too,' added Felicity. 'There must be something else that's causing a problem.' She walked over to another official, who was standing where the flags should have been hoisted and we watched her having a relatively heated exchange, then throwing her hands in the air. As she returned I tried to steel my nerves for whatever happened next. I would contest it. I'd won.

She came over. 'You're going to love this, Lucy.' She had a huge grin on her face and I felt hope surge. 'They were so sure, after all this week's American success, that it would be Agnes in first. They've got the American anthem and flag in place as pure routine.' Phyllis gasped.

'No way, that's inexcusable – oh, Lucy, you've upset the apple cart, they didn't even plan for a British winner.'

I bent over in relief, my breath coming out in huge gasps.

'They must be feeling quite dismayed. Well, I'm expecting a flag in first and third position,' I reminded them all, I was just as pleased for Gladys as myself.

'Oh, they've got a flag, but Lucy... just remember, it's not the size that matters – it's what you do with it that counts,' Felicity said, smiling wickedly. I frowned, but as she spoke I saw them raising a small British flag in the centre, with an enormous USA one in second position and another small British one in third. It looked ridiculous, but funny.

'Small, but perfectly formed – just like our country,' Gladys said with pride and I grinned.

'Indeed.'

We both stared up at the flags and I felt the tears creep into my eyes. Gladys squeezed my hand as we walked to the podium to collect our medals and I remembered to bob a curtsey to the lady who put mine over my neck.

Our anthem began, and I struggled to allow it to sink in that I'd won an Olympic gold medal. Not just that, it was a first for an individual woman on the Great Britain team.

People cheered and took photos while I just stood there, breathing it all in. Remembering it all.

The weight of the medal was substantial and it felt like the world was on pause as I looked at it, took in the image of all the sports engraved upon its shiny surface and smiled.

I had won.

Epilogue

Blackpool Gazette & Herald

B RITAIN'S SWIMMING CHAMPION

MISS LUCY MORTON'S RETURN

CIVIC WELCOME.

Blackpool's wonderful reception on Tuesday.

Miss Lucy Morton, the British swimming champion, fresh from her great triumph at the Olympiad arrived home on Tuesday evening.

She received a welcome which showed how proud Blackpool was of her great victory.

Over ten thousand people crowded approaches to Central station, lined to the streets and waited at the town hall for the civic reception.

AT THE STATION

World's Champion Startled By Ovation

Visitors and residents vied with each other in giving the champion a real homecoming welcome.

When the train drew up at the platform on Central Station there was a wild outburst of cheering, and the band played "See, the Conquering Hero Comes!" Miss Lucy Morton stepped lithely from the compartment.

The ovation startled her for a moment and she caught her breath. An instance later she stood erect, and one saw the badge, the blue blazer, and the Union Jack necktie – symbols of Britain's physical might and majesty, which she had upheld against the world.

Her mother stepped forward. "Lucy," she said with quavering voice. They kissed each other, and as they remained clasped in each other's arms Miss Morton's eyes filled with tears she could no longer restrain.

She was Miss Lucy Morton, the modest, unassuming, charming Blackpool girl again.

And it was thus that one who has won honour for her town and country came home again.

Miss Morton was accompanied from Preston by Mr G L Swarbrick, the Blackpool baths superintendent, who has acted as her trainer; Mr H F Wolstencroft, president of the Blackpool Swimming Club; and Mr F Heywood, secretary of the South Shore Swimming Club.

Among those awaiting her arrival at the station were Mr and Mrs A Morton (her father and mother), Miss A Morton (her sister), Mr H Heaton (her fiancé), and other personal friends.

Major Eric Read (representing Mr W J Read, (president of the South Shore Club), Mr J Waterhouse (secretary of the Blackpool Swimming Club), Mrs Craven and Miss Burtoft (representing the local ladies' swimming clubs) were also present, and warmly greeted Miss Morton.

TRIUMPHAL PROGRESS

Miss Morton, seated in the Mayor's car, which bore the greeting, "Our Olympic victor", was driven to the town hall, preceded by the band.

Outside the station, the dense crowds cheered and cheered again, and all along the promenade, which was lined with crowds, the triumphal progress was continued.

Talbot Square was packed with people and again there were cheers when Miss Morton was greeted at the entrance to the town hall by the Mayor (Councillor H Brooks).

By a remarkable coincidence, Miss Morton was being welcomed home in the literal sense of the word, for her father is the Mayor's attendant, and she lives with him at the town hall.

Mr Wolstencroft presented Miss Morton to the mayor. "I have the honour to present to you Miss Lucy Morton, the champion lady of the world, who has won the two hundred metres breaststroke Olympic championship, and is the only British representative to bring back a swimming championship," he said.

Then, little Miss Dorothea Brooks and Master Seville Brooks, the Mayor's grandchildren, presented handsome bouquets to Miss Morton, bouquets which had been given as his tribute by Mr A E Clarke of Market Street.

REMARKABLE SCENES

The Mayor escorted Miss Morton into the town hall. "Come along, Lucy," he said proudly, "you are mine today, you know."

The town hall staff, assembled near the grand staircase, cheered Miss Morton as she passed, and in the Council Chamber, taking her seat next to the Mayor, Miss Morton was again cheered by a crowded assembly of the members of the corporation and friends. The scene was certainly remarkable.

"I have the greatest pleasure in introducing to you this wonderful young lady," said the Mayor, "who went forth from our midst, not to fight as our boys did, and to lay down their lives, but to fight a battle of a more pleasurable kind. It is a pleasure to us to know that she is the victor out of the something like four million swimmers in the world." (Applause).

It was a really wonderful performance, added the Mayor, and he was well justified in arranging a reception.

Immediately he knew Miss Morton was going to compete he told her father she must be given every encouragement, because it was not only for herself that she would strive, but for Blackpool. She had done very well, and they will be able to show to the world something more wonderful than carnivals. (Laughter and applause).

JUSTIFIED

She had proved to them the value of their baths, and they felt they were justified in spending the money they had done on their beautiful baths. It was one of the greatest advertisements Blackpool could ever have had for it again proved what Blackpool could do.

Miss Morton had done what she had done without any idea of personal gain – (applause) – because she was an amateur swimmer, and was satisfied with the honour of having won the competition.

Her achievement was all the greater when they realised that she and other lady swimmers met with a motor car accident on the Saturday before the contest, and that they had to be given sleeping draughts in order to enable them to obtain rest.

Miss Morton did not really recover consciousness until the next day, and yet in spite of that, she had gone forth and in a wonderful way had run against the whole world.

Miss Morton was the only one to bring back to Blackpool a championship for sixteen years, male or female; and they all felt very proud of her.

A SECRET

The Mayor then revealed the secret. He said that when Miss Morton went away, he gave it to her, keeping something which had been in the archives of his family for many years.

It was a mascot, an old jet bead, and when he gave it to her, he hoped it would bring her success.

Success had come and he would now ask her to exchange that mascot for a souvenir that was his personal gift to her as a token of his regard.

The Mayor, amid loud applause, handed to Miss Morton a beautiful gold brooch, a replica of an English white rose; and received back his treasured mascot.

387

Then Miss Mary Hamer on behalf of Christ Church Girls' School, presented a bouquet to Miss Morton, who was formerly a scholar at the school.

Miss Morton, who was evidently feeling the effects of her long journey and the excitement of her public welcome, was called upon for a speech.

"I thank you very much for the reception you have given me," she said, "but I would rather swim than make a speech."

Afterword

I was inspired to write this novel after watching *The Antiques Roadshow* when Lucy's granddaughter brought her medals on to be valued. She told the story of how Lucy was in an accident before her Olympic title, and all the incredible achievements she had. I couldn't shake her story from my mind and the more I researched her, the more I could hear her story needing to be told. It felt poignant too, that this year (2024) in August, it would be one hundred years since she won her gold medal in Paris, and the Olympics are again in the French capital.

Lucy Morton was a real swimmer from Blackpool. All of her achievements listed in this book, from her local wins to the Olympic one, are true. As is the fact she almost drowned the first time she tried swimming.

So, too, are the articles in this novel, copied word for word from *The Blackpool Gazette*, with thanks to the newspaper group for their inclusion.

I have made every attempt to adhere to Lucy's timeline, sourced from a variety of references but have, on occasion, taken liberties to make it fit the narrative.

Likewise, with all the locations in Blackpool, I have done my utmost to replicate what life was like, and apologise now as a softy southerner if I've got any names or places wrong. I've spent many hours researching but I am human, and all errors will be mine.

Lucy's win was incredible, but I didn't want hers to be the only story I told. All the women competing in the Parisian Olympics are given mentions in this book, using their real names in a bid to ensure their successes are celebrated too (and yes, Lucy really did have a tiny flag on the podium!).

I don't know Lucy's thoughts on the suffragettes, but it was an important time for women and I felt it made sense to bring it into the existing narrative discourse in the novel about a woman's place.

She did indeed marry Harry Heaton, though I must confess I did take liberties with their storyline too – but I hope they loved each other just as much as they did in my version.

Those who learnt swimming in Blackpool any time from 1930-1972 may have learnt their lifelong skill from Lucy Heaton (nee Morton). By all accounts she was fairly formidable as a teacher and didn't mention her Olympic win. Many of her students would have had no idea what their teacher had achieved.

I have tried numerous ways to contact members of the family to let them know I was writing a fictionalised telling of Lucy's story, sadly with no success. It is my great hope that if they see this book they'll recognise it for what it is. A fictionalised account of an incredible woman who deserves all the accolades, and a celebration of trailblazing women in general.

Lisa Brace, May 2024.

Acknowledgements

Firstly, I want to thank Lucy. If it wasn't for her incredible achievements I wouldn't have been set out on this path to write this book. You unlocked something in me which wants to celebrate more incredible women who have, for the most part, been forgotten.

Thank you to all the wonderful readers, bloggers and reviewers who ensure our stories get into readers' hands. Thanks in advance for your reviews and ratings of this!

Thank you to all the people I've talked to in a bid to get this as right as possible, including Hannah Stewart for her swimming advice, Dr Mike Esbester from Portsmouth University who helped me work out what route Lucy may have taken from Blackpool to Paris, and the staff at Showtime in Blackpool.

Thanks to Simon West for the beautiful front cover design, I'm so thrilled with how it's turned out.

Thank you to writing bestie Daisy White. She may not write historical fiction, but she's happy to read it and let me know if it's good or not (thankfully it was!).

Thanks to Ian Skewis who has edited two of my books now. Both *completely* different, but who seems to get my writing and who I enjoy reading the cheering comments from – it's like getting your work back from a teacher!

Many thanks to my lovely agent, Annette Crossland at A For Authors. She encourages me to write what I enjoy, which means she gets commercial and historical fiction manuscripts sent her way (and even a thriller or two!). Thanks for giving me freedom.

Thanks to my mum. My first reader of *Swim* who described it as a 'beautiful, quiet book', which were heartening words for me when I was writing something so different to my other work.

Thanks to my children who are, frankly, bored of me taking them to museums so I can get things 'just right', but who are my biggest cheerleaders.

Finally, thank you to my husband who always celebrates my success (and has a lot to say about commas). Love you.

Milton Keynes UK
Ingram Content Group UK Ltd.
UKHW051841300624
444901UK00005B/171